CHRISTOPHER CARTWRIGHT

OMEGA DEEP

PROLOGUE

Ω————————Ω————————Ω

NORWEGIAN SEA–SIX WEEKS AGO

IT WAS 10:15 P.M. EXACTLY WHEN the cold, rigid plane of the submarine's sail deck broke the icy surface of the Norwegian Sea. The rounded belly of the steel predator — a heavily modified and experimental *Virginia* class block VII nuclear-powered fast attack submarine — slowly rose until she was resting on the almost glassy surface. In the calm and moonless night, the sea looked like a series of fragmented shards of jet-black shale being slowly jolted together.

The darkened sail deck made a silhouette barely the length and breadth of a small whale, but even that would be visible to the prying eyes of enemy satellites. A test like this would likely draw the attention of any number of enemy and friendly nations. In fact, they had made sure of it. Not letting the enemy know one's capabilities was as absurd as trying to maintain a nuclear deterrent without acknowledging one has nuclear weapons.

Inside, the command center was abuzz with action.

Commander Dwight Bower planted his feet in a wide stance, closed his eyes, and breathed deeply. The air smelled vaguely of warm electronics, black coffee, and amine — the chemical used to scrub carbon dioxide from the air on board. It was the smell that had enveloped him for most of his adult life, the familiar scent of home.

Beneath his feet he could sense the life in her, the activity of the men, the nuclear propulsion unit easing the 7,900-ton vessel silently along the surface of the sea.

As the weight of expectation grew, conversations took place in subdued tones between crew members at their stations.

The commander's mind was sharp and focused. Eyes from around the world would be on his submarine now, and if all went well, they would be provided with one of the most impressive feats of modern engineering since Thomas Edison publicly demonstrated the power of electricity in Menlo Park, in December 1879.

He pictured his behemoth craft, longer than a football field and seven stories high, her sail and bow carving the surface waves. She was dark and formidable—an embodiment of intimidation and strength. She was unmatched for firepower, technology, and maneuverability by any other ship on Earth. At his word, she could effortlessly shirk the crushing weight of the Atlantic, diving to a cruising depth unfathomable in days gone by, disappearing into the deep waters below.

A silent, deadly predator.

Commander Bower was still as trim as he was in his early twenties. A lifetime of discipline and calisthenics had given him the physique of a much younger man. The only sign of his sixty-three years of age was slight accents of gray in his dark hair.

He raised the Universal Modular Mast to its maximum height and brought its view piece up to his eyes. Unlike a traditional periscope, it incorporated eight separate components—two photonic masts, two tactical communication masts, one super-high-frequency SATCOMs, one snorkel, one AN/BPS-16 surface search and navigation radar mast, and one AN/BLQ-10 Electronic Support Measures warfare mast used to detect, analyze, and identify both radar and communication signals from ships, aircraft, submarines, and land-based transmitters.

Bower examined the view piece for the photonic mast. At the

mast's core, it was a very powerful digital camera, which fed back to the Command Center via a fiber optic cable. Although he was already on the surface of what appeared to be an empty sea, he wanted to get a better view of the area immediately surrounding him. The device rotated 360 degrees, and at its maximum height out of the water, could provide a range of three miles on a clear night.

He made a slow arc in a counter-clockwise direction. The sea was calm and clear of any visible vessel. His thick eyebrows drew together. It was impossible to think that no one had taken notice of his new command. Changing the view feed to radar, he grinned.

Yes. He found two surface contacts.

One at eight miles to the north and another at six miles to the southeast.

He fixed in on the contact eight miles to the north. It had the outward appearance of a large offshore fishing trawler. Its nameplate was Russian, almost undoubtedly a spy-vessel. The sight relieved him.

What was the point of possessing the Omega technology if one couldn't terrify one's opponents with a demonstration of power? He made a note of the vessel's name, *Vostok,* and rotated to the southeast.

The second vessel looked like an old ice-breaker, with a helicopter on its aft deck. Due to its large array of radar instruments, it was more likely another spy vessel. It was angled straight on, making it impossible to read the ship's name. Commander Bower rotated the digital camera upwards, stared at the starlit sky above, and wondered who was staring down upon his submarine.

Let them watch.

It was for them that he'd brought the submarine to the surface.

The *Omega Deep* project had been his brainchild and his baby for as long as he could remember. It had taken him twenty years in the Navy to convince anyone that the leap from such difficult and obscure science could be made into this game-changing technology. Then it had been another twenty years before the technology caught up with his goals. In the end, it was luck that had delivered to him the materials required to achieve his aspirations.

Something not even from this world.

Nearly thirteen thousand years ago a large meteorite struck the earth. Upon impact, millions of tons of rock and soil were sent into the atmosphere, triggering the last mini-ice age, known as the Younger Dryas. Nobody knows from which region of the seemingly infinite universe, or from what solar system the asteroid once originated. Subsequent darkness decimated the Earth's flora and fauna.

The human race was hit hard, and the event stalled the fledgling process of domestication, in what would soon become the Agricultural Revolution that transported mankind from its humble hunter-gatherer existence into the permanence of modern agriculture.

Ancient technology and skills derived over the eons were nearly lost in its entirety.

The world's knowledge was not forgotten by all. A small group of ancient scholars and astronomers, known as the Master Builders, set about building a series of stones in a temple which appeared set to record the movements of the stars. The temple was called Göbekli Tepe, and its remains were discovered in the 1990s within Turkey's Southeastern Anatolia Region.

But it didn't just record an ancient event—it predicted the future return of that same asteroid on its eccentric orbit. The same celestial body from which the earlier meteorite fell.

Twelve months ago, the asteroid returned, threatening to achieve what it had failed to do some thirteen thousand years earlier, wiping out the remains of the human race by causing cataclysmic and widespread changes to the weather globally.

Thankfully, the ancient scholars of that era had kept a small amount of the original meteorite's strange material for the purpose of stabilizing the magnetic poles.

What few people knew was that 13,000 years ago, there wasn't just one meteorite, but two. A secret team from the U.S. Defense Advanced Research Projects Agency, located the second meteorite. After doing so, it harvested the rare material found inside, known as *blackbody*.

Once only theoretical, the material absorbed all energy.

Omega Deep's hull was a unique combination of advanced metallurgy, biomimicry, and advanced projection technology. The hull was coated with *blackbody*. In addition to its unusual appearance and long list of rare qualities, the unearthly element absorbed electrons and flattened soundwaves. The result was to make an entirely silent chameleon out of a four-hundred-foot hull, making her the deadliest nuclear predator to ever stalk the seven seas.

Eyes wide and glittering with satisfaction, Commander Bower's lips curled into a proud grin. He took a deep breath in through his nostrils, as though, despite not yet opening the hatch, he could already smell the fresh air.

It was the first time the *Omega Deep* had surfaced in three weeks. It would be a short stay, an hour at most, in order to upload information regarding their testing so far, and also to receive any incoming communications. Particularly, whether or not the President was to give the final approval for *Omega Deep* to complete its final phase of sea trials.

Six miles away, a salvage ship sent out a constant barrage of sonar pings. The commander glanced at the radar operator's notes. "Do we know whose vessel that is? If it's a spy ship, it's the worst one in history because it's making a hell of a lot of noise."

"It's a private salvage vessel, allegedly owned by an American. The name on the AIS transponder is the *Maria Helena*."

"The *Maria Helena?*" A wry smile twitched the commander's lips. "What's she doing this far north?"

"I believe she's searching for something on the seabed."

"Here? Now?" The commander asked. "That seems like one hell of a coincidence."

The sonar operator—a sharp, twenty-five-year-old brunette he'd hand-picked after she achieved the highest marks to ever come out of Fleet Sonar School–shrugged. "It might be."

"What the hell are they supposed to be looking for?"

"Do you recall that sound we identified forty-eight hours ago?"

Dwight cocked an eyebrow. "The possible explosion? You finally found a report on that?"

"Yes, sir. It wasn't an explosion, but it was close to it. More like a ship being dropped from a height. Whatever it was, the vessel eventually struck the seabed—we picked up two sounds. The original impact with the surface of the ocean, and the subsequent impact on the seabed nearly twenty minutes later."

"What are you thinking?"

"My guess is it was caused by a large aircraft slamming into the sea. At least a 737, but maybe even bigger—possibly even a 747 or A380, God help them."

"A commercial jet?"

"Possibly, although there is no report of any aircraft going off the radar from Air Traffic Control."

"If you're right, why did it take so long?"

The operator asked, "Take so long for what, sir?"

"You said there were two distinct impact sounds. One when the aircraft or whatever it was struck the surface of the sea, and a second one when it hit the seabed."

"Yes."

"So, why did it take twenty minutes? I mean, if an aircraft struck the ocean this far north—where even on a good day, the seas were ten feet high and rough — it would almost certainly break apart on impact, wouldn't it?"

The operator took a deep breath, briefly closed her eyes. "There's a chance it got lucky."

"Can't be too lucky, it still ended up on the seabed."

"True, and if anyone got out alive, they'd probably freeze to death. But I don't think anyone survived."

"Why?"

"Because, according to our surface buoy, no one made any radio transmissions after the aircraft was on the water."

Commander Bower nodded and closed his eyes. He knew what that meant. Everyone on board was already dead.

"All right. When we receive our orders, we'll find out if there's anything to it. They won't let us test the Omega Cloak if there's an international search underway in the region. It would be far too dangerous."

He opened his eyes and took in the scene.

Turning on his heel, the commander surveyed his ship and his crew.

Banks of colored monitors were fixed desktop-to-ceiling above control modules. Sailors surrounded him in oversized ergonomic office chairs at their stations. The operations center of the *Virginia* class block VII experimental nuclear attack submarine looked more like something from the stock exchange than the bridge of the submarines he commanded as a younger man.

Instead of outboard watch-standers in jumpsuits manning the helm, dive, and ballast controls, there sat a pilot and copilot at computer touchscreens. Sonar, combat control, navigation, and command all worked together in the open-plan war room of the modern attack sub. With 34 feet of beam, there was plenty of space.

They had come a long way with this project. His project. And now, after so many years, he was pleased to have lived to see it reach fruition.

The world would soon see what the *Omega Deep* was capable of.

James Halifax, the submarine's Executive Officer, approached. At five-foot-two, he was a short, wiry, and a somewhat unhappy fellow. The XO had a permanent chip on his shoulder, something he unsuccessfully attempted to conceal from his CO. He'd been overlooked for the past three command positions that had come up. It wasn't his fault. The U.S. Navy had plenty of good men and women who were keen to do the job. Just not enough submarines to go around.

Dwight Bower didn't like the man. Nothing personal, except for a personality clash. But Bower respected him plenty and was glad he was on board the *Omega Deep*.

Halifax was intelligent, if a little too wily. He was arrogant, but his ability justified that. Dwight and his XO had clashed a number of times over the years. Bower had very nearly been the cause of the man's discharge three years ago after an incident, resulting in a court-martial, at which Bower had been called upon to give his expert opinion. In the end, the court-martial had been overturned. Halifax had been reinstated as an XO on the USS *Alaska* until Bower had personally requested him on board the USS *Omega Deep*.

Despite their personal differences, Halifax's intelligence and steadfast determination — edging toward belligerence — made him a prime choice for the role of XO. Bower didn't need a sycophant — he needed a competent ally to help command the world's most advanced nuclear attack submarine.

Traditionally, the U.S. Navy's fleet of nuclear attack submarines was armed with conventional weapons, but the *Omega Deep* was the first of the American attack submarines modified to be equipped with nuclear-armed cruise missiles — 42 of them to be exact.

It was a lot of responsibility. Bower was happy to share this honor and this burden with someone like Halifax. It was for this reason Bower singled the man out for the position.

Halifax met his eye and handed him a small piece of paper. "Communications have received a coded message from the Pentagon, sir."

"Thank you, Mr. Halifax." He took a breath. "Any news regarding that explosion?"

Halifax's lips thinned to a hardened smile. "Yes. It was a Boeing 747 Dreamlifter cargo aircraft, en route to Quonset Point, Rhode Island."

General Dynamics Electric Boat — one of the companies used by the U.S. Navy to build submarines — was based at Quonset Point. "The cargo aircraft was one of ours?"

"No. British owned. I'm not sure what sort of cargo it was carrying."

"Okay." Bower sighed. "Any survivors?"

"No. Three crew. None found. All presumed dead."

"Does the Pentagon want us to assist in the search?"

"No. Apparently, the *Maria Helena's* located the wreckage and the British Air Accidents Investigation Branch have requested the *Maria Helena* begin the retrieval of the flight data recorders."

"Understood," Commander Bower said, as he took the note and unfolded it onto the navigation table.

His eyes swept over the note.

The words were little more than gibberish. In addition to its array of digitally secure communication systems, Bower had insisted the *Omega Deep* retain a unique unbreakable code to be used for open communication. This one relied on a secret key cryptography to obscure its meaning. This type of code was a variation of the one-time pad — the only truly unbreakable code in theory. To decode the message, a listener had to have both the book and the key.

Cognizant of the abundant interest in their new technology by friendly and hostile nations, the decision was made early on to use this cryptography for communications regarding the Omega Cloak.

Secret key cryptography employs a single key for both encryption and decryption. In this case, a message was sent by the Pentagon using the key to encrypt the plaintext and send the ciphertext to the receiver. The receiver applies the same key to decrypt the message and recover the plaintext.

Because a single key is used for both functions, secret key cryptography is also called symmetric encryption. When using a cipher, the original information is known as plaintext and the encrypted form as ciphertext. The ciphertext message contains all the information of the plaintext message—yet isn't in a format readable by human or computer without the proper mechanism to decrypt it.

Halifax patiently waited as Dwight began the complex process of decoding the message.

From the navigation table, Bower removed the book—Tolstoy's *War and Peace*. From his pocket, he withdrew the key to the code. Today was October 2—thus he had to add the year, ignoring the first two digits, to the day's date. So, 2 and 18 made 20. He then turned the book to page twenty. October was the 10th month, so every 10th letter on the page would be discounted.

Using the key, he slowly continued this process, transcribing the letters on the pad Halifax had handed him until they became a recognizable series of words.

When Bower was finished, the lines around his face deepened for a moment. Then, abruptly, his wrinkles seemed to disappear as his face broke out in a surprisingly boyish smile.

"The team of dedicated and highly intelligent men and women behind the Omega project back stateside are happy with our preliminary notes, and confident in our success," Dwight said. "We've been given formal approval for silent running by engaging the Omega Cloak. We have been authorized to then complete our primary mission."

"Very good, sir." Halifax looked at him. "May I ask the

mission destination?"

"I'll explain that after we've dived, once the Omega Cloak is protecting us from all listening devices. They're all focused on us now."

The XO firmly set his jaw. "When do you want to sail?"

"We'll dive as soon as we have visual confirmation of the Omega Cloak."

Ω**Ω**Ω

The bow of the *Vostok* sliced through the icy swell of the Norwegian Sea with ease.

In the darkness, a large diesel powerplant hummed, as more than five miles of longline fishing hooks were slowly retracted onto their drums housed on the stern. It appeared to be a poor catch, with little visible in the line. This type of fishing was a lot like gambling. A large factory fishing trawler could spend a fortune hunting a particular school of fish in the remote regions of the Barents and Norwegian Sea into the Arctic Ocean and be rewarded with nothing. At the same time, one good catch could see them all rich.

Svetlana Dyatlova examined her monitoring station with alacrity, keen not to miss any detail.

Her face was a study of jarring contrast. She was attractive — stunning in fact, yet there was a cold, calculating, hardness in her gaze that gave people pause. Her lustrous dark hair was smartly tied back in a single plait. She had pale, smoky blue-gray eyes and a strong nose. Her jawline was prominent, with high cheek-bones, leading to a rosebud mouth and full lips, that appeared set just shy of a permanent scowl.

Suddenly, her scowl broadened into a menacing grin as she acquired her target, revealing a set of small, even white teeth, like a Cheshire cat. Her sharp eyes were wide, and despite an outward display of cold, calculating, reservation, her countenance would have made any man stare. Svetlana's heart was pounding in the back of her ears — because she had just made the best catch of her career.

Despite their appearance, those longlines that trailed from the *Vostok's* stern into the shale-like sea were never designed to catch fish. Instead, they were used for hunting submarines. Embedded into their nearly five miles of high tensile cables, was an advanced, long-range, all-weather, sonar system with both passive and active components, operating in the low-frequency band between 100–500 hertz and capable of perceiving the slightest of sounds from her quarry. And Svetlana's line had just located the U.S. Navy's latest experimental submarine.

The *Vostok* was Russia's most advanced spy ship.

At a length of 354 feet, a beam of 56 feet, and a hull displacement of 5,763 tons, she was similar in size and capabilities to her sister ship, the *Yantar,* which, although widely acknowledged as a spy vessel, operated on the auspice of the Russian Navy's Main Directorate of Underwater Research. While *Yantar* was launched in 2015 and openly applauded as one of the most capable instruments of espionage and counter-espionage, *Vostok,* started her life as a fishing trawler.

Unlike her sister ship, which had been stalked by satellites, submarines, and high altitude unmanned surveillance drones since she was first launched, the *Vostok* had quietly launched a year later at Murmansk. Designed and built to enter the Barents Sea for prolonged fishing expeditions, they had no evidence the vessel's cover had been breached.

Good deception, any Russian operative well knew, took time to develop.

As such, the *Vostok* spent the first two years fishing on the edges of the Arctic Circle away from the rest of the world, while all eyes on Earth tracked the *Yantar* as she performed low-level espionage and counter-espionage missions. At times, *Yantar* followed fictional submarine cables, and zigzagged for no reason other than to distract the world's surveillance machines, while the *Vostok* prepared to perform the most clandestine and vital spy operations for the Russian Navy.

Svetlana Dyatlova's career had just taken a giant leap.

Three weeks ago, Svetlana had broken an encrypted transmission from what appeared to be a U.S. experimental nuclear submarine, named *Omega Deep*. The breakthrough meant they now knew the exact location of the next surfacing for its next set of communications. Despite being a fairly low-ranking recruit, she was flown to the high-tech spy vessel, *Vostok*.

This was what Svetlana was born for.

Everything in her life had been leading up to this single event.

Her father had been a senior Russian Intelligence Officer back when it was still the Komitet Gosudarstvennoy Bezopasnosti — AKA, KGB. After the dissolution of the USSR, the KGB was split into the Federal Security Service and the Foreign Intelligence Service of the Russian Federation. He moved into Foreign Intelligence, and when he got too old for that, he moved into education at *The Institute* in Moscow until his retirement ten years ago. Svetlana, as a baby growing up in the Mikhail Gorbachev-era Soviet Union, had watched her country go through many changes.

It was because of her father that she was drawn into the field of intelligence. For his part, her father never intended her to become a spy, but none the less that's what happened. As she was growing up, Svetlana had watched with fascination, impressed by the respect her father commanded. The fact his deference was founded on fear didn't bother her in the least.

When she graduated from Lomonosov Moscow State University with an arts degree, majoring in cryptography and foreign affairs, it was only natural for her to follow her father's footsteps into foreign intelligence. There she excelled in every aspect from code-breaking to foreign affairs, languages, through to covert operations, athleticism, and fieldwork.

Her father had been somewhat of a legend around *The Institute*. One would have thought it might have changed the way her trainers treated her. As it was, it had — but not in the way she might have hoped. Instead, she had a target on her back as someone who didn't belong, and could never measure up to her father's ability.

Her father would have been proud of her effort today — if he was still alive.

Svetlana was positioned in the dark bowels of the hull where the cold fish storage would have been had the ship been a fishing trawler. Instead, it was the elite ship's command center. Dozens of complex instruments covered the walls, an array of technology included long and short-range listening devices, radar, sonar, and satellite hacking equipment.

Lost in thought, Svetlana remained quiet for awhile. Her eyes darted from monitor to monitor. Like a member of the audience at a magic show, she felt something was being mysteriously concealed from her. It was a simple ruse, nothing more. But until she spotted it, she might as well admit her opponent had won.

And in this case, her opponent was the U.S. Navy.

It was hard to believe she'd let that happen.

The *Vostok's* commander, Kirill, climbed down the steep set of stairs, moving fast, breathing hard. She knew exactly why he'd raced down to the command center. Svetlana looked up, careful not to react when she saw his face. It was not a brutal countenance, but when angry he could be frightening.

Kirill was ill-equipped for and unused to failure. She had no intention of becoming his casualty in this battle, a punching bag for his fury.

Her commander's eyes were piercing, "Well, what have you found?"

"Nothing, sir." She turned her palms skyward. "I don't have anything that can scientifically explain it."

He swallowed. "Nothing?"

"Not a thing. It's like the damned submarine just vanished."

"That's impossible. At least we know it definitely didn't disappear." He closed his eyes and bit his lower lip. She could see his mind ticking over all the possibilities like a computer. His lips settled into a sly, somewhat cunning smile. "Are we certain it was there to begin with?"

Her brows drew down. For an alarming moment, the possibility occurred to her that he was suggesting it was best to report that there was no sub. "You saw it as well as I did, sir."

"Yes. But now I'm trying to look at this from a different angle."

"A different angle, sir?"

"If a magician wanted to use sleight of hand to remove a 7900-ton submarine, or in this case, make him think it was moved, wouldn't he have more easily placed something else in front of us to begin with?"

She cocked an incredulous eyebrow. "You think the submarine was a fake?"

"Don't you?" he countered.

"Absolutely not," she said emphatically but held her breath as she waited to see how her CO would take the news.

"How certain are you that what just happened was real?"

"I'd swear on my life that it wasn't counterfeit."

"You saw it." His eyes lit up suddenly, his imagination caught by fantasy instead of science. "The entire submarine disappeared!"

"And yet it didn't. I'll show you." She turned to a digital recording of the footage taken from the event, moved her mouse, clicked through each image, frame by frame. "Look at this, here's the entire submarine in this frame, and now it just disappears. If it were a magic trick — even a very good one involving a holographic projection or a cardboard cutout of a submarine — it would be impossible to change it in a single frame."

Standing with deference, she studied her commander's face. It was hard and stern, with a firm-set, thin-lipped mouth, and a coldly intolerant eye. She was relieved that she saw no sign of rage.

"All right," he said.

"Sir?"

"I believe you. If you can't work out how they've done it, or what has even happened, then the most logical explanation is that they've developed a concealing technology we're decades from reproducing."

She said, "I'm sorry, sir."

He stood up and shook his head. "Not your fault."

"Would you like to watch it again?" she asked.

He nodded, without taking his eyes off the screen.

She pressed play. Her lips curled into an incredulous grin.

There it was. The stars and stripes of the American flag. Nothing tremendously spectacular about such a thing proudly displayed off the sail tower of an enemy submarine. Only, in this case, it wasn't attached to anything at all. Its edges luffed in the passive wind, just shy of twelve feet above the water, as though it was being mysteriously pulled by some invisible force at six knots.

But no submarine was visible.

If this was where the video ended, she might have assumed that the entire thing was nothing more than a clever ruse or a magic trick done by strings—albeit a very good one.

She clicked pause.

Commander Kirill stared at the image. "How are they doing it?"

She cocked a well-trimmed eyebrow. "You know how they're doing it."

"Yes, but we were told the technology was decades away."

She clicked play.

A submarine's hatch, roughly ten feet above the sea, appeared to materialize out of thin air. A sailor climbed through, and then another—apparently standing on nothing at all. They moved along above the water — before going through the careful process of lowering and then folding the flag away, as though being suspended in space concerned them not at all. With the flag creased into a triangle, the sailors glanced at the calm seawater below their feet.

Svetlana's eyes widened as one of the men's legs and torso disappear, frame by frame, as he descended into oblivion. The process was repeated for the other sailor, and at the very end, he took one last look around, and closed the hatch, leaving nothing but air and seawater in his place.

"Well?" she asked. "What do you think?"

Kirill said, "I think we should have let them have space and concentrate on this technical knowledge instead."

She agreed with him.

Invisibility was the Holy Grail of the military industry, for both its defensive and offensive advantages. But like the grail of the crusades, it seemed far out of reach to mere mortals. Cloaking technology itself was nothing new. It had been around for years. Basically, you take an image with a series of digital cameras on one side of whatever it is you want to hide and display it on the opposite side. Even their own engineers had developed such techniques within the Ministry of Defense. In terms of camouflage, the process was pretty good, but no one had been able to achieve anything like the perfect level of invisibility she'd just witnessed.

The red satellite phone started to ring.

The commander swallowed hard, picked up the phone and answered the call.

Without preamble, he said, "You have my attention."

He listened for a few minutes and then whistled.

"No," the commander said. "The price is fine. Russia will pay. Just deliver us that submarine."

Ω☐Ω

PRESIDENTIAL EMERGENCY OPERATIONS CENTER – WHITE HOUSE, WASHINGTON, D.C.

The PEOC was a blast-resistant bunker, situated deep beneath the East Wing of the White House. During emergency operations, it could be utilized by the president as an operations center capable of withstanding a direct hit by a nuclear weapon. In peacetime, the room was often utilized for training or in this case, its secure video-conferencing capabilities.

Despite being in the middle of one of the most prolonged periods of relative peace throughout the world, the occupants of the PEOC were hard at work, and a tangible tension permeated the room.

The secretary of defense set her jaw firm and breathed deeply. It was a practiced state of serenity, without which, she probably would have resigned her position years ago.

The overhead LED lights had been dimmed, and the video feed transferred to one of the PEOC's six large video monitors which continuously displayed an image of the Norwegian Sea. The water was dark and glossy in the minimal light, like shards of obsidian, as the crest of each wave gently collapsed, leaving the small ripples of whitewater in its wake.

The president stood up from across the table and looked straight at her. "What just happened to our video feed?"

"Nothing, Mr. President," she replied. "It's still in working order."

"Then can you please tell me why in God's name my submarine just disappeared?"

She swallowed, hard. "It looks like they've activated the Omega Cloak, sir."

The president smacked the table with the latest situation report. "I know what it looks like. I thought I made myself quite clear after the British Dreamlifter went down. Surely, it was a dangerous time to test the device? The *Omega Deep* needed to utilize its array of high tech and expensive scouting equipment to locate the plane wreckage, not to continue testing."

"Your directive was clear, Mr. President," she confirmed.

The president's eyes shifted toward Painter, his chairman of the joint chiefs of staff. "And?"

Painter spoke in a confident, measured rate, without hesitation. "We relayed information to Commander Dwight Bower, Mr. President. The mission was to be canceled and the submarine to join the search for the missing 747 Dreamlifter."

The president's eyes narrowed, darting between the secretary of defense and chairman of the joint chiefs of staff, before finally setting angrily on her. "Are you suggesting he misunderstood my order?"

A flash of alarm lit the secretary's intelligent, emerald eyes. "No. I'm afraid we're worried he might have intentionally disobeyed it, sir."

ΩΩΩ

TWO WEEKS LATER

The *Omega Deep* moved slowly through the submerged chasm, like an ancient predator.

Commander Bower examined the bathymetric charts of the seafloor. The *Omega Deep* was currently tracking along a south to southwesterly direction through remnants of an ancient submerged valley. The basin was most likely the remnants of the breakup of the supercontinent Pangea which saw the supercontinent separated and fragmented into multiple continents more than 248 million years ago and the Permian mass extinction, which killed approximately 96 percent of all species on Earth.

The low area of land between higher cliffs was three miles wide and nearly half a mile deep. *Omega Deep* was currently at a depth of 300 feet, leaving a cool 500 feet below her keel. Coming off the main valley was a series of smaller vales, the remnants of tributaries that once flowed into the ancient river system.

Bower had taken the *Omega Deep* here to test her maneuverability in confined spaces with the cloaking device engaged. A rift in the rocky plates three miles wide appeared much smaller when you were threading a submarine of such immense length. Besides, this was the first time any of them had tried the new navigation system.

Traditional submarine navigation systems rely on inertial guidance that keeps track of the ship's motion from a fixed starting point by using gyroscopes, or through active sonar to map their surroundings using echolocation, like a bat. The *Omega Deep* was different. It was fitted with a series of digital video cameras providing real-time footage in a 360-degree arc in all directions around the vessel.

Inside the command center, this live-feed was projected onto a central dome, which allowed the crew inside to view their surroundings. In clear water, it appeared more like looking out a glass window.

At this depth, with limited ambient light, and poor visibility, the system used LIDAR — Light Detection and Ranging — as well as infrared night vision — the same sort of technology used by ground soldiers equipped with night vision goggles. Basically, a set of lights projected infrared light, so that even in pitch dark, the sensors could then detect their surroundings.

If needed, immensely high-powered LED lights were capable of illuminating the darkest abyss. Again, because most traditional submarines, particularly Navy submarines, don't have any windows, producing light didn't reveal their position to other predator submersibles.

Belinda Callaghan, one of his junior sonar technicians, said, "Sir, we have a contact approaching from 47 degrees north-northwest."

Commander Bower felt a slight prickle in the hairs on the back of his neck. They were more than five hundred miles from any major land sources. "What have we got?"

"A submersible. Very small. No more than ten to fifteen feet in length. Shaped more like a miniature plane, flying underwater at a speed of twelve knots, sir."

"Is it approaching from above the valley or within?"

"Within, sir."

"Range?" Commander Bower asked.

"Three miles and closing," she said.

"That's close," he observed, in a tone of displeasure. In the middle of a shipping lane, with hundreds of sounds, he could have forgiven her for not noticing it before now, but where they were, the high-pitched whine of the submersible's twin engines should have been spotted immediately. "Where's its surface ship?"

"There isn't one, sir."

"Impossible." Bower glanced at the sonar operator's monitor. "A small submersible like that needs a mothership out here. There's no way it would have the range to make the journey by itself. Locate the mothership."

Callaghan stood her ground. "There isn't one, sir. The closest ship is the Antarctic Solace — and she's nearly 200 miles away."

That jolted Bower. "All right. If there's no ship nearby, the mini-sub is attached to something. That means there's another submarine prowling around here."

"I'm on it, sir," she confirmed, adjusting her sonar monitoring to target the small telltale signs of a large submarine running silent.

"Pilot, bring us to a full stop," Bower commanded. "No reason to risk someone picking up our wake."

The XO's deep-set eyes were hooded with concern. "Should we increase our depth and put some more room beneath our keel just to be on the safe side?"

Bower turned to Callaghan. "What depth are you tracking the

submersible at?"

She replied without hesitation. "Four hundred feet, sir."

Bower nodded. "All right Mr. Halifax. That's a hundred feet to spare. I'm happy to stay at this depth and let the sub pass beneath our keel." Meeting his XO's eyes, and valuing the man's input, he asked, "What do you think?"

"Agreed, sir. Let's sit it out and see what she does."

"Very good." Bower turned to the pilot and copilot. "Pilot, maintain all, stop."

"Maintaining all, stop, sir."

All eyes within the command center watched the large digital monitor, which displayed a synchronized image of the sonar screen. It counted down the distance of the approaching submersible. At first, it registered miles.

As it came closer, it recorded feet.

Despite the hull's soundproofing, the crew became naturally silent.

Commander Bower smiled. "It's all right, everyone. The *Omega Deep* was built for this. There's no reason to remain silent. Nothing you can say inside the hull will be picked up outside." Then, as if to prove a point, he shouted, "Woohoo!"

The sound echoed throughout the submarine.

No one followed suit.

And soon the command center was completely silent once more, the shallow breaths of the men and women who served were the only sounds that remained.

A slow smile curled Bower's lips. Once a submariner, always a submariner. The need to run silent was etched deep in every submariner's psyche.

Callaghan broke the silence. "Sir, it should be in visual range any second now."

"Thank you," he acknowledged.

Bower turned his gaze toward the downward-facing dome

beneath the Perspex flooring. Like the one above his head which showed the area above, this one showed a 360-degree half-sphere vision of the area below the keel.

Twin bright lights appeared in the speckled darkness below.

At that distance, it could have been nothing more than a strange sea-creature of the deep, like an anglerfish—you know the type that holds a light above their head?—but as the range diminished, the lights increased, revealing the slightest shape of an underwater vehicle.

Commander Bower said, "Lieutenant Callaghan, can you please play any external sound received by the hydrophone on the overhead speakers."

Callaghan adjusted her control and removed her headset. "Yes, sir."

The gentle electric whine of twin thrusters filled the command center. Bower stared at the light. From a hundred feet, it was impossible to make out the shape of the submersible, but he recognized the whine of the electric motors—although he didn't quite believe his ears.

Bower turned to his left. "Navigation, can you please get me a visual of that sub using LIDAR?"

"Yes, sir."

A moment later, a clear image of the submersible came up on one of the overhead display screens. The submersible's exact dimensions were: 20 feet of length, beam 14 feet—with a 7-foot wingspan—and a height of 5 feet. There were two glass bubble domes positioned forward and aft of each other, where a single pilot and copilot were housed. The overall shape of the submersible was sleek, like a sports-car, or more accurately, a sports underwater airplane, with narrow wings and a V-shaped tail-wing. The wings even had two large thrusters fixed, one to each wing, like jet-engines on an aircraft.

It was the sort of toy a billionaire would purchase.

Commander Bower breathed out, consciously feeling any

tension that had developed slip away. A broad grin pierced his otherwise stern face. "My goodness, what the hell is a lone Orcasub doing all the way out here?"

The XO asked, "An Orcasub, sir?"

Commander Bower nodded. "It's basically what it looks like. A two-person, flying submersible. It's built by Nuytco Research—the same people who build our atmospheric dive suits. Look at that thing. It's the ultimate luxury item for a billionaire. They are small enough to be easily lifted off the deck of a pleasure yacht."

The XO's eyebrows narrowed. "Which begs the question, where's the pleasure yacht?"

Bower turned to face his junior sonar operator. "Lieutenant Callaghan, any sign of another submarine or a ship?"

"Nothing."

Commander Bower turned to his XO and shrugged. "How about we follow it and find out?"

"Yes, sir," The XO replied expressionlessly.

The CO was not known for reckless or fickle behavior. It was for this very reason that the XO was surprised to receive the order to pursue the unidentified submersible. It appeared that the old man's curiosity had finally gotten the better of him.

No one aboard the *Omega Deep* could have guessed that they might end up paying for his decision with their lives.

Ω**Ω**Ω

The promotion had thrilled Belinda Callaghan, Sonar Technician, Second Class. With it, came a position on the highly secret, experimental, *Virginia* class block VII nuclear attack submarine, *Omega Deep.*

Everything about her experience on board the *Omega Deep* had exceeded her expectations. She sat at her console, manning the large-aperture, bow-mounted sonar array. A state-of-the-art set of devices, it could glean the faintest of sonar impressions from the ocean near and far.

This was her second posting, but the first assignment to a new asset. Her exceptional results at submarine "A" School in Groton, Connecticut, had seen her fast-tracked on board the North Carolina when natural attrition yielded an STS—Sonar Technician Submarine.

During that tenure, she detected and correctly identified a Chinese Type 094 submarine in the South China Sea at a distance of 18,000 feet. She earned herself a founding position on the *Omega Deep* right then and there. Captain Bower took careful note of her talents, and when the time came, he chose her.

She knew that sonar was an art. A good sonar technician must be dedicated to that art. They must think, dream and live sonar all day, every day while on board. Listening to that feed and reading the screen takes a nuanced approach because it's the subtleties that make the sonar *image.*

Callaghan's exceptional attention to detail and her methodical approach made her successful, and her dedication to continuous training made her competitive to a point. Her fellow techs knew they would one day be under her command—she could out-chart, and out-plot any of them with the roughest of data. She wanted to be the Navy's first female Sonar Chief, and anybody that worked alongside her figured out pretty quickly she had the tenacity to get there.

All she needed was the chance to prove herself.

Right now, she'd been given that chance.

The CO had asked her, specifically, to search for the Orcasub's mothership or submarine, and she was determined to find it.

Belinda Callaghan made a digital recording of the Orcasub's soundwave. Like fingerprints, these could be used to identify an individual ship or submarine from any others in the water. She adjusted the computer system settings to remove all sounds associated with that submersible. In doing so, it allowed her to concentrate on her search for a second vessel.

Belinda felt the *Omega Deep* change direction, as her CO ordered the pilots to set a course to follow the strange yellow Orcasub. She placed slightly more pressure on her right foot, as a means of stabilizing herself. Mentally, she detached herself from the submarine's movement and from attempting to gain a visual. Instead, she focused on her sonar screen, and let her ears search for any abnormal sounds hidden within the noise of the deep, which constantly bombarded her headphones.

It was a little over thirty minutes before she heard it.

The anomaly started out like a tiny smudge on her screen, and the sound she heard was unlike any other she could place. Her entire body went rigid like stone as she adjusted the volume on the feed and scoured the image for another trace of it.

There it was again!

She allowed herself a thin-lipped smile.

Tiny, infinitesimal—but definitely there. The image reflected a skinny worm for a fleeting moment, and then it was gone.

Was it man-made or natural?

Belinda closed her eyes and listened. She made the conscious effort to control her breathing and slow her heart rate. With everything amplified in her headphones, it was easy to end up listening to the sound of her breaths, and her heart beat instead of what was out there.

She opened her eyes and frowned. Because what was out there, had stopped. Scrolling back to her original recording of the sound's waveform, she replayed the alien sound.

What were you?

When you first start out as a sonar technician and put the hydrophone headphones on, all you hear is a discombobulated world of more than a thousand marine sounds, both artificial and natural. But as you progress through your training, it becomes easy to differentiate between the artificial sounds of a submarine or the natural sounds of marine-life. Soon, you can train your ears to differentiate between individual marine life sounds and artificial sounds. After more than three thousand hours at the sonar station, it was unusual to find anything completely alien to her ears.

She shook her head. Frustrated, she continued to search for the strange sound and the second submarine.

Then she heard the alien sound again.

She smiled.

You've come back, have you?

This time she was certain it was artificial.

It was man-made, it must have been. No animal sounds like that. She dithered.

Is it man-made?

Do I interrupt the commander, yet?

She waited. Silent as stone and motionless. She checked the log, four minutes passed, and still, she waited. Nothing. She cursed herself. She tried to breathe silently and strained to listen over the sound of the blood slamming in her eardrums. She slowed her breathing, in a technique she'd picked up in yoga as a means of slowing her heart rate, reducing her blood pressure, and being more in the present.

Then there it was. Unmistakable. Louder this time.

She turned to the tech next to her just as he said it. "Did you get that?"

"What is that?" she asked, excited now.

"I've no idea," he replied. "but we'd better tell the Chief."

"I'll start plotting it," Belinda said, hopeful of an opportunity to prove herself again.

Callaghan squelched the controls on her sonar station to hone in on the heading given by the mysterious sound. The monitor she primarily used was a computer-generated visual representation of the soundtrack on the feed from the sensors. It produced a three-dimensional representation similar to modern radar.

Alternatively, she could switch to an old-fashioned *waterfall* type screen, which graphed a horizontal measure of bearing, against a vertical increment of frequency. It was this type of device that she had trained on originally, and it was this one she fell back on when exploring the murky depths that the computer algorithms couldn't diagnose.

The signal she searched was shallow. Very shallow. Which made it harder to detect and distinguish between the other sounds.

To a sonar technician, depth is a friend. The deeper the signal, the less likely it is to be polluted by interference caused by sea life or debris. If you're lucky, the sound might travel through a *deep sound channel*—the perfect conditions for sound propagation.

In this case, the sound was in shallow water. Possibly even a hundred feet. The sound image was difficult to make out because the wavelength was being bounced around through the underwater valley through which they were currently traveling.

She let her eyes drift along in time with the leading edge of the waterfall display. She pushed the gain all the way to the maximum. Static and mechanical noise from the ship built a cacophony of baseline noise in her headphones. Winding it back just a touch, she found the noise again—this time with a heading, and with a matching slug shape on the waterfall readout. A rush of adrenaline gushed from her kidneys straight down her spine—shooting into her gut like white-hot fire.

Oh my God! It's a submarine!

She hit the print detail button and continued scrambling her gear to get a precise reading. As it printed, the Chief Sonar operator reached over and tore off the glossy paper from beside her. With an encouraging pat on the shoulder, he indicated he was taking it to the commander, who was as yet unaware of the situation.

The heading was 225 degrees southwest, at a distance of approximately 7,000 feet. It was coming together for her. She was on this thing.

She took a deep breath to steady herself.

Focus.

Whose is it?

She immediately knew what she was listening to. She set the audio scanner to 60 Hz and listened, waiting. A vessel runs its electronics on alternating current at a set frequency, measured in Hertz. If the electronics on that ship become waterlogged, are improperly mounted against the hull, or damaged they emit the sound of that particular operating current into the ocean.

Ships the world over use a standardized current for their electronics — 50 Hz. There was, however, one nation that used a different current for their entire fleet of submarines run on a 60 Hz system.

The United States.

Belinda's heart sank. She was looking at a stricken United States submarine. Stranded deep in the ocean and most probably damaged. Her throat tightened, and the moisture evaporated from her mouth. She stared at the worm which was now perfectly focused on her monitor.

ΩΩΩ

Commander Bower stared at the two enlarged images of the Orcasub pilot and copilot. Their faces were distorted by the glass dome, but he hoped someone from one of the digital intelligence teams, back stateside, might be able to improve the image and then identify them.

He put the two images back down next to the navigation table and turned his focus to the downward-facing digital dome.

His eyes swept the surreal environment beneath the *Omega Deep,* taking in the deep trench, sharp and vertical edges of the sea valley, and finally fixing on the glowing light of the Orcasub. It was moving at a spritely twelve knots — its two occupants, apparently unaware of the massive submarine's overhead pursuit.

Behind the visual dome, the *Omega Deep's* pilot and copilot maintained a course just fifty feet behind and twenty feet above the Orcasub. The water was crystal clear, and the light from the Orcasub was plentiful enough to navigate by.

They followed the Orcasub, matching it as it banked to the right and rose to a hundred and fifty feet in order to enter a smaller tributary valley.

The pilot said, "Requesting approval to follow, sir?"

To the navigation officer, Bower asked, "Does LIDAR mapping confirm there's enough room to pursue?"

The navigation officer nodded. "The valley is two hundred feet wide and peaks at a depth of fifty feet. If we run out of room, we can ascend and maintain clearance below our keel."

Bower firmly set his jaw, his brown eyes focused. "All right. Pilot, you have approval to follow them in." Then, turning to the navigation officer, said, "Mr. Browning, I'm counting on you to ensure we maintain a safe distance from the seascape. The last thing I want to do is explain to Uncle Sam why I just damaged his 30-billion-dollar piece of hardware."

"Understood, sir."

The *Omega Deep* climbed as it trailed the Orcasub into the narrower underwater tributary. The valley's bottom rose rapidly. While the massive *Omega Deep* followed, keeping near the top of the valley, the Orcasub trailed along the ancient river.

Unexpectedly, in sudden, rapid ascent, it climbed at a near-vertical angle. Like a modern fighter jet in a balls-out, full effort blast, it powered into what appeared to be an ancient waterfall.

Commander Bower grinned as they pursued the yellow sub from a distance. Whoever was at the controls, piloting the Orcasub, knew what they were doing. Not only did they appear to move without hesitation, but they were also following the line of the ancient tributary just above the seabed. It reminded him of an attack helicopter racing below Viet Cong radar along a valley floor.

The *Omega Deep* reached the top of the ancient waterfall.

Despite his hardened appearance, and normally difficult to read countenance, Commander Bower audibly gasped at the sight.

His eyes raked the unreal seascape below.

The ancient river opened up to a shallow underwater tabletop, covered in vivid and impressive coral gardens. It was a unique tropical playground that didn't belong anywhere near where they were. Tropical fish filled the place, swimming in and out through the coral reef, which was awash with color. Hues of red and orange glowed brightly among the shifting tapestry of mustard, greens, blues, reds, and browns. A spectacular vista of coral sponges, mollusks, giant manta rays, sea turtles, and giant clams filled his vision.

Bower stared at the yellow Orcasub as a pod of dolphins raced beside it, swimming upside and by its side.

Grinning and speaking to no one in particular, he said, "Is it just me or does it look like we just entered a tropical coral reef?"

"Sure," his XO replied. "But I've never heard of a coral reef so far from the tropics before."

"Agreed," Bower replied. "Whatever underwater landmass we've come across, it's not on any maritime maps. Yeah, the geologists, marine biologists, and archeologists are going to have a field day over this when we report back."

The depth of the tabletop was roughly fifty feet, with a narrow chasm through which the Orcasub still raced, at a depth of one hundred feet.

Under the direction of Commander Bower, the pilots positioned the *Omega Deep* at a depth of forty feet. The chasm was wide enough for them to descend deeper, but he wasn't taking any chances of clipping the sharp coral sides of the valley.

Commander Bower said, "Did you know that coral reefs are some of the most diverse ecosystems on Earth. They occupy less than 0.1 percent of the world's ocean surface, but provide habitat for at least 25 percent of all marine species?"

The crew, used to his erudite lectures, called him the "Sea Professor," but never to his face.

His XO obligingly replied, "That's fascinating, sir. Can you tell us more?"

Bower smiled. He had a reputation for being a scholarly bore at times, and he didn't care. One thing he'd learned after forty years at sea, was that being CO had certain perks. This was one of them. His crew was a captive audience when he wanted to share his knowledge. And why shouldn't he educate them in marine biology? They'd joined the Navy to see the world. He was damned sure his crew was going to really see the world, not just watch it go by.

"Did you know most of the coral reefs around the world were formed during the last glacial period when melting ice caused the sea level to rise and flood the continental shelves? This means that most modern coral reefs are less than 10,000 years old. As communities established themselves on the shelves, the reefs grew upward, pacing rising sea levels. Reefs that rose too slowly could become drowned reefs. They are covered by so much water that there was insufficient light."

The XO, happy to play the game, said, "And yet there appears to be plentiful coral life here, at a depth of 100 feet?"

"Well spotted, Mr. Halifax." Bower nodded. "Sometimes coral reefs are found in deep sea, away from continental shelves, around oceanic islands and atolls. You'll find the vast majority of these islands are volcanic in origin. The few exceptions have tectonic origins where plate movements have lifted the deep ocean floor on the surface. But even in those conditions, the coral never survives as deep as 100 feet, which is why a lot of scientists are going to be pretty excited by what we've found here today."

His XO said, "Not what we found, sir. The owners of that private submarine appear to have known about it."

"Indeed, Mr. Halifax."

In the crystal-clear waters, through which crepuscular rays reached the seabed, the Orcasub became perfectly visible.

Bower squinted as he examined the now clearly visible faces of the pilot and copilot, encapsulated in their first-class seats on board the Orcasub as it flew quietly through the secret tropical rainforest.

The commander glanced around the Command Center. "Can anyone tell me what causes the unusual clarity of tropical waters?"

Mr. Browning, his navigator, answered first. "Tropical waters contain few nutrients. Thus, no drifting plankton, which equates to clear water visibility."

Bower nodded, continuing his lecture on marine biology. "They call it *Darwin's Paradox*. How can so much marine life flourish in such nutrient-poor conditions?"

Macintyre, the copilot on shift—a gentleman in his twenties from Wyoming who was on his second year out from receiving his coveted submariner Dolphins—dutifully asked, "What's the answer, sir?"

Bower shrugged. "I've no idea."

The crew laughed at his honesty.

There seemed to be an uncanny air of relaxed joviality on board. And why shouldn't there be? The world's most advanced predator was stalking a billionaire's private sports submersible and had now located an ancient marine wonderland in the most unlikely of places.

Up ahead, the Orcasub headed to the end of the chasm, where it ran straight inside the mouth of a large underground chamber, roughly twenty feet high by thirty feet wide. Bower scanned the seascape for signs of where the submersible might have come out. There were none. The cave formed out of the mouth of a small rocky outcrop on the coral tabletop, like a monolith, with no sign of any place in which the Orcasub might disappear.

Bower said, "Pilot, all stop."

"All stop, sir," the pilot confirmed.

The command center remained silent while they waited patiently for the small sub to come out again, which it didn't.

"What the hell is it doing in there?" Commander Bower asked.

"It could be trapped, sir," the XO suggested. "You know, it's gone inside only to get its multiple thrusters snagged on something inside."

"I doubt it. You watched the pilot. He knew how to fly. Someone like that didn't enter a cave on a whim. He knew what was in there. No way he was going to get trapped."

The XO nodded. It was a valid point. "Or, it could be waiting?"

Bower's eyebrows narrowed. "For what?"

"For us to leave it alone."

Commander Bower met him with flat eyes. "Are you kidding me?"

The XO shrugged. "They might have spotted us. It's possible."

"How?" Bower asked. "With the *blackbody* coated hull, it should be impossible for the most advanced acoustic systems in the world to locate us, let alone some billionaire's private submersible sports craft."

The XO shrugged again. "I'm just suggesting the possibility, sir."

Commander Bower's vision narrowed, fixed upon that single image of the mouth of the cave. The pod of dolphins leisurely raced out again, as though bored by what they'd discovered inside. The coral, which surrounded the opening was a florid mixture of rainbow hues and tropical fish.

He ran the palms of his hands through his thick hair.

For a moment he contemplated the idea of sending a team of Navy SEALs out the lockout locker in dive gear to investigate.

Or he could just wait the Orcasub out. The *Omega Deep* was a nuclear sub with a near infinite endurance and a little under 90 days' food supplies. The Orcasub had less than 80 minutes dive time. He could wait. But something was bothering him.

What if Halifax was right? What if the pilots of the private submersible had spotted them?

It would mean that nearly 30 billion dollars of research grants had been wasted. By him.

A moment later, he forgot about the problem, because Sonar Technician Callaghan interrupted his thoughts. "Sir, I've got a contact for a second submarine. It's laying on the seafloor with a cracked hull."

"How close?"

"Four thousand feet. At a course of 220 degrees." Lieutenant Callaghan's face had paled. She swallowed, hard. "And, sir, it's American."

ΩΩΩ

Belinda held her breath, waiting for the commander's response.

Despite the implications of a sunken U.S. submarine, Commander Bower moved with a kind of considered grace, calm and contained. He leaned in next to the young STS, with his left hand on the console beside her, and his right on the back of her chair. He took a deep breath in and out and nodded his head in confirmation. He knew exactly what he was looking at.

He tapped the screen lightly with his index finger where the readout showed "60HZ," and asked, "What depth do you have it at?"

"Hard to say for certain, sir."

"Hazard an educated guess?"

"It could be somewhere between one and three hundred feet."

He frowned. "Nothing more accurate than that?"

"No."

"What's causing the difficulty?"

Despite the circumstances, she smiled. He hadn't asked her why she couldn't do it. "We're not getting a direct line of sight from the sound. It's being blocked and bounced around some sort of submerged valley."

"All right. You said it appears to be transmitting a repeated sound?"

"Yes. It's similar to Morse Code, but I can't decipher it."

"Really?" The CO was already reaching for a second headset. "Can I hear it, please?"

She plugged the second set of headset leads into her hydrophone audio output. "You're good to go, sir."

She watched as he listened to the playback of the alien sound.

His focus was shifting fractionally in and out, his brows rising and falling a little, the shape of his mouth always changing, as if he was constantly thinking. He studied the sonar screen and listened, simultaneously taking everything in, as though there was a computer behind his eyes, running at full speed.

This was another reason the crew sometimes called him *the Professor*.

Every member of a submarine crew, of any rank, knew a little about every single station on board. It was set up so that in battle, particularly in the event of a hull breach, you never knew where people would end up. It was vital that people knew how to perform tasks and operate in roles they were not normally commissioned to work. This went double fold for a commander of a U.S. submarine, who needed to demonstrate leadership at every level of the ship.

The human ear of a healthy young person can hear at a range between 20 and 20,000 Hertz, but by the time a person reaches forty, their high-frequency range diminishes to below 12,000 Hertz. Professor or not, it seemed impossible to her, that the CO could discern and identify the sound that appeared alien to her well-attuned ear.

The CO bit his lower lip and removed the headset, handing it back to her. The lines in his face seemed to deepen and darken in the bare light. He took his time before he spoke. "I've heard that sound before…"

She cocked a well-plucked eyebrow. "Really?"

"Yeah. You were right. It's similar to Morse Code but different. In fact, it is Morse Code after its been broken down using a cipher. The code is relatively simple. It had to be. You see, it was designed to be used by senior submarine officers, ranked XO and above, as a means of top-secret communication during an emergency."

"Do you know what it says, sir?"

Commander Bower sighed heavily. "It says, we've been sunk by hostiles. Have tried to escape. Unable to reach surface due to attackers."

ΩΩΩ

Commander Bower was not known for reckless or fickle behavior.

Nor had he reached such a height in the U.S. Navy's command structure by being careless. He understood the only fight you were ever certain to win was the one you didn't enter. He would have never needlessly endangered his crew and the 30-billion-dollar piece of military hardware under his command. He should have surfaced to make an immediate satellite report to the Pentagon, who would have sent him another two submarines and an aircraft carrier at the least.

But for some reason, one he would never have the time to understand, he made the worst decision of his career.

In another three weeks, he'd complete his initial evaluation of the experimental stealth submarine. It would be his last command and a fitting send off after an exemplary career.

Commander Bower had always followed protocol. Forty-three years in the Navy—nearly thirty of those in Command—and he'd never broken from standard operating procedures…

until today. It could have been because retirement was around the corner. In another four weeks, after the completion of the initial testing of the unique stealth technology and his brainchild, the USS *Omega Deep* would return stateside, marking the end of his final command.

In the back of his mind, all he could hear was the hull number at the end of the encrypted message:

SSN23 — The USS *Jimmy Carter*.

His first command.

Now, he was witnessing her first hand, destroyed at the bottom of the ocean. His submarine. His men and women. If it wasn't for the chance discovery of the *blackbody* material used to construct the USS *Omega Deep,* he too might have been among those lost.

Either way, he made a decision then and there that went against the Navy's protocol. Instead of surfacing to alert his superiors, he gave a very different order, the biggest mistake of his career.

"Pilot. New course, bearing: 220. Full speed." Commander Bower swallowed hard. "Let's come around and see if we can find any survivors."

"Copy, setting a new course. Bearing: 220 degrees, full speed, sir."

"Weapons control," Bower said in a cool and even voice, "I want all available torpedoes ready to fire on my command."

"Understood, sir."

The *Omega Deep* raced toward the stricken American nuclear attack submarine. Inside, the command center was silent. Every member of the crew focused on the task at hand within their respective stations. They were riding near the surface, their keel just twenty feet shy of the massive submerged rocky tabletop.

Commander Bower turned to Lieutenant Callaghan. "Have you found our enemy target yet?"

"No, sir," she replied.

"Keep looking. I know the CO of the *Jimmy Carter* personally. If he and his crew haven't reached the surface in this shallow depth, mark my words, there will be an enemy submarine in these waters preventing him."

"Understood, sir."

To the navigation officer, he said, "Have you got a LIDAR map of the wreck site?"

"It's just coming up now, sir," Browning replied, pointing to an image — similar to a bathymetric map of the seafloor. "The *Jimmy Carter* appears to be at the bottom of this shallow ravine here, at a depth of 100 feet."

"Is there room for the *Omega Deep* to descend to that depth?"

"Yes, but we won't have a lot of room to maneuver if we get into trouble."

"Understood," Bower said. "I think it's fairly safe to say, we're going to encounter trouble."

The *Omega Deep* slowed to a stop directly above the wreck site. Commander Bower stared through the downward facing spherical viewing dome. There, his eyes swept the scene below. A relatively narrow ravine — approximately one hundred feet wide and fifty feet deep — came to a rocky conclusion. The seabed was mostly black sand. Embedded in the middle of that sand were the wrecked remains of the USS *Jimmy Carter*.

Bower felt the bile rise in his throat at the sight, and his face twisted into a mask of incognizant fury. The submarine appeared intact with its keel deep in the sandy seabed.

"Sonar. Anything?" he asked.

"No, sir," she replied. "I've got good visuals up to three miles with no contacts. There's a chance a submarine is hiding inside one of the trenches farther out than that, but right now, we're on our own."

One of the modifications on the Omega Deep compared to traditional attack submarines, was the addition of a lockout trunk above and below the main hull. This allowed for deep sea rescue missions to be carried out if needed by direct connection to the other submarine.

Dwight Bower grinned sardonically. "Pilot, can you see their forward escape hatch?"

"Yes, sir."

"Think you can line up our keel-based lockout locker and make a connection?"

"Yes, sir."

Bower glanced above at the upper viewing half-sphere. There were no boats or submarines in view. "All right. Weapons, let's be ready for any attack."

"Understood, sir."

Ballast control took on some more water, and the *Omega Deep* sank toward the wreck of the *Jimmy Carter*.

The pilot and copilot adeptly maneuvered the bow thrusters until the *Omega Deep* was directly above the stricken submarine.

A Navy SEAL team, positioned within the keel lockout hatch said over the internal radio, "We're not getting a seal. We need to descend a little deeper. Maybe another foot."

Commander Bower nodded at the pilot. "All right, take us down gently."

"Copy that, sir."

The *Omega Deep* dropped another half a foot.

Bower said, "SEAL team, report?"

"No good, sir. We're still not making contact. We're going to have to come down lower."

"All right, will do." Bower stared at the downfacing viewing sphere. Their keel was so close to the damned submarine—he felt he could reach out and touch it through the sphere. "All right, pilot. Nice and easy, it's time to bump shoulders."

The pilot took the *Omega Deep* gently downward.

Commander Bower's eyes widened as they appeared to continue their descent. He held his breath and braced for the inevitable collision. His eyes focused on the viewing sphere below.

But there was no collision.

Instead, the *Omega Deep* kept descending.

It passed right through the wreck of the USS *Jimmy Carter*.

They descended through a layer of sediment like fog and kept sinking.

Commander Bower was the first to regain his composure. "Ballast, take us up."

"I'm trying, sir, but the controls aren't responding."

Even as Commander Bower saw what had happened with his own eyes, he didn't believe it could be real.

"Emergency ballast blow!" he ordered.

The navigation's officer was the closest to it. He pulled the emergency main ballast blow lever.

No effect.

The *Omega Deep* crashed into the soft seabed below.

Bower searched their new environment. But, both the upper and lower viewing half-spheres were a complete whiteout in the murky gray silt.

"Sonar, give me one ping—I want to know exactly what's coming for us!"

"Copy, sir," Lieutenant Callaghan said. "One ping."

The active sonar made an audible ping.

Commander Bower's eyes were fixed in disbelief at the sonar screen as a clear outline of the surrounding seabed right through to the edge of the submerged ravine rapidly came into view. The seabed was clear, but more than a hundred small shapes approached. They were small. Much too small and plentiful to be other submarines. They were moving in a direct line toward his ship. Much too direct to be fish or any other marine life.

The commander gritted his teeth and knew in an instant that he'd been caught by one of the cleverest, yet simple ruses in the book. He oscillated between anger and acceptance, believing that he could muscle the *Omega Deep* out of her predicament or, at the very least, contain the fallout.

Commander Bower gripped the onboard microphone and gave the order he'd never expected to give as a submarine commander. "Prepare to repel boarders!"

CHAPTER ONE

———Ω———

BARENTS SEA–120 MILES NORTH OF NORWAY–PRESENT DAY

THE *MARIA HELENA* SWAYED HEAVILY under the large swell of the Barents Sea, some hundred and twenty miles above Norway. This close to the Arctic Circle, the seas were rarely gentle, and even if they were, Sam Reilly wouldn't have waited any longer. There simply wasn't enough time to do so. Every day they lost was another day where they were guessing what caused the bizarre crash of the Boeing 747 Dreamlifter. Another day of playing Russian roulette with some thirty thousand commercial jets in service that may have the same critical fault with the aircraft's software.

No one knew for certain if it was a one-off fault or the outcome of a coordinated cyber-attack. If it was intentional, someone had achieved the extraordinary and compromised the highly-secure computer controlling the most advanced and reliable flight and navigation system on board any modern jetliner, causing it to crash into the sea. Thrumming in the back of his head was the same terrible fear.

Next time, it might not be a cargo carrier.

Sea spray lashed the aft deck. It would be a miracle if they didn't lose their latched-down Sea King helicopter to any number of the tremendous waves. Sam wore heavy wet weather gear to defy the near-freezing environment and stood outside the pilothouse door, facing aft. He watched as another wave lashed across the deck and glanced up at Veyron who was manning the purpose-built crane fitted to the aft deck.

He met Veyron's eyes, planted his palms upward and mouthed the words, "What the hell's taking him so long?"

Veyron simply shrugged.

It was out of his control and most likely out of all of their control. It should have been ready to bring up nearly twenty minutes ago. However, these things seldom worked as smoothly or simply as expected. Sam pulled the hood of his rain jacket tight so that it cradled his face. His cold blue eyes watched as another wave broached the deck. The icy spray stung his unshaven face. He waited for the water to dissipate over the sides, as the deck shifted more than thirty degrees in either direction—and then fought his way across the aft deck to the crane's small pilothouse.

He climbed inside and closed the door. "Well, Veyron... what's the problem?"

"I don't know..." Veyron slouched in his chair, his face set with indifference, enjoying the heated comfort of his station. "Tom's having trouble fitting the cradle."

"All right. Did he give you an ETA?"

Veyron shook his head. "All he said was he'd let me know the second it was ready."

"All right... let me know as soon as you get word it's on its way up."

"Sure will, boss."

Sam waited for the crest of two waves to crash against the *Maria Helena*. She rode them surprisingly well, and he took the opportunity to climb out and return to the ship's main pilothouse to check on Matthew.

He quickly climbed up the three sets of internal stairs, removed his wet weather gear and entered the bridge. His skipper, Matthew wore a blue Hawaiian shirt and had the temperature cranked up on its highest setting so that it made Sam feel like he'd just stepped straight out of the arctic freeze into the tropics.

Matthew was standing up, steering the *Maria Helena* manually. Despite the phenomenal advancements in autopilot technologies, nothing could beat the careful and studied manipulation of a ship through a rough sea like an expert skipper. Almost working as a sixth sense, the man had developed an uncanny ability to predict the movements of the swell and where each wave would strike his vessel.

Sam asked, "How's she riding out the swell?"

"She's holding together." Matthew kept his eyes focused on the upcoming wave. "I'd rather not keep her here a minute longer than I have to. Any news about when Tom and Genevieve are going to be finished?"

"No."

"They're taking their time," his eyebrows narrowed a touch. "Do you think they realize what the weather's like up here?"

Sam nodded. "I know. I just checked with Veyron. They're having some problem with the cradle."

"Right." Matthew adjusted the wheel to take a giant wave on at a slight angle. "You might want to tell Tom if he doesn't have it sorted soon we might need to drop the cable and wait until the weather eases."

Sam pursed his lips slightly. "You know we can't do that."

Matthew sighed. "And we can't stay here being bombarded by the waves indefinitely, either."

Sam said, "Just a little while longer. There's too much at stake to give up now, and you know as well as I do that it might be a number of weeks until the sea gives anyone any respite."

"I'll do my best."

Sam slipped into his wet weather gear again and returned downstairs. He stepped outside and faced the aft deck once again. The series of cables riding over the end of the crane was taut. His heart raced, and he found himself holding his breath for a brief moment. *Had Tom and Genevieve managed to get the cradle fitted and attached to the lift cable?* He stared at the cable, and a moment later he heard the whine of the electric winch start to turn—and the lift cable started to move.

On the side wall at the back of the pilothouse the ship-to-ship phone rang.

He picked it up on the first ring. "Tell me the news?"

"We're in business," Veyron confirmed.

"I'll let Matthew know."

Sam flicked the ship-to-ship call to the bridge. "Matthew, we're finally bringing her up."

"Great. I'll reduce throttle and try and keep her steady in position, but you'll have to let me know if I start to drag backward."

"Okay, I'm on it."

Sam watched as the wet cable retreated from the sea and ran across the long arm of the crane and smoothly through a series of pulleys and neatly around its holding drum. He breathed easily. The hardest part of the job was now complete. Any second now the massive aft tail of the Boeing 747 Dreamlifter would open, and then Tom would make short work of locating the aircraft's black box.

The phone at the wall behind him started to ring. Not the ship-to-ship one, but the satellite phone that could send and receive information anywhere in the world. Sam let it keep ringing. He had a fair idea who wanted to reach him and what it was about. He took a deep breath and sighed. The secretary of defense would have to wait until he had answers to give her.

She would just have to wait.

The phone kept ringing.

Elise opened the door. "Sam?"

"Yeah?"

"There's a gentleman from Phoenix Shipping after you," she said.

He could barely hear her through the external noise of the electric cable motor and the cantankerous seas.

"Who?" Sam asked.

"Gene Cutting," she shouted above the roar of the wind and sea.

Sam glanced at her. He searched his memory for the name but came up empty.

Elise sighed. "Says he works for a shipping company… but not in shipping though. Something about insurance."

"I've never heard of him."

She persisted. "Says he needs you to go over a recent shipping accident. Something about an expert opinion for the insurance companies?"

Sam had been called in as an expert to give his opinion to various maritime disasters and events in the past. He didn't mind when the information gathered was used to improve the safety of the industry and all those at sea, but in most cases, it became a field trip into bureaucracies and the idiosyncrasies of technical language. In the end, it was the lawyers who won, as they went head-to-head in the court. Sam knew exactly why this man from the insurance company wanted to talk to him, and he wasn't interested.

He made a dramatic sigh. "Get rid of him for me, will you?"

Elise nodded. "Sure thing."

Thirty seconds later, the cable winch stopped turning. It hummed louder for a few moments. Sam's gaze quickly swept the end of the crane's arm. The pulleys were intact, and the cable appeared taut. The pitch of the electric motor suddenly increased, and the winch began to turn again.

Sam swore loudly because the cable had come loose—and they had lost purchase of their haul.

The blue phone rang. This one used a communications cable

along the lift cable—allowing ship-to-diver communications.

He picked it up before it finished its first ring. "What the hell are you doing down there, Tom?" Sam asked. "Are you trying to break my lines?"

"No, boss. The tail appears to be a hell of a lot heavier than we gave her credit for."

"Can you do it?"

"Sure we can. We're just going to need a much larger cable…"

"You want me to bring you up?" Sam asked.

"No. Genevieve and I will stay longer."

"You'll overstay your decompression times."

"I know. Tell Elise to warm up the hyperbaric chamber."

"You sure?"

"Yeah. It's safer than waiting around for another go at this."

"Agreed."

"Oh, and we'll need another cradle."

"Ah Christ, I'm going to have to come down there, aren't I?"

CHAPTER TWO

—Ω—Ω—Ω—

SAM CHECKED HIS FULL-FACE dive mask, regulator lines, and tank one last time before climbing into his infrared-heated thermal undersuit, followed by a thick dry suit. He was diving with a single air tank. There was no need for elaborate dive gas mixtures at such a shallow depth, and he didn't intend to stay down very long. The Dreamlifter wasn't particularly deep at 100 feet, but the topside conditions were horrendous, and the Barents Sea was not known for its hospitality, above or below the surface.

The *Maria Helena* bucked and rolled as Sam discussed the plan with Veyron on the intercom, whilst he was suiting up. Veyron had just returned from the deck after spooling the heaviest cable the *Maria Helena* could hoist on to the crane drum, with the largest cradle on board attached. Considering the conditions, he was nothing short of a magician—a master of his craft.

Sam stood behind the door and gripped the handle with his right hand. In his left, he held his fins and mask. Beads of water raced down the small window on the door, and he peeked out across the deck. He turned to face Elise, who was barely visible beneath her cord-closed hood and life jacket ensemble. He smiled at her. "You ready?"

"You bet," came her muffled reply.

Sam pushed the door out into the howling wind and spray. As he and Elise scrambled out on to the aft deck, the elements assaulted them. Dark clouds had closed in while Sam had made ready, and rain now joined the sea water that strafed them as they crossed the slippery, rolling deck surface toward Veyron and the crane box.

There was just enough room for the three to squeeze into the control room and close the door. Veyron sat at the crane controls, relaxed as ever. Sam and Elise were saturated from the brief exposure to the deck and tried not to get water over everything as they finalized the ad-hoc plan for the dive. With Tom and Genevieve waiting below, time was not their ally if they wanted to get it done today.

Moments later, Sam stood at the starboard toe-rail of the aft deck in his fins and mask, holding tightly to the lifeline. To his right he watched the boom of the crane as it dipped and swayed toward the broken swell, accentuating the uneven movement of the ship. The dark green foaming sea reached up to his feet with the troughs between waves, and then sucked away deeply as the boat climbed another peak. He ensured his shoulder strobe was flashing and checked again for his pocket EPIRB. Rain and sea spray whipped at him as he checked his air supply once more.

Time to go.

Sam waited for the moment when the *Maria Helena* was at her lowest in the water at the aft. He planned to step out into the water, descending as quickly as he could and getting as far from the boat as possible.

Veyron prepared a running line for the 8 inch thick steel cable that Sam would bring down with him with the attachments to make the new cradle.

Sam ran his eyes across the cable, appraisingly. "You're certain it will carry her?"

Veyron nodded. "That'll carry as much as the *Maria Helena's* capable of lifting.

"All right. Let's get this thing done."

Elise came out again, with the sat phone in her hand. "Sam, it's Gene Cutting."

"Who?"

"The guy who wants your expert opinion for the insurers..."

Sam shook his head. "Tell him I'm not interested. Tell him I'm diving."

"I already did. He didn't want to listen. Said he appreciates you're busy. Says his company's willing to pay big, just for your insight. Nothing formal. Doesn't want to drag you through the courts—just wants some expert opinion on what could have possibly gone wrong. Apparently the *Buckholtz*, a large container ship ran aground under some fairly unusual and mysterious circumstances as it was leaving Hamburg this morning."

Sam sighed. "What happened?"

"Apparently the *Buckholtz* came out of its shipping lane while leaving the Elbe River, turned ninety-degrees and ran aground into Neuwerk Island."

"Neuwerk Island?" Sam confirmed, with an incredulous grin. "How the hell does a large cargo ship manage that?"

"No idea. That's what Gene Cutting wants you to find out."

Sam held his palms upward in supplication. "We're already racing to raise the tail of the Dreamlifter and gain access to the main fuselage so that we can retrieve the damned black box. If this isn't an isolated incident, and there's a generic virus or fault with the program, we're going to see a lot more 747s crash—and next time we might not be so lucky—it might be a commercial passenger jet that gets hit, so I'm afraid we just don't have time for him."

"He says he'll come to you..."

"I'm not interested!" Sam placed the full-faced dive mask over his face, gripped the eye of the 8-inch cable with its hook, and dropped over the stern of the *Maria Helena*, disappearing into the dark waters below.

CHAPTER THREE

$$\Omega \text{———} \Omega \text{———} \Omega$$

THE ICY WATER ENVELOPED SAM'S body in an instant.

Despite his protective layering, the extreme temperature shift was enough to shock him into focus. He didn't wait on the surface to check his dive equipment. In the violent seas, the safest place for him would be deep below the raging waves.

Without any air in his buoyancy control device, he immediately started to sink. The weight of the hook and cradle afforded Sam a gentle descent, at the measured rate of the crane's cable. He had attached a lead-line to keep the lifting tackle at a comfortable distance, to allow for the rise and fall of the boat on the swell above.

He swallowed as he descended, allowing his ears to equalize to the new pressures. On his heads-up display, he watched as the depth increased rapidly. His eyes swept over the other gauges, confirming that his air supply readings remained where they belonged.

The stormy conditions at the surface denied the sea much of its ambient light, making it difficult for Sam to see very far as he trailed the hook into the deep ocean water, but after closing half the distance to the bottom, he could start to make out the Boeing 747 Dreamlifter on the seabed. From his high viewpoint, the great jet already started to fill his entire vision. Tom and Genevieve's flashlights danced off the fuselage far below, like tiny stars as they prepared for the arrival of the new cradle.

Sam took a deep breath and exhaled slowly. He took in the surrounding vista, just being present. Lifting the tail of the submerged juggernaut would be complex, and he wanted a clear mind. Even after thousands of hours spent diving, he still loved every minute of his time underwater. He allowed the chilly embrace of the water and the serenity of the seascape to engulf his thoughts, just for a moment. As the white mass of the aircraft loomed ever larger from below, the scale of the task at hand hit home.

At 235 feet in length, and a wingspan of 211 feet, the bulbous Dreamlifter was a beast of the air. Originally created to transport the pieces of the huge Boeing Dreamliner passenger jet to assembly locations, it is a monstrous creation. She had a payload over 840,000 pounds fully loaded, the largest capability in the air.

The entire front section of the airplane was compromised during impact, bashing in the nose of the plane like a squeezebox. This had rendered the side doors useless leaving only one point of access, the articulating tail section of the aircraft. During normal operation, the entire rear end of the plane opened like a huge door. It swung away to the port side, facilitating full access to the cavernous 65,000 cubic feet of cargo space.

With the first lift, Tom and Genevieve had successfully broken the suction of the fuselage from the seabed, so Sam hoped that they could hover the tail section a couple of feet off the sea floor using lifting bags and the new cradle. The *Maria Helena* would then drag the cargo door open after the divers manually disengaged the locking mechanism. It was a complicated and difficult maneuver, but Sam knew his tech diving crew well and trusted them to perform at the highest level.

Veyron had sent the lifting bags down ahead of Sam, and when he arrived at the bottom, Tom and Genevieve had attached almost enough to hover the fuselage with the nose down. Genevieve was filling the second-to-last float to half full, and Tom was attaching the final bag. The aquatic lifting bags looked like two rows of miniature hot air balloons, assembled for a race.

"How long have you guys been down now?" Sam asked over the radio mike.

"About two hours," Tom replied, consulting his watch.

"I hope you put a good book in the decompression pod, you're going to be in there for a while!"

"Yeah well, I've got good company, so it could be worse," he said, grabbing the compressed air tool line from Genevieve and filling the last lifting bag.

"Too bad I can't say the same thing!" Genevieve chimed in, swimming back to the other side of the sunken airplane.

A puff of silt clouded up from the body of the aircraft where it met the ground, and the huge cargo plane's tail lifted ever so slightly. "We have lift-off!" Tom said.

"Nice! I'm hoping that the wings will stabilize this baby enough in the mud for us to swing the tail open. Let's leave her as low as we can now that she's off the floor." Sam said.

"Genevieve, are you okay to check all the bags are secure? Tom and I are going to see about these locks." Sam said.

"Sure thing."

On the underside of the fuselage on both sides, there were emergency release levers for the hydraulic locks that keep the tail closed under normal conditions. Not requiring power, the releases break the seal on the closed fuselage, allowing emergency crews access to the stricken airplane. Sam and Tom took one of the levers each and broke the tail. The seal cracked, and a small amount of air escaped from the top of the body as the giant rear section opened about two inches.

Step one.

Tom and Sam swam the cradle around the bottom of the tail

section and the top edge of the fin, securing the crane hook and cable into the open loops of the sling, and adjusted it to fit securely on the starboard side of the aircraft.

Sam reached up and toggled the switch on top of his mask. It adjusted the readout on the heads-up display inside to show a compass. "Okay Matthew, she's laying almost due west. The heading is 268 degrees. When we're ready, if you can edge forward at the same heading for around fifty yards, with a bit of luck, we should see some movement on the tail."

"Copy that. Heading of 268 degrees."

"Okay Veyron," Sam said into the radio, "Pull the hook in just enough to take up the slack."

"Copy that Sam, I'll luff around to mid stern and take it up slowly. I've set my weight limit alarm, but let me know when it's tight. I can't feel much up here with all this movement."

Sam watched as the thick steel cable started edging away toward the surface, "Just there Veyron." It came to a stop, curved, but taught.

"Okay everyone, let's clear out down here. Give it a good fifty feet. Genevieve, are you still happy with all the bags?"

"They're all good. I've tech screwed all the saddles to the fuselage so they won't move now. Good to go."

"Great. Tom?"

"I'm clear."

"Okay Matthew, power on."

"Copy that, throttle to fifty percent."

The *Maria Helena*'s mighty twin screws took up the strain on the cable, and with her stern laying low under the strain from the crane boom, she dragged herself forward, displacing the swell and crashing through the breakers on her bow.

"Okay guys, that's getting close to my maximum weight alarm," Veyron said into the radio with the sounds of high pitched alarms following his voice in the transmission.

"Matthew? How are you going?"

"She's laying pretty low, but I've still got a little way to travel."

"It's your call buddy, no movement down here yet, though."

"Okay, I'm going to dump some ballast, and power up a little. Pumps up and engines to seventy percent."

The *Maria Helena* dragged herself a little lower in the water, and the sea boiled angrily behind the stern as she ripped through the water, trying to produce some forward motion. Like a tugboat pulling a container ship, her stern swam side-to-side, heaving against the line.

Far below, the metal cable twanged and pinged out a metallic whale-song as it straightened up, straining under 40,000 horsepower of torque from the twin diesel power plants at the surface.

Bang!

The divers were startled as the cradle slipped a little higher on the plane's tailfin, finally seating itself, and then a mighty groan issued from the cavernous belly of the fuselage as the tail swung open.

"We're in!" Sam shouted. "Okay Matthew, that'll do it. And Veyron, you can drop the hook now. Great work team, really. Great job."

"That's why we get paid the big bucks, hey Sam," Matthew said over the mike, powering down the ship. "I knew she could do it. I'll take back some ballast now, and we'll hold steady topside. It's still pretty hairy up here in case you'd forgotten, so feel free to be quick."

"You got it, buddy. Tom, Genevieve — let's see what's in this plane, shall we?"

CHAPTER FOUR

S AM SWITCHED ON HIS FLASHLIGHT, shining its beam directly into the now open fuselage, before quickly swimming inside. Tom and Genevieve entered the gaping space at the rear of the aircraft. They swam single file into the gargantuan freight area. It was 65,000 cubic feet in volume and all of it empty. Their flashlights bounced around the cavernous void as they entered, lighting up numerical distance markers on the wall, and inactive emergency lighting strips that ran the length of the internal fuselage.

Tom's beam flashed throughout the empty hold. "I thought this was meant to be fully loaded?"

"It was," Sam said. "Some sort of heavy machinery. I wasn't told any details."

"Looks like someone got the aircraft's cargo manifest wrong," Genevieve pointed out, matter-of-factly. "It's not like the heavy machinery's managed to fall out of the cargo hold without damaging the rest of the aircraft."

"You're right." Sam kicked his fins, swimming toward the cockpit. "Someone must have got the manifest wrong."

He felt dwarfed by the awesome capacity of the room. It was like standing in the center of a deserted motorway tunnel, but 100 feet under the water. Freight rollers lined the floor, stretching away into the distance, their perspective joined on the visual horizon like train-tracks on a prairie. The diver's lights seemed tiny as they beamed from one end of the aircraft to the other. The beams were uninterrupted by anything in the visual field they illuminated. The cargo bay was completely empty. There was nothing in the plane at all.

"Were we expecting this thing to be loaded?" Tom said.

"As far as I know, yes. I was told it was carrying a payload of machine parts." Sam answered.

"Well there's nothing here now, that's for sure," Genevieve said.

"Good thing we're not here to retrieve its cargo," Sam said. "We've been hired to retrieve the aircraft's data recorders."

"What kind of data recorders does this thing have?" Tom asked

"It should have a Cockpit Voice Recorder, a separate Flight Data Recorder, and a Quick Access Recorder. The QAR is in the cockpit, but I doubt it will have survived."

Tom nodded. "I should think it would be unlikely."

The quick access recorder was an airborne flight recorder designed to provide quick and easy access to raw flight data through a USB drive, standard flash memory card, or wireless connection. Like the aircraft's flight data recorder, the QAR received its inputs from the Flight Data Acquisition Unit, recording over 2000 flight parameters. Its purpose was to sample data at much higher rates than the FDR, and for much longer periods. Unlike an FDR, it isn't a mandated requirement by the Civil Aviation Authority and wasn't designed to survive an accident. Even so, Sam knew it would most likely provide valuable information if it could be salvaged.

Sam said, "Tom, can you and Genevieve try and locate the CVR and FDR?"

"Sure, any idea where they will be housed in the Dreamlifter?"

"Yeah, they're in the tail section, high up in the port side on an isolated tray. There should be a coarse wiring conduit to it. The box is bright orange."

"Of course, that's the color a black box should be," Tom answered, smiling in his mask.

"All right, I'll see you both in ten minutes."

"Where are you going?" Tom asked.

"To the cockpit. I want to see if I can retrieve the QAR—it's unlikely it survived the crash, but maybe Elise can salvage the data stored within."

"No problem. Rendezvous in ten minutes?"

"Sounds good," Genevieve said.

Sam consulted his diver's watch. "I've got 04:40, see you guys here in ten minutes."

Genevieve nodded, looking at her watch as Tom said, "See you in ten."

Sam watched as Tom and Genevieve swam off toward the rear of the aircraft and the open tail section. He swam the length of the fuselage to reach the cockpit, then stopped in the center of the cargo area.

Swimming forward in the empty aircraft, Sam was struck by the strangeness of the whole wreck. The interior structures were completely intact, a little askew here and there on panel joins, but with the exception of the bent-up nose, the damage to the overall fuselage was minimal.

There's no way she crashed at high speed, maybe the nose damage is from the sea floor, after a successful water landing. But why? Why wasn't there a distress signal?

Sam swam on past the curtained off crew and galley area on his right without stopping and entered the open cockpit. There was no sign of the crew. He was expecting all three of them to be inside. The Dreamlifters are only licensed to carry essential crew, no passengers—they didn't even have a jump seat. Still, the flight was about to cross the Atlantic, which meant a minimum of three pilots to rotate through the rest periods.

So, where were they?

The cockpit space seemed surprisingly cramped, compared to the massive fuselage. In the tiny room, Sam was restricted to minimum movements because of his tech-diving gear. He swept his beam around, surprised by how little the cockpit of the Boeing 747 megafreighter had changed since the 1970's. This version was updated and rolled out from 2014, yet with the exception of some multifunction monitors replacing gauges, the fit-out was entirely utilitarian and distinctly last century.

The Quick Access Recorder was right where it should have been, under a flip cover at the third officer's workstation. Sam retrieved the USB flash drive and zipped it into a storage pouch within his buoyancy control device.

He shined his flashlight around the cockpit searching for any other clues. He noticed that a gauge at eye-level had been destroyed. There was no other damage around it. He examined it closely and saw fragments of hair, bone, and blood — and just visible in the dead center of the dial — the base of a copper projectile.

He immediately knew where the pilots were.

Sam turned awkwardly in the doorway, his fins and gear obstructing his movements in the confined space. He pulled himself back along the tiny corridor with his hands and stopped at the galley. Drawing back the curtain, and looking up, he saw the bodies of two men in flight officer's uniforms. They hovered like ghosts against the roof of the galley by the lifejackets they wore, with their legs hanging down below them like giant tendrils.

Sam added a little buoyancy to his BCD and joined the men at the roof. He gently turned to the closer of the two men and came face to bloated face with the plane's chief pilot. The middle-aged man's mouth was ajar and his black eyes wide open — frozen forever in a look of surprise. A cavernous hole in the center of his forehead created the ghoulish appearance of a third eye.

The man's ID tag floated about his face and listed the name *Michael Bateman.* Anchored to his neck by a lanyard embroidered with the logo of the freight company he died flying for, Sam took the laminated card in his hand and examined it under his flashlight. Without expression and fine features, the puffy countenance bore little semblance to the man in the photograph, but enough to positively identify him.

Sam was racked with pity for these men, fellow pilots who met the same horrible, fearful end. He dropped his chin to his chest and made a silent covenant to retrieve the poor men's bodies before the *Maria Helena* left the wreck site. He retrieved the names of the other flight crew members and moved out of the galley.

The question remained, where was the third pilot? And, if he had murdered the two other pilots, where did he end up? It's not like there was anywhere else for him to go once he'd killed the two men.

He consulted his wristwatch and felt for the USB stick in his belt pouch.

04:49hrs, time to leave.

CHAPTER FIVE

SAM REACHED THE OPEN AIRCRAFT tail.

There, Tom and Genevieve had retrieved the data recorders from the tail section without incident and were already securing the data recorders into a large lift bag, which they were now attaching to the cable used to shift the aircraft's tail. Sam glanced at the two orange boxes as they hovered in the water next to Tom and Genevieve.

"Did you find the pilots?" Tom asked.

"Yeah. Two of them. Both dead. Murdered."

"Murdered?"

"Yeah, a single bullet wound to their foreheads."

"What about the third pilot?"

"He's missing."

Tom turned and quickly flashed his light down the fuselage, as though the missing man might still be waiting, hiding there, about to attack. "I don't understand. He killed them and then intentionally crashed the plane?"

"Either that or the plane crashed, and then he murdered them. Who knows? Either way, it doesn't really explain where he is now."

Genevieve said, "What if he intentionally brought the plane down, killed the other two pilots, and then stole whatever was inside the cargo hold?"

Sam said, "That's quite a scenario."

"Sure," she replied. "But it's sounding less impossible the more I look at it."

Sam nodded. "You might be right. The question is, what was inside the aircraft's hold that was valuable enough to make someone go to such lengths to steal it?"

Tom said, "Not to mention, why not just shoot the two pilots, and then fly the plane to a perfectly good runway somewhere to offload its valuable cargo?"

"Unless…" Sam started.

"Unless what?" Tom persisted.

"Whoever's responsible wanted to make certain no one would believe the cargo had been stolen?"

"Why?"

Sam said, "I have no idea, but I intend to find out."

Then, in the back of his mind, he recalled how the secretary of defense had been specifically interested in the results of the aircraft's flight data recorders.

Could her interest in the recovery of the flight data recorders have something to do with its secret cargo?

Tom let go of the lift cable. "All right, this is secure, let's head topside. Genevieve and I already have more than an hour of decompression time in the hyperbaric chamber. No reason to make it longer."

"Agreed."

"I'm good to go," Genevieve said.

Sam checked his dive watch. His bottom time was 15 minutes, with a total dive time of 25 minutes. He would need one short decompression stop, but Tom and Genevieve would need to decompress in the hyperbaric chamber on board.

All three of them ascended slowly, leaving their bounty of flight data recorders, secured to the lift bag. They would haul it up from topside. Right now, the safest place for it was to remain in the deep, and much calmer waters.

Sam exhaled slowly, keeping his eyes on his depth gauge, displayed on his heads-up display, to ensure that he didn't exceed their maximum rate of ascent.

After making his required decompression stop, he, Tom, and Genevieve made their final ascent to the surface. All three of them reached the internal surface of the *Maria Helena's* moon pool simultaneously.

The moon pool was built in the middle of the *Maria Helena's* hull and served as a diving command center, as well as a relatively calm port to launch their mini-submersibles and to dive from. In the turbulent waters of the Barents Sea, the pool was still choppy, and water was splashing over the sides, running across the internal decking.

Sam inflated his buoyancy control device and quickly swam to the edge of the moon pool. His hands gripped the ladder, and in a couple of seconds, he'd climbed out. Genevieve was next, followed by Tom.

The *Maria Helena's* dive center housed their Triton 36,000 submarine, *Sea Witch II,* just forward of the moon pool. Secured to the starboard wall were two giant atmospheric diving suits, custom made to fit Sam and Tom. The exosuits looked like something out of a bad sci-fi movie but provided an anthropomorphic submersible capable of diving to 2,000 feet. Along the port side were a series of dive lockers, with dive tanks, sea scooters, and other diving equipment. Aft of the moon pool, and fixed to the deck by heavy steel welds, was something resembling a small submarine. It was made of reinforced steel and cylindrical, with a single porthole—its purpose was an emergency hyperbaric chamber.

Elise was already at the controls. "Welcome back." Her eyes met Tom and Genevieve. "How are you two feeling?"

"Fine," Genevieve replied.

"Never better," Tom was already opening the hyperbaric

chamber's doors. "But I'd like to keep it that way."

Elise nodded. "It's good to go."

Sam removed his dry suit and wrapped a heated blanket over himself as Genevieve and Tom climbed into the decompression chamber.

Elise turned the pressurized lock and brought the pressure inside up to the equivalent of 40 feet.

The *Maria Helena's* chamber, which had originally been plumbed for commercial diving, had an identical set of controls inside and outside the chamber, although the topside controls will usually override the diver's controls. The rationale behind this plumbing philosophy is that in an emergency, divers can operate their own decompression. In the civilian world, not many chambers can be run from the inside.

Sam removed his dive booties, hood, and gloves. He dried his wrinkled, shaking hands. His movements slightly subdued by exhaustion. Deep, red lines marked his face from the mask, emphasizing the pallor they all shared — a mixture of fatigue and cold.

Elise glanced at him. "Nice dive?"

"I've had better. It was a little cold down there, and it's always sad to see the cruel fate of fellow pilots."

"Any guesses what happened?"

Sam said, "I think they landed the plane on the water successfully, and then it sank. That damage is low speed. He must have been some pilot. It would be like landing the world's biggest bus on the sea at two hundred and fifty miles an hour. Damned near impossible."

"And then someone killed him and the copilot?" Elise asked.

"Yeah. Back of the head, single shot. Both of them."

Her response was mechanical. "How weird?"

"Yeah."

Elise glanced at the pressure reading for the chamber,

confirming it was fixed at the equivalent of 40 feet. "So, what happened to the murderer?"

Sam shook his head. "No idea."

"Any luck with the flight data recorders?"

"Tom and Genevieve retrieved both of them." Sam pulled a woolen jumper over his head. "They're still attached to the lift cable. I'm about to help Veyron pull them up."

"Anything you want me to look at?" she asked.

"We've been told by the British Air Accidents Investigation Branch not to tamper with either of the black boxes." He unzipped the pouch on his buoyancy control device and handed her the soaking wet USB stick he'd retrieved from the cockpit.

Elise took it, her face distorting in a small grimace. "It's a bit wet. That was careless of you."

Sam lifted his palms outward toward the ceiling. "Hey, I didn't put it in the water."

"Is that the QAR?"

"Got it in one," Sam replied. "Any chance you can still access the data?"

"The seawater will have wreaked havoc, but I'll try my best." She smiled. "Any luck with the data and voice recorders?"

"Yeah. Tom and Genevieve found them. The team from the UK Air Accidents Investigation Branch were adamant we're not to open its casings and disturb the data."

She nodded. "That seems fair. It's their show. We're just here to retrieve it for them. So what's the plan for it?"

"As soon as Genevieve's decompressed, she's going to fly it to Finland, where it will be taken by a commercial jet to Heathrow, where the UK AAIB will take it apart, see what it has to say and commence their investigation."

"All right. I'll have a look at the QAR as soon as we're done here."

Sam pulled up his wet weather pants, zipped up his work

boots, and zipped the wet weather jacket up to his face.

"Where are you going?" she asked.

"Up on deck to help Veyron pull up the flight data recorders."

CHAPTER SIX

Ω———————Ω———————Ω

SAM WATCHED AS VEYRON OPERATED the heavy winch, as it pulled the lift bag containing the twin black box recorders onto the aft deck of the *Maria Helena*. As soon as it cleared the deck, Veyron adeptly maneuvered the crane across inward until he successfully lowered the load onto the deck.

As soon as the bag was on the deck, Sam stepped forward, disconnected the winch hook, and secured the lift bag so that any broaching wave wouldn't sweep it away again.

He met Veyron's eye and gave him the all okay signal.

Veyron secured the hook to the deck and made his way across the deck to greet him. "Well done, Sam."

Sam shook his hand firmly. "Thanks. It was Tom and Genevieve who did most of the heavy lifting."

"All the same. You got it done."

Behind him, standing at a half-open door at the base of the pilothouse, a stranger said, "Good man, well done!"

"Thank you." Sam glanced at the stranger. He was moderately overweight, and his shortness accentuated that weight. The man wore a crisp, white beard, and a well-practiced, deceitful smile. At a guess, the man was one of three types of people—a politician, lawyer, or a banker. None of which he had any interest in speaking to today. "I'm sorry, who are you?"

The man held out his hand. "I'm Gene Cutting."

Sam accepted the hand and gave it a curt, but firm shake. "Right. I'm sorry, who?"

"Gene Cutting."

"So you said. From where?"

"I own Phoenix Shipping, and I need your help."

"I'm afraid you'll need to get in line. I have a lot on my plate right now. Are you a friend of my father's?"

"No. I'm afraid I've been a competitor to your father over the years. Our dislike of one another has been entirely professional, I assure you. Your father's an amazing man."

Sam glanced at the second helicopter, this one on the generally unused forward helipad. "Then what are you doing here?"

"I have a problem."

Sam nodded. "So, you said."

Gene continued. "One of our ships ran aground yesterday. We need your help."

"Sorry, buddy. You should have called ahead. I could have told you I'm not interested in taking on extra work currently." He looked at the Dreamlifter's black box. "As you can see, I have a lot of work to do, here."

Gene ignored him. "I did call."

Sam stared at the man through narrowed eyes. "You're the guy who's been trying to call me all day?"

"Yeah."

An incredulous grin crept up on his lips. "That makes you an asshole or a fool. Which one are you?"

"Hey, I need your help. We're willing to compensate you well for your time," Gene replied, nonplussed.

"I already told you I wasn't interested."

"I know. But this is important."

"What I'm currently doing is important!" Sam sighed and shook his head. "Can't you get one of the other experts to have a look at it?"

"I already have."

"What did they say?"

"They said they have no fucking idea what to make of it."

"Make of what?"

"What went wrong with the *Buckholtz*?"

"I thought you said it ran aground."

"It's a little more complicated than that. Let's just say, the events related to this accident are a little more mysterious than simple error."

Sam shook his head again. "Come into my office. We're heading off in less than an hour, after a British Air Accidents Investigation Branch vessel arrives. You've got until then to convince me."

CHAPTER SEVEN

S AM OPENED THE DOOR TO the briefing room.

With his hand, he gestured for Gene to take a seat across from him. Gene nodded a cursory thank you and took a seat.

Sam opened the forward door and yelled, "Elise, Matthew, Veyron… come into the briefing room… our new friend here wants to tell us a story."

Gene narrowed his eyes. His thick curly brow closed together. "I'm sorry. The images I'm about to show are of strictly proprietary knowledge…"

Sam crossed his arms. "Hey, you came to me?"

"And I want just your opinion. If this gets out, we might be in some real trouble…"

Sam took a deep breath and nodded at the rest of his crew. "All right. I'll hear you out, but if I accept the job, it means you take my entire team on, and no more secrets. Agreed?"

"Agreed."

Sam said, "All right, Elise do you want to start preparing the black box for its flight?"

"All right," Elise said.

Sam turned his attention to Gene, "When Tom is out of the hyperbaric chamber, I will need to discuss this with him."

Gene opened his mouth to protest. "But…"

Sam interrupted him. "I don't work without him. That's not negotiable."

Gene opened his mouth to protest, took one look at Sam's hardened face and closed it again. "The ship was the *Buckholtz*. She was leaving from Hamburg on her way to the U.S. port of Quonset Point, Rhode Island. The captain was a veteran for the company with more than thirty years' experience and had made this particular voyage multiple times a year for the past three years."

Sam sat a glass on the table and poured a small amount of water in without asking whether his unwanted guest wanted one or not. He took a small sip of the drink and then looked at the stranger sitting down in front of him. "So, what happened?"

"The ship ran hard aground on Neuwerk Island."

Sam studied the map and location of the accident. "What did the captain say went wrong? Anything short of a hurricane shouldn't have affected the *Buckholtz* so much to send it on a direct collision course with the island."

"He says he was following the channel and simply ran aground—only it wasn't just mud, it was rock—and it took a fifty-foot gash out of her backside. She sank stern down within minutes with the bow dry and above water."

"Any chance the captain was intoxicated?"

"No. He was tested for alcohol and drugs an hour after the accident. Everything was done by the book. He had three witnesses who confirm what he saw on three different systems. Depth gauge, radar, and GPS-based navigational maps all confirmed he was traveling through the channel at the time."

"Do you think the sandbar moved?"

"No. Everything was exactly where it was meant to be. I'm telling you, it looks like the captain, second in command and watchman all just made a massive mistake."

Sam leaned back in the big leather chair. "So, what would you like my help with? Are you having trouble getting the insurance company to pay or something?"

"No."

"So, let the insurance company do their mandatory checks. They'll perform a root cause analysis and come up with an answer. Sometimes these things really are just an accident."

"Yeah, that's what we figured. But…"

"What?"

"There's something else. A camera inside the bridge records everything that happens. Like an aircraft's flight data recorder, this can be used in the event of an accident or collision with another vessel to determine the cause and who was ultimately at fault. The recording provides crucial clues, including the position of the controls, the functionality of the engine, and bow thrusters."

"And what did it say?"

"It confirms exactly what the captain and his two witnesses said — they were traveling up the middle of the channel, nowhere near the rocky beach."

"Any chance the tapes could have been switched?"

"Not a chance in the world. The system has heavy security to make it difficult to do just that. If the crew had hours between the event and one of the company's boarding parties arriving — I would have assumed that was the case — but there was less than five minutes between the accident and one of our helicopters dropping a team on board."

"Five minutes?" Sam met him eye to eye. "That's a pretty quick response for anyone."

Gene shook his head. "No. Our engineers were on their way out to the vessel to perform some routine safety checks while the *Buckholtz* was on her way out to sea when this happened. It's a fairly common procedure. Every day the ship is in harbor costs the company more than a million dollars in lost revenue and demurrage, so it works out cheaper simply to fly out our engineering teams to perform the tasks, where possible, usually on the ship's outward journey."

"Did they see anything strange from the air?"

"Nothing. It was night time. Not much could be seen from the air."

"What time was this?"

"Nine p.m. Just under twelve hours ago."

Sam asked, "Any chance one of the channel markers were out?"

Gene shrugged. "Sure. But not all of them. And besides, the island stands out like a giant shrine on the horizon. No way the captain could have missed its silhouette against the shore."

"Stranger things have happened."

Gene's satellite phone rang. He answered it and swore. "All right. This changes everything." He nodded his head to himself, hung up, and turned to Sam. "We have another issue, this one a little more pressing."

Sam said, "Go on."

"The *Buckholtz* was carrying an experimental piece of equipment inside one of its shipping containers. It was stored in the section of the hull that is now nearly sixty feet below the sea. We're going to need your help to retrieve it. What's more, it's vitally important that no one know that it was on board."

"Why?"

"The item is the culmination of many millions of man hours and more than two billion dollars spent on research and development. If it's believed that the engine was lost due to the negligence of the captain, the news would wreak havoc on the company's share price."

Sam nodded his head. He understood how these situations worked. Such companies had stretched their financial reserves to the breaking point, only to have bad luck bring them down just as their big risk was about to pay off.

"What's happened?"

"I've just been informed that one of our more important shipping containers, which until now we hoped was still dry, is now below the waterline."

Sam said, "I would think the replacement cost of any single shipping container is a lot less than the value of the likely salvage and repair cost of the *Buckholtz?*"

"Not this one." Gene's tone was emphatic.

"Why?" Sam asked, studying his response. "What's inside that's so special about it?"

Gene shook his head. "I'm afraid that really is proprietary knowledge. I would be remiss in my duty to the owners who have paid well to maintain its secrecy. All I can say is that we are willing to pay well to have it retrieved."

Sam said, "All right. We'll accept the case on one condition."

"Shoot."

"What's this really all about?"

Gene frowned. "All I can say is that if that container gets damaged, it won't just be money that we've lost."

CHAPTER EIGHT

Ω ——————— Ω ——————— Ω

S AM MET TOM AT THE hyperbaric chamber.

There was a gentle hiss as the internal gas equalized with the pressure outside. The hatch at the end of the tube-shaped device opened, and Genevieve climbed out first, followed by Tom.

Sam said, "How are you both feeling?"

"Never better," they replied in unison.

Tom then looked up at him. "I hear we're going somewhere?"

"Yeah," Sam replied. "Both of you, but not the same places." To Genevieve, he said, "The Sea King is fueled and loaded with the Dreamlifter's data recorders, which I need you to deliver to an airfield in Norway, where they will be picked up by a private jet and flown to the Air Accidents Investigations Branch's headquarters in London."

Tom smiled. "And where am I off to?"

"Neuwerk Island, at the mouth of the Elbe River, Germany."

Tom nodded. "Obviously. Sounds lovely. What's there?"

"A whole heap of mud and a container ship that's run aground."

"You're heading up the salvage operation?"

Sam shook his head. "They already have another company coming out to help pull the ship into deeper waters after repairs are made below her waterline."

"So, what are we doing there?"

"I've been asked to locate and retrieve a specific container in the hold in the off chance we're not able to get the ship afloat easily."

"They just want you to retrieve a shipping container?"

"Yes."

"What's in the container?"

"No idea. He won't say."

Tom grinned. "Why did you accept the case?"

Sam shrugged. "Why not?"

"Because we've got plenty of work, and you're not interested in a simple recovery case. So what's this about?"

Sam smiled. "I want to know how the ship ran aground."

"Why? Accidents happen. It's a busy shipping lane."

"Yeah, but this captain turned his ship ninety degrees and ran straight into the clearly visible island."

Tom cocked an eyebrow. "You think he did it intentionally?"

"No. I've seen the video from the bridge. It looks like he was following the navigation markers."

"Then what happened?"

"I have no idea." Sam grinned. "But that's what I intend to find out."

CHAPTER NINE

Ω——————Ω——————Ω

S AM AND TOM GRABBED TWO small crates, pre-packed with all the equipment they would need to make the dive and assess the wreckage of the *Buckholtz*. The equipment was loaded onto Gene Cutting's Eurocopter EC 155m, where the man's pilot was waiting to take the three of them directly to the site of the accident. The *Maria Helena* made its way behind, working its way down the Norwegian coast, to meet them the following day.

It was a long flight.

The Eurocopter made a slow circuit of the wrecked *Buckholtz* in a counter-clockwise direction. From the air, his eyes swept the landscape. Neuwerk Island was a little oasis, surrounded by more than ten miles of mudflats. To its north, were the two smaller orbital islands, Nigehorn and Scharhorn. The helicopter banked farther to the south, where the mudflats reached Cuxhaven at the mouth of the Elbe.

A row of poles, supporting steel cages thirty feet above the mud flats, marked the way across, where tourists from the mainland can navigate on foot for six hours of the day during low tide. The path's elevated cages were rescue pods. Should high tide catch a walker far from shore, the walker can climb into the pod and wait for the tide to recede.

The Eurocopter circled the island again to the wreck site.

The *Buckholtz* had a length of 1,312 feet, a beam of 193 feet, and a gross tonnage of 210,890. Her bow was high up along the beach at the northern tip of Neuwerk Island, leaving her lower third submerged beneath the deep water of the North Sea, with the exception of the aft bridge and pilothouse forming an artificial island, nearly five stories above the sea.

Sam stared at the sight, struggling to imagine how an experienced captain, with a veteran channel pilot on board, could possibly make such an enormous mistake. It was almost impossible to believe the mistake was accidental.

The Eurocopter made its final circuit of the stricken vessel. Gene, who was sitting up front next to the pilot, looked over his shoulder, and asked, "Have you seen enough?"

Sam nodded and pointed his thumb downward. "Yeah. Take us down and let's get a better look at the ship."

"All right," Gene replied, turning to the pilot. "Take us down."

The pilot nodded, banking sharply toward the *Buckholtz*. The Eurocopter settled into a hover directly above the cargo ship's five stories high pilothouse. Its skids touched the steel roof, which now sloped gently back toward the sea. The helicopter's rotors continued to whine, as the pilot took up most of the pressure, in case the pilothouse became unstable.

"End of the road gentlemen," came the pilot's voice.

Sam thanked the pilot, slid the side door open and climbed out.

The steel platform where the Eurocopter had put down toward the aft of the *Buckholtz* provided firm ground beneath his feet, despite its not-so-gentle 10-degree downward gradient. His eyes swept the platform. The place had been designed to be used as a helipad under normal circumstances. Right now, he guessed the Eurocopter could have shut down the engines on top, but it would have left the helicopter perched on an uncomfortably steep angle.

Inside the Eurocopter, Tom pulled the two large crates to the edge of the door followed by their two duffel bags which contained overnight clothes, laptops, and toiletries. Sam lifted them to the ground. Gene Cutting stepped out of the front passenger's seat, and Tom slid the side door shut. Overhead, the rotor blades whined, their pitch changing as the pilot took off again, sending several tons of downdraft on top of them, before banking quickly and heading south to an airport in Hamburg to refuel.

Gene Cutting glanced at Sam and Tom. His deep-set and sullen eyes still in despondent awe of the scene. An unbelievable accident that would cost his company many millions to repair. The man's eyes took in the entire area, before settling on Sam. "What do you think the project will take?"

Sam made a thin-lipped smile. "I'm not sure. It depends."

"On what?" Gene asked. "I'm told you're the best. Time is money — a lot of money — so the sooner we can get the *Buckholtz* afloat, the happier I'll be. So, what does it depend on?"

"It depends on what sort of damage we have below decks. If we're lucky, we can make simple repairs by welding a sheet of steel over whatever gash lies below the waterline, pump the water out of her, and float her again on the next high tide. If we're lucky, all of that can be achieved in the next week. She's already resting firm on her keel, so after that, it's just a simple matter of setting up a rigging system of oversized pulleys to drag her off the muddy beach."

Gene frowned. "And if we're unlucky?"

"Then the gash has ripped a hole spanning multiple bulkheads. It might require extensive welding and engineering work beneath the water level. That can be difficult and time-consuming. Every day the hull remains beneath the water, the longer the Buckholtz will remain out of action, being repaired at the shipyards."

"Do you have a timeframe in mind?"

Sam shrugged. "It could be months. But I doubt it." Sam ran

his eyes across the muddy beach. "You said this entire area is full of mudflats?"

Gene nodded. "Yes."

Sam smiled. "I think you'll be fine. Tom and I will make a dive today and get a preliminary idea of the damage. It won't take long. I'd say by this afternoon, we should have a rough idea what's involved."

"That's great." Gene took a deep breath in, held it, and swallowed. "Look. There's a container on E deck of particular value. If this is going to be longer than a week, I want to ask you something that might just sound crazy, but hear me out."

A wry smile formed on Sam's lips. "All right. Shoot."

Gene handed him the engineering schematics for the *Buckholtz,* rendered in 3D with shipping containers set throughout the ship. On E deck, the lowest level, toward the aft of the ship and now the deepest section, a single container had been circled with a red pen. "See this here?"

Sam studied the map and nodded. "Container E85. Right in the middle there. What about it?"

"It needs to be in Quonset Point, Rhode Island before the end of two weeks." Gene met Sam's eye. "Can it be done?"

"If we get lucky and we refloat the *Buckholtz* by the end of the week, I don't see why it can't be removed in Hamburg and flown to Quonset Point within the fortnight. It will be expensive, but by the looks of things, the money's not an issue at this point."

"That's right. It just has to be done. But what if you can't refloat the *Buckholtz* within the week?"

Sam squinted his eyes, as though he was failing to see the point of the question. "Then, container E85 doesn't make it to its destination on time."

Gene set his jaw firm. His eyes fixed on Sam's like steel. "That's not an option."

"Really? I'm afraid it's out of our control."

"What if you cut a larger hole in the hull?"

Sam let that sit for a moment. He studied Gene's face. The man was serious—there was no doubt about it.

"You want me to cut a giant hole—significantly larger dimensions than the shipping container so that we can extract the container E85?"

"Yes. If you have to," Sam said. "It could be done. It would potentially add weeks or even months to the long-term salvage cost of the *Buckholtz.*"

"That doesn't matter."

Sam made a thin-lipped smile. "What's inside the container?"

"I'm sorry, Mr. Reilly. That's a proprietary secret."

Sam swept the ship, partially visible below the waterline, with his eyes. "All right. Let's hope we can get the ship off Neuwerk Island in time."

CHAPTER TEN

TOM SLID HIS ARMS THROUGH the shoulder strap of the duffel bag and ran his eyes across the unique environment of the *Buckholtz,* whose keel was buried hard into the muddy bottom. In the space between the bow and the bridge, the neatly stacked shipping containers reached five stories above the deck, with nearly half of them now submerged beneath the water. The cool breeze across the Northern Sea predicted the last remnants of fall. If they were going to raise the *Buckholtz,* they would need to do so quickly, or wait until winter had finished.

Looking at Sam, he asked, "Where do you want to set up for the dive?"

"Let's set up in the bridge. I'm keen to get a better look at the command center and try and see for myself what the captain saw last night." Sam looked around, searching for a way down. "Besides, I'm told from inside the bridge there's an internal stairway that leads all the way down to the engine room below. It should be an easy way to get access to the internal hull."

"Sounds good. Should we come back for our diving equipment?"

Gene glanced at the two heavy pre-packed crates. "Leave them there. I'll have some of the engineering team come and move those into the bridge for you."

"Okay, thanks," Tom replied. "Lead the way."

At the edge of the pilothouse, the tip of a steel ladder was visible just a few feet above the starboard side of the helipad. Because the *Buckholtz* had settled into a 10-degree list to port, the ladder now leaned inward, making it an easy climb down toward the entrance of the internal bridge.

He climbed down arm over arm, before stopping at the landing space directly outside the main bridge. A narrow and open deck ran on the outside of the bridge to the port and starboard side, like a slim wing.

There were multiple engineers and mariners working within the upper decks of the pilothouse, securing the emergency power systems, running diagnostics on the damage, and planning repairs, as well as trying to stabilize the ship from listing farther to port side.

Tom stepped into the bridge from the external port wing.

His eyes ran across the bridge, from port to starboard side. The digitally fortified bridge was a far cry from the command centers of bygone merchant ships. Controls, displays, and instruments ran the entire length of the bridge, with the helm placed at the center, in a position of command.

Along the portside instrument panel stood the navigation station with GPS, digital maps, and Admiralty charts. To the right of which, stood a large monitor with the Electronic Chart Display and Information System (ECDIS), a geographic information system used for nautical navigation.

The first three forward computer screens showed Radar 1, 2, and 3. Directly in front of the helm, and displayed above eye height were the ship's primary indicators, which showed the ship's course over ground, compass, depth, engine RPM, rate of turn, clock, and barometry.

To the starboard side was a second ECDIS digital display map, which precisely mirrored the one seen at the navigation station.

Tom stood next to Sam at the helm and stared out across the bow, more than a thousand feet ahead of the bridge, and riding high up on the mudflats of Neuwerk Island.

His eyes darted across the series of controls and displays. The helm still used a small wheel with a compass directly ahead. The controls for the engine's RPM and bow thrusters were within reach to the right.

He let his eyes search ahead, where the bridge overlooked row upon row of now-submerged shipping containers and more dry containers toward the bow of the ship.

Tom closed his eyes and tried to imagine what it would have looked like at nighttime. The port channel markers were clear and would have been flashing their warnings that the shallow mudflats of Neuwerk Island were nearby. Even if they had failed, the island itself had a lighthouse and a series of small homes that would have lit up the otherwise empty coast.

He opened his eyes and glanced at Sam. "How does an experienced captain and Hamburg Port pilot get things so wrong?"

Sam shook his head. "Beats the hell out of me."

Tom turned around. Behind the helm, through a green door, was an elevator that could be taken down to the engine room nearly ten stories below. Next to that was a red door, which led to the internal stairwell, leading to the flooded engine room.

He swept his eyes across the radar and radio rooms behind the helm. The radar room had another series of monitors that displayed the radar images of the area ahead and to the side of the ship. Radar 1 displayed anything nearby that might impede their passage, while Radar 2 and Radar 3 processed information from up to ten miles away at the edge of the horizon, including any weather systems which they might want to avoid.

The radio room had a combination of MF and HF radios, Sat C and Sat F, and a satellite phone.

Sam turned to Gene, who had remained silent throughout, letting them examine the bridge like a detective might scrutinize the scene of a homicide. "Do you know where the gash in the hull is?"

Gene shook his head. "No. There's a small gash on the starboard side, but it's too high and too far forward to cause the stern to sink so quickly."

"So, where's the damage to the stern?" Tom asked.

"We don't know."

"Have you sent a diver to investigate?"

Gene said, "Sure. Of course."

"And what did they find?"

"Nothing. There's a thick combination of mud and sludge in these waters. Right now, several feet of the stern are buried in the muddy bottom of the Elbe River."

"But you're certain there's a gash down there?" Sam persisted.

"Yes. How else would the stern sink so quickly?"

Sam said, "I don't know. But Tom and I will find out soon enough."

"What are you going to do if you can't see it from the outside of the hull?"

"The only thing left for us. We'll have to have a look at it from inside."

"The hull is split into sixteen watertight compartments. You might need to search all of them?"

Sam smiled. "That's all right. I have a simpler way to find the leak."

"Really. Where?"

"Through the duct keel."

CHAPTER ELEVEN

Ω——————Ω——————Ω

SAM LAID A SET OF engineering schematics for the *Buckholtz* across the navigation table.

Pointing to the keel, he said to Tom, "A more recent addition to the modern cargo ship is the addition of a set of double-bottom tanks, which provide a second watertight shell that runs the entire length of the ship. In this case, the double-bottoms hold fuel, ballast water, and fresh water. Between the two shells is a hollow keel called a duct keel."

Gene smiled. "That's right. If we can't find the leak from the outside, you should be able to find it by going through the duct keel. It's going to be hard as all hell to get to, and you couldn't pay me enough to follow you down there. That area's damned tight, and if you have even a hint of claustrophobia, it's bad. With the flooding, it's a nightmare.

Tom ran his eyes across the schematics and smiled. "You sure can pick them, Sam."

"We've been in worse." Sam shrugged. "Besides, a nice narrow tunnel like that, running the length of the hull is far safer. Almost impossible to get lost in such a tight space."

Gene laughed. "You two can keep your jobs."

Sam said, "All right. Your company owns this ship, so what can you tell us about her layout that might help us locate the opening?"

Gene started off, slow, like a university lecturer, breaking everything down to its simplest form. "The *Buckholtz* is classed as a Very Large Container Ship, meaning that it holds more than 10,000 TEU — that's twenty-foot equivalent units, by the way."

Sam and Tom nodded in unison.

Gene continued. "Her hull, similar to bulk carriers and general cargo ships throughout the world, is built around a strong keel, set upon a complex arrangement of steel plates and rigid beams for strength. Resembling ribs and fastened at right-angles to the keel are the ship's frames. The ship's main deck, the metal platework that covers the top of the hull framework, is supported by beams that are attached to the tops of the frames and run the full breadth of the ship. The beams not only support the deck, but along with the deck, frames, and transverse bulkheads, strengthen and reinforce the shell."

"In other words, she's a standard piece of naval architecture for her class," Sam said. "Do you know where the access port is for the duct keel?"

"At the bottom of the engine room, which is directly below us here. It houses the main engines and auxiliary machinery for the fresh water and sewage systems, electrical generators, fire pumps, and air conditioners. It's also entirely under water at the moment."

Sam nodded. "Okay. So how do we reach it?"

"It's accessible either by taking the lift behind that green door straight down — when it isn't flooded — or by following the stairs over there."

Sam glanced at the internal stairwell. "Well, that makes it easy enough."

"Anything else?" Gene asked.

"What about this secret shipping container?" Sam asked. "Where's it located? I suppose we should have a look at it while we're down there."

"You won't find it by going through the duct keel, but it

should be relatively easy to access heading forward of the engine room, into the main cargo bay. There are a series of internal passageways and gangways that you can take to reach it."

"Do you have a map of those?"

"Sure." Gene rolled up the first set of schematics and unfurled a second set. "The *Buckholtz,* like most container ships, uses a system of three dimensions in its cargo plans to describe the position of a container aboard the ship."

Sam said, "Go on."

"The first coordinate is the bay which starts at the front of the ship and increases aft. The second coordinate is the tier, numbered from the bottom of the cargo hold. The third coordinate is the row. Rows on the starboard side are given odd numbers, and those on the port side are given even numbers."

"Right," Sam acknowledged. "And the rows nearest the centerline are given low numbers, and the numbers increase for slots further from the centerline."

Gene scrutinized his face, trying to determine how he'd come up with the answer. "That's right. I was about to ask how you knew, but then remembered, that your father owns Global Shipping. You must have spent plenty of time exploring container ships as a kid, am I right?"

"Yeah, a fair bit of time." Sam grinned as he recalled some of the trips. "During a crossing from Panama to Gibraltar my brother and I played some of the longest games of hide and seek in history, stretching through the entire length of the nearly 1400-foot cargo ship."

"What a playground for a couple of kids, hey?" Gene returned his focus to the task at hand. "As you probably know, container ships only take on 20-foot, 40-foot, and 45-foot containers. The 45-footers only fit above deck. The 40-foot containers are the primary container size, making up about 90% of all container shipping and since container shipping moves 90% of the world's freight, over 80% of the world's freight moves via 40-foot containers."

"And what type of container are we looking for?" Sam asked.

Gene smiled, as though they'd achieved some monumental task. "It's a custom built 60-foot container."

Sam pictured the container. "So, it's a 40, and 20 joined together?"

"Basically."

"And where did you store something that shape?"

"At 10/14/08."

Sam mentally pictured this. "That's bay 10, about sixty feet forward of the bridge, row 14, that's right up against the portside, and tier eight, that's about forty feet below the waterline right now, isn't it?"

"That's right."

Sam made a couple of notes on the digital notepad, and said, "All right, let's go have a look."

CHAPTER TWELVE

A T THE LAST DRY LANDING space within the *Buckholtz's* internal stairwell at the sixth deck, Sam laid out the twin dive packs. The kits were set up for rapid deployment on short notice for cave rescues or overturned and flooded ship rescues. The supplies were far from extensive but would allow at least two dives before the *Maria Helena* arrived.

He unzipped the heavy lining and examined the tools of his trade.

Inside were two closed-circuit rebreather dive systems, a series of underwater tools, and two sea scooters. The packs were stocked with a variety of breathable gasses, including oxygen, helium, and nitrox. Today's dive would be considered shallow in terms of pressurized depths, and so they would dive with a combination of oxygen and air via the rebreather system to maximize their available dive times.

Sam and Tom quickly went through the rigorous process of setting up and testing their equipment. Sam opened the aluminum backpack. Inside was an axial type scrubber unit filled with the granular absorbent used to remove CO_2 from the closed-circuit during the dive. He removed the half-used cartridge and replaced it with a brand-new unit, filled with five pounds of sodalime and then reinserted it, locking the lid with a heavy-duty thread.

He worked his way through, testing two times for leaks. These are the positive and negative pressure tests, and are designed to check that the breathing loop was airtight for internal pressure lower and higher than the outside. The positive pressure test ensures that the unit will not lose gas while in use, and the negative pressure test ensures that water will not leak into the breathing loop where it can degrade the scrubber medium or the oxygen sensors.

Sam and Tom methodically and efficiently worked their way through their dive equipment, going through the laborious process of preparing each part for the dive.

Confident that their systems were in working order and that their multiple redundancy systems worked too, they finally donned their thick dry suits.

Sam pulled the hood of his neoprene dry suit over his head. "Are you good to dive, Tom?"

Tom had already slipped his arms through the aluminum backpack of his closed-circuit rebreathing system, that was designed to mold to his back. "I'm good whenever you're ready."

"All right."

Gene stepped down to the platform with one of the engineers. "How long are you going to be?"

"Shouldn't be long," Sam replied. "Under an hour."

"And what do I do if you take any longer than that?"

Sam shrugged. "Any of your engineers capable of diving in confined spaces?"

"No. We have two commercial divers on board who can do some steel welding if required, but they're working with atmospheric dive suits, so there's nothing they can do for you if you get stuck."

"All right. I guess you're back to waiting."

"For what?" Gene persisted.

"Until we get ourselves out of whatever trouble we found."

With that final thought, Sam donned his full-face dive mask.

He took a deep breath and started pre-breathing the unit—a process of breathing normally for about three minutes before entering the water to ensure the scrubber material gets a chance to warm up to operating temperature, and works correctly, and that the partial pressure of oxygen within the closed-circuit rebreather is controlled within the predefined parameters.

Sam inhaled effortlessly.

The gas he breathed was humid and warm, rather than the dry, cold air divers are used to with compressed air and a scuba cylinder and regulator set up. In the frigid waters of the Northern Sea, that would be a welcome bonus.

He checked his gauge for two things.

One, that CO_2 levels weren't rising, meaning the new sodalime scrubber was doing its job correctly and two, that the partial pressure of oxygen within the closed-circuit remained within the initial setpoint of 1.3 bar.

Sam ran his eyes across the top reading, where a nondispersive infrared sensor showed that the CO_2 levels weren't elevating.

Below that, his glance stopped to examine the reading from the oxygen analyzer. It showed the partial pressure of oxygen as 1.3 bar.

Three minutes later, he radioed Tom, "I'm all good to go."

"Sounds good," Tom replied. "Let's go see what went so disastrously wrong."

Sam slipped his dive fins on, switched on his flashlight and slid into the narrow space of the *Buckholtz's* flooded internal stairwell. The water was cloudy with mud, but the visibility was good enough to clearly make out the shapes of the steps and walls which made up the flooded stairwell. The beam of his flashlight was able to reach the engine room three decks below.

He deflated his buoyancy wing until he was negatively buoyant and started his descent in a counter-clockwise direction, following the stairs to a depth of thirty feet and stopped. There, he checked his gauges, confirming on his heads-up display that his CO_2 levels weren't climbing and that the partial pressure of oxygen within the fully closed-circuit remained within the predefined parameters.

Sam glanced at his buddy. "How are you doing Tom?"

"Good," came Tom's cheerful reply. "All gauges in order."

"All right, let's continue down into the engine room."

Sam swallowed, equalizing the pressure in his ears and sinuses and occasionally inserted a small amount of gas into his dry suit to prevent its compressed air from squeezing him tight. At a depth of sixty feet, the stairwell opened onto a level steel gangway.

The engine room sprawled across four full decks, making it the largest open space on board the entire ship. He flicked his flashlight around the engine room, its beam striking a series of large turbines and the massive prime mover engine, used for the *Buckholtz's* primary propulsion, before finally settling on a closed hatch at the very bottom.

Sam said, "That's it."

Tom fixed his beam on it. "That hatch there?"

He descended quickly, as the flooded compartment allowed him to skip what would have otherwise been a ladder spanning four decks.

Sam played with the steel lever until the hatch came free, and he opened it fully. "That's our opening to the duct keel."

Tom said, "Why's it shut?"

"What do you mean why's it shut?" Sam asked. "It's meant to be shut. It's designed to be water-tight. Otherwise, what's the point of having it."

Tom tilted his head to the side, as though Sam had already answered the question. "That's exactly why I'm wondering why its closed."

Sam swallowed. "You're right. If it was water-tight, and the damage was done inside the duct keel, none of the water should have reached the rest of the engine room. And if the flooding occurred elsewhere, there shouldn't have been any water inside the duct keel."

"Exactly. Any ideas?"

"None. Unless there are two damaged sections of the hull?"

Tom shined his light into the dark tunnel. "Let's hope there are some answers down there."

Sam pulled himself through the manhole.

It was small enough that he had to consciously position himself so that his arms and larger closed-circuit rebreather system could squeeze through, the same way he might during a cave dive. The entrance led to two sets of vertical ladders, which descended another twenty feet.

He made the descent, carefully diving head first because the ladders didn't allow for anything else. At the bottom, there was a second manhole. Sam quickly maneuvered the hatch and swam through.

The duct keel was an internal passage of watertight construction, comprised of two longitudinal girders spaced precisely eight feet apart to form a narrow tunnel running just shy of the entire 1400-feet length of the *Buckholtz*.

Two sets of large piping took up most of the space. One pipe to shift the storage of the heavy fuel oil used to drive the large shipping vessel, and the second one, to maneuver the ballast water to maintain an even sail and to compensate for swell.

Tom's flashlight flickered past Sam's shoulder, disappearing far into the distance.

Tom said, "Any idea how we're going to get across the length of this thing?"

He fixed his flashlight on a pair of horizontal carts that looked awfully similar to old mine carts, with a single set of narrow railway tracks that disappeared into the blackness of the tunnel. At the back of the cart was a simple mechanical arm — known as a walking beam—that pivots, seesaw-like at the base, which the passengers alternatively push down or pull up to move the cart.

Beneath his full-faced dive mask, Sam grinned. "How about we use that?"

CHAPTER THIRTEEN

TOM COULD BARELY CONTAIN HIS laughter as he and Sam started to vigorously pump the mechanical arm, sending their submerged iron handcart racing through the flooded tunnel, and making him feel more like a torpedo.

They quickly picked up momentum, and the heavy iron handcart rushed through the water. Ahead, Sam's headlamp lit up the tunnel like the headlights on a train.

The duct keel appeared sound and intact.

Tom said, "Any chance the *Buckholtz* grounded her bow on the muddy island, only to slide backward into the water and slice the side of her hull, above the keel, with an uncharted reef?"

"It's possible," Sam admitted. "Unlikely, but possible. Let's get to the end of this and then we'll have a better look."

Their trip across the flooded section of the duct keel ended approximately two-thirds of the way along the length of the *Buckholtz*.

The hand-cart broke through the surface of the water, marking the end of the flooded section of the ship. Tom kept pumping the arm, and the cart continued its journey into the progressively shallower water until they were running along dry rails.

The cart picked up speed, despite the slight incline.

Tom said, "Think the air's breathable?"

"Not a chance," Sam replied, shining his flashlight across a set of rusty pipes. "Oxygen is depleted by oxidization of steel. Without access to the outside air, my guess is the air here contains well under 21 percent oxygen required to sustain life."

"I suppose, on top of that, carbon monoxide, inert gasses, and methane from the breakdown of carbon within the ballast water are all potentially present to form a lethal cocktail."

"Yeah, I think I'll keep my dive-mask on."

Tom kept pumping the cart's arm.

The tunnel never seemed to change. There were three large pipes running parallel to the handcart — one for fuel and two for ballast water.

Tom studied his surroundings as he moved, without finding anything that appeared out of place.

"You see anything?"

"No. Not a thing."

"Which means, we will have to go back to searching the external hull."

Sam lightly pulled the brake, and the cart came to a stop.

Tom said, "Did we reach the end?"

"No," Sam replied.

"What is it?"

Sam stood up, stepping off the handcart. He swept the area with his flashlight before settling on something lying on the middle of the tracks. "That."

Tom looked at the body. It seemed fairly intact, with little sign of decomposition. A male approximately fifty to sixty years old, overweight, but not obese. The body was lying prone so that he couldn't see the face. Tom leaned over and felt for a pulse, almost expecting to find one.

The body was cold.

Not like ice, but no warmer than the inanimate steel it was

lying on.

"The guy's dead," Tom confirmed.

Sam rolled him onto his side. "There's no sign of any injuries."

"What do you think killed him?"

"My guess, he got trapped down here while doing his routine maintenance check of the duct keel, only to become trapped, and then suffocated."

"That makes sense." Tom barely suppressed a grin. "Although, I'd like to know why Gene denied any injuries or fatalities when the *Buckholtz* ran aground?"

"Yeah, me too. Maybe he genuinely didn't know yet."

"Or, he was murdered," Tom suggested.

"What makes you say that?"

Tom shined his headlamp on the man's hand. It still gripped a notepad. He picked it up and handed it to Sam. "Read that."

Sam took the note and ran his eyes across it. "I'M SORRY, SVETLANA. THEY MADE ME DO IT."

CHAPTER FOURTEEN

SAM STEPPED BACK ONTO THE handcart.

He committed the name, Svetlana, to memory. It was a common enough Russian name, but maybe Elise would be able to put the name and the dead man's face together somewhere. She could be quite the magician when it came to locating unknown people.

"You don't want to go to the end?" Tom asked.

"No. We already know it doesn't lead anywhere and any damage farther toward the bow can't possibly have caused the flooding, because it was out of the water the entire time." Sam glanced at the body one last time. "No. The duct keel hasn't told us anything about where the water came in from—only that someone used it to murder someone."

"So instead of answers, we got more questions."

"Yeah, like what he knew got him murdered."

"Exactly."

Sam flicked the gear lever downward, changing the direction of the handcart to run toward the stern. He and Tom started pumping the arm until they built up speed and then alternated between one another every few minutes.

Sam glanced at his gauges. Everything was as expected. They had been on the dive for 41 minutes, and their maximum depth was 51 feet. Using their closed circuit rebreather system, they still had more than three hours of dive time available.

He glanced at Tom. "How are your gauges looking?"

"Good," Tom replied. "At current consumption, I still have three hours and fifteen minutes of gas before I'm going to need to hit the reserve. Why? Did you want to search the internal hull throughout each of the individual bays?"

"No. But if you're up for it, I wouldn't mind eyeballing Mr. Cutting's precious secret shipping container. Maybe it might reveal a clue to the murder."

"Okay, I'm keen."

It took nearly twenty minutes to reach the engine bay.

Sam was happy to leave the narrow confines of the duct keel, and happier still, to be on the outside of the watertight doors through which they had entered.

On his heads-up-display, a compass was projected in front of him. He glanced at it, setting a heading for south-southwest at 220 degrees — the same direction in which the *Buckholtz's* keel ran aground toward Neuwerk Island.

Beneath the compass, was a digital image of the ship's schematics superimposed on what Sam was looking at to provide a sort of augmented reality. His computer system updated instantly providing their predicted location and mapping, based on what Sam was able to see. It made diving within the massive cargo ship much more achievable.

He kicked his fins, swimming directly over the top of the large diesel powerplant and through a closed set of blue doors.

Sam pushed through the doors, which opened to Bay 9. Rows of shipping containers were stacked to the ceiling. A narrow steel gangway formed a platform to walk throughout the containers, with a series of ladders to take sailors up or down a deck.

He followed the passageway all the way to port side and then followed it toward the bow in the next bay.

Sam's display popped up with his location, *10/14/08.*

Sam mentally retrieved the precise location of the secret shipping container.

Bay 10/ Row 14/ Tier 08

He gently kicked his fins, moving slowly forward.

A small marker on the gangway below him was the only evidence he'd passed into the 10th bay. He stopped and shined his light through the series of intricate tunnels formed by the placement of multiple shipping containers, stacked upon themselves.

"Do you see it?" he asked Tom.

"Not yet. It should be directly below us."

He searched for a way to get down. The passageway they were on didn't allow them to descend. Instead, they would need to get much lower. Swimming another twenty feet forward, he turned right to follow an internal passageway toward the *Buckholtz's* centerline.

Sam fixed his gaze on the row of shipping containers beside him. A tiny camera mounted within his dive mask took in the image. He held his attention on the first of the shipping containers for a moment longer until it triggered his augmented reality to spit out the shipping container's position.

10/14/10

Sam said, "It should be directly below here."

"Great. Can you see how to get down there?"

Sam adjusted his heads-up-display, so that he zoomed out from the ship's schematics, allowing him to see what he was looking for — a set of stairs and ladders, which would allow him to drop down to the 8th tier.

"Got it!" he said. "There's a set of ladders that run all the way to the bilge."

"All right," Tom said. "I'll follow you."

Sam continued to swim toward the ladder. It wasn't that he

needed a ladder to get down, but with the rows upon rows of shipping containers secured so close, it was impossible to move anywhere. Even the gangway and passageway that he was traveling above didn't have railings—it didn't need to; the shipping containers formed a natural barrier.

He glanced at another shipping container. The location flashed across his heads-up-display. *10/08/10.* Sam kept swimming until he reached the internal ladder system. There, he released a small amount of air from his diving buoyancy wing until he slowly sank downward.

It took only a few seconds to descend to the 8th tier.

Sam followed the narrow gap between the rows of shipping containers, heading toward the port side, and then stopped.

A dark void filled the portside.

He shined his flashlight around and then swore—the 60-foot, specialized shipping container was missing.

CHAPTER FIFTEEN

S AM STARED AT THE NOTE being displayed by his heads-up-display's augmented reality.

10/14/08 – shipping container: missing.

He shined the beam of his flashlight across the dark, empty space. It almost certainly matched the dimensions of the shipping container at 60-feet by 8-feet wide. Directly surrounding its edges were rows upon rows of shipping containers.

Sam's lips formed an incredulous grin. "All right. I'll bite. Someone's stolen the damned thing."

"Looks like it," Tom agreed.

"The question is, how did they do it?" Sam flashed the beam across the bay. There wasn't even enough spare room for him or Tom to swim freely, without following the narrow passageways. "It's not like they could have stolen the shipping container but left the other twenty between here and the deck."

"No. Which means, they needed to get out through the side of the hull."

Sam's head snapped around to Row 14. His eyes hadn't given it any thought before because he knew that he was at the last row on board the *Buckholtz,* but now, as he glanced toward the port hull, he spotted it.

Sam stared at the opening. "I don't believe it!"

Tom moved to follow him. "That's impressive. A lot of work went into stealing that shipping container. It makes you wonder why?"

"You mean, what's inside that shipping container that's worth sinking the entire ship for?"

"Exactly."

Sam fixed his flashlight on the opening. It was a little over 8-feet wide by 11-feet tall. Almost the same dimensions as the specialized shipping container.

The edges were razor sharp angles, forming a wound of surgical precision rather than a gash made by the sinking of the *Buckholtz*. There was one thing for certain, the steel had been cut with a powerful piece of hardware.

Sam kicked his fins and moved toward the opening.

There was something about it that caught his eye. Water appeared to be flowing through the opening.

A small eddy had formed, where the murky waters of the Elbe were mixing with the stilled water of the interior hull. That would have made sense if someone had cut the opening moments ago, but surely the damage had been caused nearly twenty-four hours ago when the ship first ran aground?

He swam out through the opening to get a better look and formulate some sort of explanation. The water outside the hull was slightly warmer and the visibility obscured by clouds of mud.

That's when he stopped.

There, thirty or so feet away, lying on the muddy seabed was the specialized shipping container. From what he could see, the purpose-built container was still intact. According to Gene, it had been designed to withstand significant pressures in the event of water damage.

"Over there!" Sam shouted.

"I see it!" Tom said, without making any move toward the

massive hold.

Sam kicked his fins and swam toward the shipping container.

He was nearly there. Maybe five feet shy of placing his hand on it, when the shipping container started to move.

The massive structure jolted forward.

It looked like a magic trick, until he looked up, and spotted the dark fin of the large submarine.

CHAPTER SIXTEEN

Ω————————Ω————————Ω

A SERIES OF DIVERS HAD secured the shipping container onto a buoyant sled and then attached the front of that to the submarine.

Mentally, Sam tried to orient himself to the shipping lanes. There was deep water to the north of Neuwerk Island, where the North Sea began. Even a large submarine could conceal itself indefinitely in its depth.

He had no way of knowing just how valuable the contents of the specialized shipping container might be, but that didn't matter to him. What counted was the fact someone had gone to such extreme lengths to steal it, and for that, he was willing to put his neck on the line to stop them.

Sam kicked harder until he reached the side of the shipping container. A series of thick nylon cables enmeshed the entire thing like a spider's web.

He grabbed his dive knife and started to slice through the first one he could find.

The container jolted forward again. It was a tentative movement, like someone was testing it and making certain its cradle would hold. They didn't have much time to cut it free, or the submarine would drag it off into the North Sea — where it would disappear for good.

"Quick!" Sam shouted. "Tom, try and cut the other side."

There was no reply.

"Tom?" Sam looked over his right shoulder.

Still no response.

Holding on with his left hand, he flashed the beam of his light behind him, toward the razor-sharp opening of the *Buckholtz.*

The void was dark, and visibility nearly impossible beneath the recently disturbed muddy waters, but Sam spotted the series of large bubbles as they drifted toward the surface.

There were too many, and they were too large to be the natural result of Tom releasing excess gas from his buoyancy wing.

Had he been injured somehow?

The fleeting thought dissipated as quickly as it had arrived. Sam's heart raced and the lines of his face creased with concern.

Those bubbles looked like what you'd expect to see from a traditional scuba as the expired air bled into the water.

In fact, those bubbles had come from three scuba divers.

Sam forgot about the specialized shipping container and its precious secret cargo. He let go of the remaining nylon tiedown, switched off his flashlight and raced toward the *Buckholtz* in cover of darkness.

He took in the scene at a glance.

They had caught Tom as he swam out of the hold, and in the process had somehow damaged his underwater radio—thus explaining why he hadn't called for help. It had taken three divers to get Tom down, but Sam couldn't see what they were trying to do to him.

All he could see was that Tom wasn't going down without a fight.

He struggled and fought like a frenzied fish. Hand-to-hand fighting is difficult in enclosed spaces, like the interior hull of the *Buckholtz,* but it was next to impossible in thick dive gear, while submerged in narrow spaces. The viscosity of water forces every move to slow down. Numerous weapons still fired under water, but bullets rapidly lost their momentum, rendering any shots ineffective unless the barrel of the gun was pressed up against an enemy. Kicks and punches were mostly useless too, for the same reason.

A sharp, streamlined weapon, like a speargun, was the most lethal.

The fact that Tom was still alive suggested to Sam that the divers weren't expecting trouble and thus weren't equipped to fight. They had most likely spotted him and Tom and tried to kill Tom while he was on his own.

Right now, they were working to physically maneuver Tom until he was face down and they could easily close off his oxygen supply.

Sam gripped his dive knife firmly in his right hand.

There wasn't much time.

Three of them versus him and Tom. They had the advantage, but he might still surprise them—and once Tom was free, it would be a much fairer fight.

Sam reached the diver closest to him. The diver had his back up against the internal wall of the *Buckholtz*. He was trying to work out how to shut down the oxygen supply to Tom's closed-circuit rebreather system. It was nearly impossible without dismantling the aluminum backpack, but the sight gave Sam an idea.

The scuba diver's tank was directly in front of him. Sam reached forward and closed the attacker's regulator valve.

Confident it was now closed, he positioned himself backward in the dark and waited for a few seconds. Sam watched as the diver realized something was wrong, and unable to do anything about it, broke free from the fight and headed toward the surface.

The second diver turned to see what was going on. Sam watched as he peered out the opening in the hull, where the first diver was now making a rapid ascent to the surface.

When the diver turned again, to face Tom, Sam slid his knife into the diver's throat.

The blade was razor sharp, designed for slicing ropes and anything else that he might become entangled with, and he drove it straight through his attacker's windpipe. The diver frantically, reached for his throat, as though he could somehow protect himself.

Sam twisted the blade, causing further damage, and then yanked it free.

It was a disturbing way to kill a man, but there was nothing else to be done. It was either the scuba divers or Tom and him. Kill or be killed. Given the options, Sam was happy with his choice. He stared at the diver. Sam's knife had inflicted a fatal wound, and the man knew it. His eyes were wide with terror, and his arms flailed frantically, searching for some sort of support.

Sam stared at the stranger's eyes. There was something else there, too. Concealed within the man's death throes, was another emotion, something that took Sam by surprise— triumph.

Sam tried to back away, out of reach, but he wasn't quick enough. The dying man's hand connected with Sam's full-faced dive mask and the man yanked it free.

In an instant, his visibility was taken from him.

Sam tried to orient himself, but there was little he could do. The second his mask was ripped free, murky water gushed over his face, flooding his mouth and blinding his eyes. He forced himself to open his eyes. In the darkened mess, his eyes swept the environment, trying to distinguish the darkness of the internal hull of the *Buckholtz* and the radiant light from outside.

His only chance was to reach the surface, but until he got control, and knew in what direction that was, he would end up doing nothing more than racing toward his death.

The seawater turned white with bubbles gushing out of the end of the piping that should have formed his closed-circuit rebreather system—a system no longer closed with the destruction of his mask.

Still, he needed to reach the end of that tubing. It wouldn't last long, but the air inside might sustain his life long enough to reach the surface.

He groped in the dark for the end of the pipe and then pulled it toward his mouth. The bubbles went everywhere. He couldn't seem to form a seal. *Why not?* Mentally, he struggled to come up with an answer. *Had his attacker managed to rip the piping down the middle?* It seemed impossible. He tried a second time to form a seal over the end of the tube but failed.

Next solution, locate his pony bottle.

A pony bottle was a small tank with 50 bar of compressed air. It encompassed a small regulator and single mouthpiece. It was generally attached to his right leg as a last resort, emergency, breathing source.

Only now, he couldn't reach it.

He ran his hands all the way down his torso and thighs.

It wasn't there.

Could his attacker have managed to knock that off, too?

Sam shook his head. It didn't matter. Right now, he needed to surface. But the darkness was overcoming him.

He thought he saw the light and started swimming toward it, only when he reached it, his world got darker again. The problem was that without vision or an air supply it was almost impossible to determine in which direction the surface was. He followed the light, as his chest burned with the tightness of suffocation.

Sam felt his ears ache and swallowed to equalize the pressure.

He should have been near the surface. *Was he going deeper?* The thought horrified him. He gritted his teeth and kept swimming. The world in front of him was bright like he was nearing the surface. He reached his hands forward expecting to break the surface of the water.

Instead, they slammed into something metal.

Sam stared at the light in disbelief and grabbed it.

In an instant, full understanding dawned on him. It was a flashlight. Not his, but the other diver's. The light must have fallen free, dropping to the lower levels of the *Buckholtz's* internal hull. He'd followed the light all the way down to the bottom, which meant he was now what... 50...or possibly 60 feet from the surface?

Terror stripped at his hardened resolve, and part of him was ready to take a deep breath and end it all then and there.

But he'd never been a quitter and didn't plan to make this the day of his death. So, instead, he gripped the flashlight and kicked off the bottom of the hull in a desperate race to the surface. He kicked both of his legs in a slow and continuous motion.

Despite his tenacity, Sam couldn't stay submerged without air indefinitely — his vision started to darken.

He felt his world come apart as his oxygen-deprived brain struggled to make sense of his environment.

Above him, Sam's hands struck steel. It was possibly the internal deck of the *Buckholtz,* or even simply a gangway or passageway.

It didn't matter.

There was nowhere else for him to go.

Sam stopped kicking. And why shouldn't he? It was now impossible for him to reach the surface. A ghost, or was it simply a figment of his imagination, told him to have a rest and take it easy. Everything was going to be just right.

The ghost was big and friendly. It handed him something and told him to breathe. Sam kept pushing it away. *No thank you... I'm quite all right, dying here without your help.* But the ethereal specter was insistent, until Sam finally felt something forced into his mouth.

The creature patted him heavily on his back, encouraging him to breathe.

I can't breathe this, it's just water.

I'm dreaming, but I know I can't breathe water!

He felt two more heavy blows to his back. The ghost was persistent if nothing else. Sam no longer had the strength to resist. He took a deep breath in and waited for his lungs to fill with water. The breath was followed by another one.

It felt good. Cold but good. Not at all like what he expected drowning, or even death for that matter, to feel like.

A moment later, he started to move.

The creature was pulling him downward. Sam no longer had any fear. And why should he? Nothing can harm the dead, can it? It didn't take long, and he was pulled through an opening, and dragged to the surface.

Sam felt his head broach the sea. The mouthpiece was removed from his mouth. He closed his eyes he took a deep breath of fresh air. It tasted salty but fresh.

Next to him, the ghost was removing something that covered its face.

He opened his eyes and stared at the specter.

"Tom?"

Tom suppressed a grin. "Who the hell else did you expect to save your sorry ass from the bottom of the hull?"

CHAPTER SEVENTEEN

S AM CLIMBED THE LADDER ON the side of the *Buckholtz* until he reached the bridge. It was a quarter past two in the afternoon, and the sun shined warmly on the deck. Once there, he laid down over the warm external wing, taking in the radiating heat. He was exhausted and could have slept there for a week.

Instead, he turned to Tom. "Thanks."

"No problem. Like I said, if not me, then who? Besides, you came back for me in the first place." Tom crossed his arms. "Obviously, I could have taken care of the three attackers by myself, but you did help speed the process up a little."

Sam smiled. "About that. Last I saw you, you were still fighting one of them. So, what happened?"

"It was easy. While you cleverly distracted him by losing your dive mask, and nearly drowning, I knocked him off me. In the subsequent fight, he took one look at me and decided to swim after the container."

Sam sat up. "We should try and find it."

"I wouldn't bother. That team was filled with pros. The container was already being towed by a submarine. That submarine's well on its way into deep water, and we're never going to see it again."

"We might get lucky and spot it from the air if we get on the helicopter."

"Sure. But we'd need a helicopter first, and the *Maria Helena* won't be here for a few hours."

Sam said, "Maybe we can resume the search once they get here?"

"What?" Tom laughed. "And get lucky finding a submarine that's had a three-hour head start?"

"You think it's unlikely?"

"Unlikely?" Tom shook his head. "It's impossible. If you know of a way to do that, you should talk to my dad. He's spent his life trying to locate submarines that wanted to remain hidden."

"All right. That's fair. So, we lost the container."

"Yeah, now we just need to see Gene and find out what he wants us to do about it."

Right on cue, Gene Cuttings approached. "I see you two made it back okay without any trouble?"

Sam suppressed a grin. "Yeah, you could say that."

Gene sighed heavily. "Well? What's the damage? How bad is it?"

Sam ran a towel over his face, running the palm of his hands and fingers through his thick, wavy, brown hair. "I'm sorry, Gene. You've got big problems."

"That bad?" Gene's eyebrows narrowed. "How long will it take to retrieve?"

Sam shook his head. "No. You misunderstand me. It's not just difficult to retrieve. I found the storage room."

"And?"

"It's missing. There's a 20-foot gash in the hull, where someone has attacked it with surgical precision to remove your specialized shipping container."

"How long ago do you think it was stolen?" Gene asked.

Sam shrugged. "About twenty minutes ago."

"Jesus! Why don't you get back down there? Didn't you try

and stop them?"

Sam crossed his arms. "We did."

Gene noticed the small scratch marks on Sam's face. Lines of tension creased his hardened face. "What happened?"

"We were attacked. They, whoever they were, fitted the shipping container onto a large cradle and were in the process of towing it out to sea with a large submarine, when a group of divers attacked us."

"So the whole accident was set up as an elaborate plan to steal it?"

"It would appear so," Sam replied.

"How?"

"I have no idea, but I'm still keen to find out. I'd like to have a look around the island, to see if I can spot anything that might reveal what went wrong. At first, I would just assume that your crew was involved, but those digital recordings were pretty convincing—someone set the *Buckholtz* up to crash into Neuwerk Island."

"What about my ship?"

"It won't take much to seal the gap in the hull and then pump out the water. Once we do that, she'll mostly float off on the next high tide. Tom's already contacted the *Maria Helena.* She will be here by tomorrow morning, along with two tugboats, and will be able to coordinate the operation to bring her back into the water. Once we do that, they will be able to tow her into dry dock in Hamburg for more extensive repairs."

Gene visibly relaxed. "That's something at least. Thank you."

One of the engineers shouted something to Gene, which Sam couldn't quite hear. He turned to Gene and asked, "What did he say?"

Gene frowned. "There appears to be a dead scuba diver floating in the water."

Sam said, "Sorry. That's my fault. You'd better send your guys out to retrieve the body. The German police are going to want to examine it. If we get lucky, we might find out who stole your cargo, too."

Gene sighed. "All right, I'll organize it. Anything else you want to let me know about?"

"Yeah. You have another dead guy in your duct keel. This one has a note."

Gene's eyes narrowed. "What did the note say?"

"I'm Sorry Svetlana, they made me do it." Sam squinted his eyes. "Does that mean anything to you?"

"Not a thing."

CHAPTER EIGHTEEN

A FTER SOME DISCUSSION ABOUT WHO was responsible for the retrieval of the body, Sam and Tom ended up climbing onto the rubber Zodiac and making the retrieval themselves. Sam opened the throttle, and the little 2-stroke engine whined, sending the Zodiac skipping off the wavelets. It took less than five minutes to round the stern of the *Buckholtz* and then spot the body.

Twenty feet out from the body, Sam released the throttle, and the bow of the Zodiac dropped into the water again. He idled to a stop on the starboard side of the body. Tom reached over and pulled the scuba diver on board.

The man's throat had been slashed, and there was no doubt he would not have survived.

Even so, Tom checked for a pulse, before confirming, "He's dead."

"It was him or me," Sam said.

"I don't blame you."

Sam pulled off the diver's facemask. He looked about 45–50 years old, with a gray beard, steely blue eyes, and no distinguishing marks.

Tom folded back the diver's hood and read the brand name. "It's a British brand."

Sam glanced at it and suppressed a grin. "It looks decidedly British, doesn't it?"

"It isn't?"

"No. This was made for the Russian SVR—Foreign Intelligence Service—formerly known as the KGB."

"Really?" Tom was skeptical. "What did they want with the container?"

"I have no idea, but I suppose that would all depend on what exactly was stored inside."

Sam opened the throttle, and the Zodiac skipped toward the muddy beach once more. They rounded the stern of the *Buckholtz,* and the propeller snagged on something, sending the 2-stroke engine into a high-pitched whine.

Sam closed the throttle and then took it out of gear.

Tom asked, "What's wrong?"

"I don't know. The propeller got caught on something."

Sam killed the engine and tilted the outboard so they could get a good look at the propeller. It was fouled by something metallic. He pulled at it, and a large chunk of reflective metal came free.

Sam examined the material. "Aluminum?"

"Looks like it," Tom replied. "I wonder if the *Buckholtz* was carrying a container full of the stuff."

"Why?"

"Just look at the water, the place is riddled with the stuff."

"Really?" Sam squinted his eyes and swept the water. Broken and partially submerged were dozens, if not hundreds of separate pieces of aluminum—giant sheets of foil—scattered throughout the water. "Beats me."

Sam finished freeing the propeller, dropped it back into the water, and then carefully idled toward the shore. They pulled the Zodiac up on the beach. The beach was lined with a type of black cloth. At first, Sam guessed the material was used to protect the island from erosion, but the more he studied it, the more out of place the material appeared.

Tom said, "What is it?"

"This stuff," Sam said, picking up the material. "It doesn't look like it belongs here."

"It's not here to stop the runoff from the island?"

"That's what I thought, but I don't think so."

"Why not?"

Sam pointed toward the larger rocks and small buildings on the island. They were all covered in the same material. "There's no reason to cover those things."

Tom grinned. "I don't believe it."

"What?"

"It looks like someone has gone to the trouble of hiding the island while building an artificial island out of aluminum out at sea!"

Sam nodded. "Of course. Aluminum would have reflected the *Buckholtz's* radar, making the pilot think he was on the wrong side of the shipping lane. A glance at the Neuwerk Island would have revealed nothing but darkness, and only confirmed the pilot's terrifying suspicion that his ship was in the wrong place. As a consequence, he turned ninety degrees, trying to avoid a direct collision with what he now thought was the island, and in doing so, ran aground."

A few minutes later, Sam climbed back onto the Zodiac and motored it across to the bottom level of the bridge. There, he explained the near impossible theory to Gene, who struggled to accept it.

It no longer mattered. The ruse had achieved its objective, and the highly valuable cargo was gone. The *Maria Helena* would arrive in two days, and then they would pull the *Buckholtz* back into the water.

Sam's satellite phone rang. He answered it. "Sam Reilly speaking."

"Mr. Reilly," came the voice of the lead British investigator for the crashed Boeing 747 Dreamlifter. "We've retrieved the data from the FDR. We are lucky this plane's FDR had a video feed."

"And?"

"You're not going to believe what happened."

"What happened?"

"I wouldn't even bother trying to tell you about it. I've emailed a copy of the FDR cockpit recording. Just watch it and let me know what you think."

Sam asked, impatiently, "Do you know how the 747 crashed?"

"Yeah, I just don't believe it."

"Why? What happened?"

"Just watch the tape. It gets really interesting at 15:32!"

CHAPTER NINETEEN

Ω ——————— Ω ——————— Ω

SAM OPENED HIS LAPTOP, DOWNLOADED the document, and pressed play.

Next to him, Tom sat down and stared at the video feed. The flight deck recording depicted the view from a camera mounted directly behind the two pilots. Its wide lens allowed for a clear view of the cockpit, including both pilots, instruments, and the view of their windshield.

Sam's eyes instantly met the thick cloud cover that obstructed the pilots' vision ahead. He glanced at the instruments. The pilot in command had more than ten thousand hours of flying time under his belt and had flown the route from Germany to New York hundreds of times before. He had intentionally diverted nearly a hundred miles north of his original route in an attempt to catch a ninety mile an hour tailwind. It wasn't an unusual detour for the company to take, despite being far from the direct route.

The pilot in command, with clear knowledge of the likely weather patterns in the region, had set up instrument-rated flight—meaning that he would rely entirely on "instruments only" for his navigation and no visual reference.

The first fifteen minutes appeared routine. The aircraft had already climbed and reached its cruising altitude of 42,000 feet. The copilot quietly completed a series of flight reports.

Although Sam had never personally flown a 747 Dreamlifter, he'd been in the one that his dad owned many times. To his ear, the aircraft's four Pratt & Whitney PW4062 engines purred nicely. There was nothing to suggest the aircraft was about to suffer a fatal fault, leading to the aircraft's demise.

At 15:32 everything changed.

It was subtle at first, and like most disasters, a series of unfortunate events led to the aircraft's demise.

Sam noted that the pitch of the four engines hadn't changed.

The pilot on the left—the one in command—looked at the airspeed gauge. It showed their speed had suddenly dropped from 560 to 470 knots. Next to it, the altimeter showed their altitude falling at 100 feet per second.

The captain turned to face his copilot with the calm authority of a man who'd spent his life in command of an aircraft. "What do you make of that?"

The co-pilot shook his head, bewildered. "Maybe we've hit a patch of icy air and a downdraft?"

Both men glanced at the artificial horizon—the instrument that showed the aircraft's attitude, which is its angle of attack relative to the horizon. The image showed them flying straight and level.

"I don't think so," the pilot replied. "You'd better check the cargo bay. Make sure we haven't had a load shift."

Sam found himself nodding in agreement. It would have been one of his first thoughts in the same circumstance. If a heavy load shifts midflight, it instantly changes the weight distribution of the aircraft, either sending it nose up causing it to stall dramatically, or nose down, causing it to run straight into the ground. Either way, it was a logical explanation.

On an iPad, the copilot flicked through a series of live video feeds showing the cargo bay. After the fourth one, the copilot put the iPad down and said, "No. The cargo's still intact."

Sam rewound a few seconds and paused the image of the

cargo bay. He felt the spiny prickle of fear pluck at the hairs in the back of his neck. There, in the middle of the massive Dreamlifter's cargo bay, taking up the entire space, was a large sphere. It sat on a purpose-built container, bolted down and secured by large cargo chains.

He stared at that image. His breathing became uneven, and he felt a knot twist in his stomach. Sam recalled the recent dive he'd made in the Norwegian Sea on board that same aircraft.

The cargo bay had been empty.

No one ever informed him that the aircraft was carrying a load. Someone was intentionally lying to him.

He closed his eyes and sighed.

Why?

Why go through the process of hiring him at all, if they weren't going to tell him what this was all about?

Sam made a digital copy of the sphere with his smartphone. He attached it to a message for Elise, with a single question — *Please identify.*

He then pressed play, and the video continued.

The pilot said, "I'm going to disconnect the autopilot and take over manual control for a minute."

"Copy that," replied the copilot.

The pilot disengaged the autopilot and took over manual control of the large aircraft. Sam watched as the man gently eased the wheel forward, dipping the nose and then pulling it toward his chest. The artificial horizon showed their nose pitch downward and then upward, before the pilot gently leveled the aircraft to straight and level once more.

The pilot shrugged. "She seems to be responding fine."

The copilot pointed to the altimeter. "We're still descending."

"All right, let's increase power and see what happens."

"Agreed."

The pilot increased power to all four Pratt & Whitney engines.

Sam glanced at the altimeter. It was still slowly rotating counter-clockwise, meaning they were still on a steady descent.

The pilot saw it, too. "I don't get it. We're not making any difference to it. One thing is for certain, all three of these instruments can't be wrong."

"I'm running through the checklist now!" the co-pilot said, opening the emergency checklist for primary flight display faults.

He scanned the boldface information. These were the actions that were absolutely critical to survival—so called because in their flight training manuals they were written in boldfaced capital letters. The term, boldface, was said to be written in blood because these critical steps, usually created from an accident investigation, were ones that should have been taken to avoid a fatal crash but weren't. These steps could, in a crisis, save your life.

"Right. I'm going through the list now." The copilot opened up his flight manual and ran through a checklist for potential faults leading to instrument disparities. In this case, specifically, the altimeter and airspeed weren't matching up.

Sam found himself impressed by the professionalism and competence displayed by the pilots. They were clearly experienced. This sort of situation was the thing of nightmares in terms of airmanship. In thick cloud cover and without accurate instrumentation, a pilot could quickly become disoriented and panic. It was a recipe for disaster. Unable to trust the effectiveness of the artificial horizon, speedometer, or altimeter, a pilot had little means of maintaining the aircraft in straight and level flight.

Yet, still. At this stage, the two pilots were working the problem in a calm and efficient manner. Such an event was a true proving ground where pilots demonstrated how well-rounded their capabilities were, but more often a crucible where pilots identify gaps in their knowledge, leading to a domino effect, quickly cascading into an irreversible disaster.

Few people survived such events.

Sam closed his eyes for a moment as he recalled that these two men, despite their competence, failed to survive the event.

The copilot said, "I'm manually checking the air driven gyroscope, GPS, and inertial navigation to get an accurate reading of our attitude."

The captain said, "Read me the numbers when you're ready."

"Okay, got it. We're flying straight and level. Our altitude is 42,000 feet, and our speed is 470 knots."

The captain shook his head. "I don't believe it. That's exactly what I have."

"Any ideas what caused it?"

"There might have been a slight glitch in the primary flight display."

Sam recalled how most information was digitally run through the primary flight display on a Boeing 747. The PFD is a modernization of older, fully mechanical displays that present the critical flight information on a fully-integrated display. This includes airspeed, altitude, attitude, and "bugs" — important, dynamically updated information calculated by the system's computer. The biggest difference with the PFD is that the underlying mechanical measurement systems — the gyroscope, the pitot barometric pressure instruments, and differential pressure gauges — are totally separate to the display.

A third pilot stepped into the cockpit.

Hello. Sam paused the image and took a copy of the man's face. *Who are you?*

"What's going on?" the new pilot asked.

He was most likely the third pilot, currently on his rotational rest time.

The captain said, "We had a problem with our primary flight display. Some of the data was being incorrectly displayed, but it seems to have worked itself out now."

"Do you want a hand?"

"Yeah, you want to plug the maintenance laptop into the BUS and run a diagnostic test?"

"Sure."

"If you find anything, let me know, and we'll switch over to the secondary flight display."

"All right, I'm on it."

The third pilot turned, and a moment later, everything changed.

A series of loud warning alarms screamed and flashed.

The captain said, "I've got fires in engines 1 and 2."

All three of their heads raced to the port window. The wing was entirely obscured by the thick cloud cover.

"Anyone have a visual?" the captain asked.

"No," came the reply.

"All right. I'm shutting down engines 1 and 2."

"Confirm," the copilot said. "Shutting down engines 1 and 2."

The pilot in command increased power to engines 3 and 4 and applied pressure to the right rudder to counteract the yaw to the port side.

The third pilot said, "I'm going to plug into the maintenance BUS and see if I can work out what's going on with those engines."

"Understood. Let me know what you find." The captain then said to his copilot, "Get me the coordinates for Oslo Airport."

"Yes, sir."

The captain was about to voice a mayday when he noticed their airspeed was decreasing and their altitude was plummeting.

He said, "We're losing altitude."

"How?" the copilot said, "Engines 3, and 4 are at maximum

power."

The Dreamlifter should have been able to maintain its altitude with just two engines running.

The captain's eyes darted across a series of instruments, trying to determine the cause of the problem.

"Could we still be having the same problem with the primary flight display?"

The copilot checked off the numbers from the secondary flight displays. The readings seemed to be matching up.

The captain was about to instruct his off-duty officer to switch over to the secondary flight displays when the warning light for engine number 4 lit up.

"We've got another engine fire!"

The copilot pressed his eyes to the starboard window. "I can't see anything!"

"Yeah, well I don't want a fire on board. I'm shutting her down."

"Are you sure you want to do that?"

The captain shrugged. "What choice have we got?"

"It might be another glitch."

"And it might not be. If we're wrong, we have nearly 50,000 gallons of aviation fuel ready to ignite."

"All right, all right. Let's shut down."

The captain checked that he had the shutdown switch for engine number 4, confirmed it, and then shut it down.

He then depressed the microphone and calmly voiced his mayday, including their rough position, and that they were going to head toward the Oslo Airport in Norway for an emergency landing, but at this stage, he believed they had a fault with their instruments, not their engines or aircraft controls.

There was no response on the radio.

He tried again without any success and then gave up.

The captain set up for a gradual descent. "Have you found

the coordinates for Oslo?"

"Yeah, but at our current descent rate, we'll be lucky to make it halfway."

"All right, we're probably going to end up ditching in the ocean. I want you and Roger back there to get in your survival suits. It's a long shot, but if we do have to put down into the water, I want to make sure we give ourselves the best possible chance of survival."

"Okay, I'm on it."

Four minutes later, both copilots returned.

The captain looked at Roger. "What did the maintenance system say was going on with our primary flight display?"

"It didn't. According to its self-diagnostics, the system's running smoothly."

"What about the engines?"

"It's recording high oil pressure in all four engines, and extreme heat in engines 1,2, and 4."

The captain turned to face him. "There's high oil pressure in all four engines?"

"Yes, sir."

"You know what this means?"

"Yes, sir. We're living on borrowed time before engine 3 gives out."

"That's right."

The fourth engine alarm buzzed.

The captain's head snapped to the right. His heart raced, and he felt fear rise in his throat. His eyes remained fixed on the warning light. The two copilots stared out the starboard window. It was a pointless exercise. The cloud cover was too dense to allow them to see anything.

"We have an engine fire warning for engine 3, sir."

"Understood."

And still, the captain remained silent.

"Sir?" the copilot asked.

"Shut it down."

"Copy that, sir. Shutting down engine 3."

The constant drone of the engines ceased, and the cockpit became silent.

The captain said, "All right. We're committed to a water landing, gentlemen. You'd better strap yourselves in tight."

"What about your survival suit, captain?" the copilot asked.

The captain smiled. It was sardonic but confident. "We're out of time. That's all right. If we survive the landing, I'm happy to take my chances."

Even as Sam watched the events unfold, he shared the same sense of disbelief as the two pilots — how could a modern Boeing 747 lose all four engines?

The captain dipped the nose until their airspeed picked up. The last thing he wanted to do was stall now. He made firm and decided movements with the control, happy to see the aircraft was still responding to his inputs.

The altimeter started to race counter-clockwise.

"Can you control our descent?" the copilot asked.

"Not a chance in hell." The captain eased the wheel forward, dipping the nose farther. "Besides, I don't think the altimeter's giving us the correct readings."

"I'll get out the manual instruments and see what we've got."

"All right, but I think we'll know for sure any second now, just as we drop below the cloud cover."

"Is that wise?"

"Not really. But it's not like we really have a choice, do we?"

The copilot shrugged. "We might slam into some sort of ground terrain."

The pilot shook his head emphatically. "Unlikely. There's nothing higher than a cruise ship for more than a hundred miles. We're good."

"What if the altimeter's right?" the copilot asked. "All you're going to do is send us straight into the sea."

"It's wrong. I can feel it."

"Many pilots have made that mistake before."

The captain nodded. "All right. There's a mug in my backpack over there. Can you please pass it to me?"

The copilot unclipped his harness and reached around to retrieve the mug. "What do you want to do with it?"

"Fill it up with some coffee from the thermos."

"Really?" the copilot cocked an incredulous eyebrow. "You feel like a coffee break right now?"

"Fill it up and sit it in the middle here."

The copilot looked dumbfounded but did as the captain had asked.

The captain grinned. "The damned thing's nearly level."

The Dreamlifter's nose punched through the cloud cover at a thousand feet, revealing an almost perfectly still sea below.

"Well, I'll be... that's really something isn't it?" the captain said.

"I've never seen it so flat!"

In fact, neither had ever seen it so calm.

It was like a millpond. Like the calm before a storm—or within the eye of a storm...

They contemplated the necessity of a water landing. In a few minutes, they wouldn't have a choice. The pilot set up for a landing and then spotted, there in the middle of the sea, a small island, with a single runway.

The captain set the flaps to their maximum setting and lowered their landing gear.

His eyes swept the primary flight display for their glide ratio. They couldn't have set up for a better landing had they known about this mysterious island an hour in advance.

"Here we go, gentlemen! Good luck!"

The Dreamlifter raced across the top of the runway, and the captain pulled back on the wheel, until the massive cargo aircraft flared, and settled onto the runway.

The windshield was covered instantly with water.

It was a perfect water landing. The tiny island and runway disappeared like a mirage.

And the FDR video feed ceased.

Sam turned to Tom. "Well. What the hell do you make of that?"

CHAPTER TWENTY

ω————————Ω————————ω

SPRATLY ISLANDS, SOUTH CHINESE SEA

ADMIRAL SHANG JIANG STEPPED OUT onto the bridge of the recently launched *Feng Jian,* a Chinese type 003 aircraft carrier of 85,000-tons. She was the crowning jewel in his exemplary career, and his ship had been dispatched to protect the territorial waters of the South Chinese Seas.

The South China Sea Islands consist of over 250 islands, atolls, cays, shoals, reefs, and sandbars. None of which has indigenous people, few of which have any natural water supply, many of which are naturally under water at high tide, while others are permanently submerged.

The Spratly Islands were originally a series of coral islets mostly inhabited by seabirds. There were a series of banks, more than a hundred submerged reefs, forty underwater banks, and twenty-one underwater shoals.

The *Feng Jian* was specifically assigned to the Fiery Cross Reef, the largest of China's military bases built upon the heavily disputed seven islands of the Spratly Islands, made permanent by land reclamation. The base on the Fiery Cross Reef was now complete and perfectly capable of looking after itself.

The artificial island was now defended by nearly five thousand permanent defense personnel. The fortifications included twelve hardened shelters with retractable roofs, missile silos, forty combat aircraft, and four long range, Xian H-6 bombers capable of performing bombing raids up to 3,500 miles away. The island itself was one of the most strategically advanced military bases in the world, with an array of manned and autonomous defense systems. An autonomous artificial intelligence system gathered information from the island's radar and sonar towers, providing the most advanced early warning system and recommended evasive actions.

It was the purpose of this AI military system, more than the artificial island themselves, which had concerned the United Nations, of which China was a permanent founding member.

Admiral Shang Jiang's hardened face was unreadable. The Fiery Cross Reef was surrounded by shallow waters, which appeared a striking turquoise in the sun. He looked at the disputed islands that he'd been sent to protect with no great pleasure. Despite their paradise-like appearance, he believed the islands had been cursed with disharmony for his people — a scar of pain for the human race.

It was only after the commencement of the reclamation of land project in 2013 that the world had really taken any notice. But their disputes weren't new. Shang Jiang would have been just as happy to have detonated the entire set of islands, obliterating them, and sending them to the seabed a thousand feet below.

For his people, they represented a line in the sand — a decision to take charge and control of the safety of their sovereign waters and shipping lanes. In a perfect world, there would have been freedom of safe passage within international waters, but with everything at stake, it's hard to maintain an altruistic view on the human race.

Shan Jiang sighed.

He believed in the good of mankind. But sometimes, that good only came after the iron might of one's military.

Mentally, he prayed that China's strong military influence within the region might be that altruistic force.

The history of people in the South China Sea went back centuries, and the conflict had been building since the 19th century. In the early days before World War II, France, Britain, and Japan had tried to claim sovereignty. In modern times, Taiwan, Vietnam, the Philippines, Malaysia, Brunei, and China all claimed all or part of the area. Commercial fishing, and considerable oil and gas reserves started the more recent rush, but in the big picture, the country that controlled the Spratly Islands controlled the South China Sea and the region's ship-borne trade, worth $5 trillion annually. The dredging and land reclamation done by China dwarfed previous efforts to claim the region. In all, China had reclaimed and militarized 3,000 acres of land, all part of a show of strength that Shan Jiang was confident would bring peace to the region.

It was a report from the AI observation system within the Fiery Cross Reef which interrupted his reflections on the past.

Admiral Shang Jiang immediately read the report. Afterward, he handed it to his commander. There were deep creases of concern embedded in his otherwise relaxed demeanor.

The note reported what appeared to be an unidentified American nuclear attack submarine in the process of surfacing to the east of their position. It had originated well within the bounds of the known international shipping lanes but was now heading much too close to the recently completed military installation on the chain of Spratly Islands.

It was most likely a show of force and a toothless appearance of disgruntlement over the island's military development. The admiral guessed that the submarine would surface, then skirt the outline of the shipping lanes, before disappearing into the deeper waters of the South Chinese Sea, avoiding any formal confrontation.

It wasn't the first time he'd witnessed such a brazen risk to peace in the region, and it undoubtedly wouldn't be the last. He sighed as he took a pair of binoculars and watched the submarine surface roughly half a mile away to his east. But it was the first time an American nuclear attack submarine had come this close.

The submarine surfaced and ran in a north-east direction, on a direct course to a section known as the Dangerous Grounds. The area to the north of the Spratly Islands was known as the Dangerous Grounds because it was characterized by many low islands, sunken reefs, and degraded sunken atolls with coral often rising abruptly from ocean depths greater than 3,000 feet — all of which makes the area hazardous for navigation.

The admiral's dark black, bushy eyebrows narrowed, as he wondered what the submarine commander's intentions could possibly be. It was an obvious display of power. If it were there merely on a reconnaissance mission, it would have remained submerged and probably undetected, but its commander had chosen to surface.

It was a brazen threat, akin to a declaration of war.

Admiral Shang Jiang ordered the *Feng Jian* to pursue the renegade American nuclear attack submarine.

The sub headed north, toward a series of shallow channels, into an area known as the labyrinth, because it represented more than a hundred uncharted submerged reefs. What was a lesser known fact, was that when the People's Republic of China commenced its land reclamation project in the region, it used underground dredging, and boring machines to deepen a series of shallow channels through the labyrinth, as well as produce shallow water traps, that would impede, if not make navigation impossible by their enemies.

And now, their enemy was sailing at full speed into a trap.

More surprising still, the purpose of attack submarines was to remain hidden. Stealth was paramount to its success, and for that, they needed the ability to dive. So then, why would its commander willingly take the submarine into a region known for its shallow reefs and almost impossible navigation, with no room to dive?

The thought rested heavily on Shang Jiang's mind, as he ordered his crew to their attack stations and warned that the Americans were doing something they shouldn't be, so to be on high alert.

He then took out his binoculars and examined the submarine again. There was no one on its deck. The conning tower was empty, which meant, presumably, its watertight hatches were closed, and despite the commander's brazen display of confidence, the submarine was ready to dive at any moment.

It was a battle of wits and waiting.

Shang Jiang breathed. He hadn't reached the age of 72 by being jittery. Nor had he done so by being complacent. He would pursue the offending submarine, careful not to start an international incident, while being prepared to fight if need be.

The submarine turned to the east…

Into the labyrinth. Into a trap.

Shang Jiang put his binoculars down.

Where do you possibly think you're going?

The helmsman glanced at Shang Jiang. "Do you want me to wait out here, sir?"

Shang Jiang hesitated. Not because he was concerned his helmsman couldn't pilot the bulky aircraft carrier inside, but because he knew once he'd entered the labyrinth, a confrontation with the American submarine was unavoidable. Both men knew the labyrinth well. In fact, they had taken the *Feng Jian* into her narrow shipping lanes previously during her sea trials.

"Sir?" the helmsman asked.

Shang Jiang's lips thinned to a hardened line. "Take us in."

The *Feng Jian* reduced speed to just two knots and turned due east on a bearing of 90 degrees, entering the narrow lanes and abundant submerged coral reefs that formed the labyrinth. The ECDIS — electronic chart display and information system — depicted the bathymetric information and a graphical representation of the mapped seabed and various channels that formed the labyrinth. As far as Shang Jiang was aware, only China possessed such navigation information. Even with the map, it would be dangerous to maneuver the Feng Jian, and almost impossible for the American submarine to do so without running aground.

The ECDIS showed that there was only one entrance that any large vessel, be it an aircraft carrier or a submarine could enter the labyrinth. That meant both vessels would need to return the way they came, but to do so, they would need to navigate all the way to the end of the main channel, before making a series of sharp, hairpin turns, until the channel finally turned back on the original channel.

Shang Jiang looked through his binoculars again. The submarine was moving much faster than they were. Faster than he would have been willing to attempt to maneuver his aircraft carrier through the narrow channel. Although the submarine was also smaller, it was still longer than a football field and navigation in these confined waters would be a challenge.

His first officer greeted him. "Sir, the observation tower at Fiery Cross Reef says it lost all signs of the American attack submarine on its radar and sonar."

"Lost?" Shang Jiang asked, incredulously. "When?"

"Four minutes ago, just after it surfaced."

"That's impossible." Shang Jiang raised his binoculars and examined the submarine. Less than half a mile away, and on the surface, he could make out the full shape of its dark conning tower and bow, where the white ripples of a bow wave broke into a nearby coral reef. "I can see the submarine with my own damned eyes."

"Our own radar crew report still seeing something out there... but whatever it is, it's much smaller than an attack submarine."

Shang Jiang met his eye. "Like what?"

"I don't know. Maybe a small boat or something."

"What does sonar say?"

The first officer said, "There's definitely something out there. It could be a submarine, but their waterfall monitors are painting a very different picture to what we're seeing."

Shang Jiang frowned. "Like what?"

"More of a sphere shape."

"Really?"

The first officer shrugged. "It's what they're saying, sir."

Shang Jiang's lips curled upward in the slightest of grins. "It's a holographic projector."

"Excuse me, sir?" the first officer asked. "I'm not sure I follow."

"The American submarine. It's nothing more than a clever ruse. A magic trick. The thing's just a sphere, projecting the image of a submarine."

Both men stared at the submarine through binoculars. It certainly looked real, as it approached a small crescent-shaped atoll which formed a navigational dead end.

The submarine slowed to a complete stop.

"Full stop," Shang Jiang ordered. Then, addressing his first officer, he said, "Now let's see where they go."

By the time the helmsman brought the *Feng Jian* to a full stop, the aircraft carrier had closed the distance between the two vessels to just 250 feet. The aircraft carrier now settled in a narrow channel west of the submarine. The passage out of the labyrinth involved a hairpin turn to the right up ahead, followed by multiple small turns, that inevitably allowed them to return to the main channel.

Shang Jiang stared at the submarine.

The coral atoll was just becoming visible on the outgoing tide. Across the bank, about two hundred feet to the north, a second channel ran parallel to the main channel. The channel was small and shallow, making it almost unnavigable by the submarine — definitely with an aircraft carrier — and impossible to reach from the submarine's current position.

The admiral made a weighted sigh. The childish game was about to reach its conclusion, and he just prayed that whoever commanded the submarine — or whatever it was — didn't decide to throw a violent tantrum because of the inevitable outcome.

A moment later, the submarine rotated on its axis in a counter-clockwise direction. It wasn't unusual for submarines to have a series of bow and stern thrusters to allow for such a maneuver. The submarine stopped with its bow facing the aircraft carrier.

Recognizing that it would be impossible to pass the *Feng Jian* in the narrow channel, the submarine turned due north. Its bow aimed directly at a coral reef that was only just now becoming visible on the outgoing tide.

Shang Jiang's eyes narrowed.

What are you thinking?

Angry white water erupted from the submarine's stern, as it powered ahead at full speed.

The submarine reached the coral reef and appeared to hover directly over it, crossing more than 200 feet of the atoll, before sinking into the water of the smaller channel that ran parallel to the main one which the aircraft carrier was using. The submarine moved fast. Much faster than a conventional submarine could possibly maneuver. It traveled more than half a mile in no more than a few minutes.

Coming to a complete stop on a second channel, this one ran in a north-southerly direction and was much too shallow for either vessel to navigate. The submarine was now stopped perpendicular to the *Feng Jian*.

Shang Jiang stared at the menacing bow of the submarine.

The admiral stared at it with incredulity. "The damned thing's a fake. Nothing more than a holographic reflection. A trick done by mirrors!"

"It would appear so, sir," the first officer replied.

Shang Jiang swallowed hard.

Because out of the bow of the submarine, the water lit up with the white froth, as something raced toward them.

"Torpedo!" The admiral shouted. "Evasive maneuvers!"

But it was too late. The mammoth *Feng Jian* was too large to maneuver in the tight confines of the labyrinth. There was no time to build up speed.

The torpedo struck the *Feng Jian* amidships, tearing a thirty-foot hole into her hull. The 85,000-ton aircraft carrier sank quickly, coming to rest in the shallow water, as though she'd merely run aground.

CHAPTER TWENTY-ONE

NEUWERK ISLAND, GERMANY

THE *MARIA HELENA* ARRIVED THE next morning. It took two days to make the repairs to the *Buckholtz* and pump out the massive amount of internal seawater. The water was pumped out to the bow, where it naturally cut a hole in the sand and muddy debris which still held the bow onto the island. It would all help with the ultimate goal, culminating at midnight on the third night, at the highest tide, when the *Maria Helena*, along with two tugboats would attempt to pull the *Buckholtz* free of Neuwerk Island.

From the aft deck of the *Maria Helena*, Sam stared up at the behemoth stern of the *Buckholtz,* where a single hawser rope — sixteen inches thick — split into three separate lines, where it was tethered to two tugboats and the *Maria Helena*. He gripped a single radio, from which he planned to coordinate the impossible. And it did seem impossible to think that the three little boats could do anything to affect any type of change on the large container ship.

In fact, it was impossible for the three little ships to pull the larger one free of the island. The *Buckholtz* was simply too heavy. Instead, Sam had decided to change the equation a little into his favor. To do this, he left the first two bays of the *Buckholtz* flooded and shifted the entire load of maneuverable ballast from the bow and amidships into the stern. In doing so, the heavy stern of the *Buckholtz* sank into the deeper waters, while its bow naturally wanted to lift.

Sam spoke into his microphone, "All right, let's gently take up the tension on the hawser."

The three pilots slowly motored forward, until the thick rope straightened as it became taut. Sam studied the angles. Everything was lining up perfectly. He checked his wristwatch. It read 00:05. They had just reached high tide.

"All right, on my mark, I want a gradual increase to full power."

Sam waited. His eyes swept the midnight scene, scanning each individual rope, and boat for any sign of chafing or incorrect angles.

He swallowed. It was now or never. "Let's go gentlemen."

Sam listened as a combined 140,000 horsepower worth of diesel engines increased their RPM, straining to extract every single newton of torque out of each propeller, as their blades cut through the seawater.

The sound was deafening.

The sea turned white with the backwash of multiple propellers. The aft end of the *Maria Helena* fishtailed as she dug so deep into the water that for an instant Sam feared she was going to pull herself under.

He gritted his teeth. "Full power!"

Sam let the cacophony of powerful diesel engines, trying their best to achieve the impossible, continue for twenty minutes before he ordered it to stop.

He ran the palms of his hands through his thick hair.

Matthew, his skipper, looked back at him. "What do you think, Sam?"

"Beats me. As far as I can tell, we're going against Newton's first law of motion — an object at rest remains at rest until a net external force is applied to it. I guess we don't have enough power to do that."

Tom stepped onto the deck. "I've got an idea, but I'm not sure anyone's going to like it."

Sam said, "Shoot."

"We've had nearly two days of running water pumped into the front of the *Buckholtz's* bow, leaving a deep crease beneath her keel."

Sam suppressed a grin as he thought he'd started to see where Tom was going. "Go on."

"Do you know there's a dam eighty feet up from there?"

Sam nodded. "I also heard it's the only source of fresh water for the island."

"Right," Tom continued, undeterred. "I'll leave it to Gene how he wants to rebuild the dam and refill it for the people living on Neuwerk Island, but…"

"You want to know what would happen if we blew the dam wall, release a quarter of a million gallons of water onto the tunnel running beneath the keel?"

"Yeah, that's the gist of my idea."

Sam said, "I think we're going to get into serious trouble with the EPA."

"That's an American organization. The Germans use the German Environmental Agency, called the *Umweltbundesamt*. They're the ones who are going to be pissed. Even so, do you think it would work?"

Sam nodded, surprised at Tom's knowledge of German environmental administration. "Sometimes it might be better to ask for forgiveness than approval. Besides, even the Umweltbundesamt would have to agree that it would be better to damage a dam and remove the *Buckholtz* than have it remain permanently here, where it could become a long-term environmental disaster."

Tom grinned. "So, we're agreed?"

"Agreed. Take Genevieve with you. She'll make sure you set it up right and don't do anything to get yourself killed. Let me know when it's in place, and we'll try again."

Tom patted him on the shoulder with an open hand. "This will work."

"I sure hope it does."

Sam looked around at the now quiet seas. The water was high and completely still. He couldn't have asked for better conditions. If the next attempt failed, the *Buckholtz* might be stuck for some time before they got another opportunity to shift her.

He spoke into his microphone, "All right, stand down, while we work the problem from the land."

It took just under twenty-five minutes before Sam got the message from Tom that everything was in place. Sam told him to wait until the three boats were set at full power and the ropes were taut before he did anything.

And then he started the process again.

All three powerplants roared, and the *Maria Helena's* stern shifted backward and forward, digging herself deeper into the water.

After three minutes, Sam said into the radio, "Okay Tom, let her rip."

The explosion rocked the northern edge of Neuwerk Island like an earthquake, followed by a thunderous roar of water racing free.

And still, the two tugboats and the *Maria Helena* continued at full power.

Sam fixed his eyes at the *Buckholtz,* where water now rushed to meet her, gushing around her keel. The hawser rope strained under the extreme pressures.

The first wave of water reached the *Maria Helena's* stern, and for an instant, Sam was worried it was going to swamp the smaller ship, but she rode the wave with the self-confident poise with which they'd come to expect of her.

The stern of the *Buckholtz* shifted in the unstable water, rising a few feet and then dipping again, but still, she remained fixed on the island.

Between the cacophony of engine noise, multiple propellers, and rushing waters, a new sound emerged. This one was far more resonant, more like thunder than anything possibly manmade. Sam squinted his eyes and listened. He mentally tried to block out the rest of the sounds and concentrate on the new sound.

That's when he saw it.

The *Buckholtz* had started to shift.

It slid slowly at first, and then picked up momentum until it was racing off the island. Sam swallowed hard as the hawser rope went loose. The container ship was moving faster than the other three smaller ships.

Sam picked up his microphone. "Get out of its way!"

At the helm, Matthew steered the *Maria Helena* to the starboard, toward the island.

The *Buckholtz* slid by, creating a massive wake. The *Maria Helena* was thrown like a toy on its side. Sam gripped the guardrail, narrowly escaping being thrown into the water. The engine whine reached a scream as the propeller came free of the water for an instant.

A sharp clanking noise of metal on metal came free, and an instant later, the *Maria Helena* stabilized in the settling sea and the growing silence.

Matthew stepped out of the bridge.

Sam glanced at his face, and said, "What happened?"

Matthew's jaw set firm, and his face set in lines of hard determination. "I think we just lost our propeller."

CHAPTER TWENTY-TWO

T HE *MARIA HELENA* ANCHORED OFF the shallow muddy beach off the north of Neuwerk Island. To the north, the *Buckholtz* was being assessed by a team of engineers before its tow down the Elbe into Hamburg where she would be put in dry dock.

Sam sat on the bridge, talking to Matthew, who had already arranged for the *Maria Helena* to be towed to a shipyard along the Elbe to repair its propeller.

Elise stepped into the room, her mouth set in a broad grin.

Sam glanced at her. "What is it?"

"I think I know what happened to the 747 Dreamlifter!"

"Really?" Sam smiled. "What?"

"It was the third man."

"The off-duty pilot?"

"Yeah."

"Sure. I'll buy that," Sam said. "It makes sense. There were three pilots on board the cargo aircraft. Two were found dead — murdered, with large bullet holes through their head, execution style. The third pilot was missing. He could have been kidnapped, or simply washed out of the aircraft, but it's most likely he was the killer. Who was he, by the way?"

"That's where it gets interesting. His name was David Townsend — obviously an alias — who was a locum pilot for the company. One of the original pilots had a minor car accident, which prevented him from flying on the day. The locum pilot was brought in last minute to fill in for him."

Sam was incredulous. "The transport company trusted a total stranger to fly their hundred-million-dollar jet, not to mention whatever secret cargo they were carrying?"

"No. The locum had been employed by the cargo company for more than a decade and was often used to fill in gaps just like this one. There's nothing untoward about David. He lives in London, with his wife and three children."

"That doesn't sound like a guy who brings down a jet plane and kills his copilots…"

"That's right," Elise confirmed. "Only he wasn't David Townsend."

Sam cocked an eyebrow. "He wasn't?"

"No. David Townsend was found dead in the trunk of his car, which had been parked in the long-term stay at Berlin International Airport."

Sam said, "Guess that answers how he got on board."

"It gets better. According to the lead investigator in Berlin, the ballistics match those of the two shots on board the Dreamlifter."

"Right. So at least we have our murderer."

"Well, the face of our murderer," Elise agreed. "And before you ask, no, I can't find it on my system anywhere."

Sam stared at the image of the murderer's face. "All right. At least it's something. Someone, somewhere, is going to recognize this man."

Tom stared at the face. "All right. So, now that we know this guy killed all three pilots. The question is, why?"

"That's obvious. They wanted whatever the Dreamlifter was transporting."

Elise said, "Sure, but when I checked with the aircraft's

CHRISTOPHER CARTWRIGHT | 163

manifest, it reports being on a dry run to Quonset Point, Rhode Island."

"No shit?" Sam asked, taking the iPad. "Let me see that."

Elise smiled. "What are you thinking?"

"I'd like to know why ever since we started investigating the Dreamlifter, everybody has been lying to us?"

Tom said, "Okay, so the bad guy causes the plane to make a water landing — which, may I remind you, is one of the deadliest procedures in aviation, with only a few successful cases in history with an aircraft of this size — for what purpose? Why didn't he just shoot the two real pilots and fly whatever secret part was stolen to wherever it is that he wanted to take it?"

"Because a Boeing 747 Dreamlifter's a pretty hard thing to lose. Radar would keep track of it during and after takeoff. It would be nearly impossible to land the aircraft somewhere without the owners finding out."

"So, instead. He set about an elaborate plan to bring the aircraft down in the Barents Sea."

"Exactly."

"All right. So how did he bring it down?"

Elise said, "I can answer that."

Sam smiled. "Really?"

Elise smiled. "Yeah, remember how he logged his laptop into the maintenance BUS, looking like he was trying to correct the fault?"

"Sure."

"He used the BUS to hack into the aircraft's primary flight display, mirroring the primary flight data with a fictional data interface from his own laptop. In doing so, he made it appear that the instruments had returned to normal — remember how he'd told the pilot and copilot that he'd switched to the secondary flight data system, and that seemed to fix the problem?"

Sam nodded his head in agreement. "Go on."

"But instead of transferring the aircraft over to the secondary flight data system, our bad guy simply overrode the primary with his own version—mirroring the real primary flight display. He then carefully manipulated the values of each instrument, forcing the pilot to alter course to meet the artificial runway."

"But the pilots should have noticed that?"

"And they might have. The third pilot used a strategy designed to foil both pilots, despite their experience and systems that might have prevented the crash. He created a situation recreating the 2009 crash of Air France 447. The pilots in control of the Airbus A330 from Paris to Rio de Janeiro were relying on a highly-automated, fly-by-wire autopilot. This advanced autopilot not only did what the pilots programmed, but interpreted those instructions into a flight normally optimized for comfort and safety. The plane went into a storm, where they had zero visibility and icing conditions that caused the planes pitot tubes, which measure airspeed, to fail. The failure in the sensors caused the stall protection to fail and the pilot's inputs were overcorrected. The pilots kept the angle of attack too high and placed too much trust in their instruments. From there, pilot inexperience and "the startle effect" left the pilots distracted, correcting the wrong issues. The plane descended in a fatal stall until it crashed."

Elise continued," The two pilots reacted very professionally—modern plane and crew experience would have brought them out safely. The third pilot manipulated the situation by inserting warning alarms into the system, so that the pilot's attention was focused on constantly treating other problems and not noticing what was really going on."

Sam shook his head. "How could you possibly have worked all that out?"

Elise shrugged. "I pay attention to detail."

Tom said, "Hey, Sam and I have been pilots for a long time, and neither of us could work it out after spending the better half of a night staring at the damned thing. Come on, how did you work it out?"

Elise smiled. "I got a phone call from someone at the British Air Accidents and Crash Investigators."

"And?"

"It turns out the QAR had an additional set of video cameras set up. One of them was set at the back of the cockpit where the third pilot used his laptop to access the BUS and hack into the primary flight display. The video recorded everything he did. It showed him guilty as hell. There's no question about it—the third pilot brought the plane down, exactly where he wanted it."

Sam grinned. "That answers that, but there's one thing I don't understand."

Elise said, "Shoot."

"Where did the island come from?"

CHAPTER TWENTY-THREE

Ω

E LISE PUT THE ADDITIONAL VIDEO footage on.

They watched the third pilot sabotage the Dreamlifter. From a different angle Sam, Tom, and Elise could see everything—from the false instrument readings through to the sequence of false engine fires.

Sam felt a surge of heat up his neck and was surprised by his own anger. "That scumbag! If we ever find him, he'll pay for this."

Elise grabbed the iPad and pressed down on the screen. "There's more." A separate video feed showed the cargo area. Light flooded in as the forward hatch opened up, and ten men dressed in military gear flooded in. Two flashes came from the direction of the cockpit and in short order, two of the men dragged the pilot's bodies into the cargo area.

The two men joined the others releasing the sphere, and assembling and inflating two large pontoons around the engine. In under a minute, the whole thing was set up. The tail door cracked open. As the camera adjusted to the new lighting conditions, a large sea barge moved toward the plane. A heavy tow line was attached to the sphere, which was rapidly floated out as the cargo hold filled with sea water.

Tom stared at the screen, baffled, "They were professionals. There was no way this was done without inside help."

"Okay, so there's the sphere being loaded onto the boat, before the aircraft sinks. I still don't see what happened to the island."

"Have a look behind."

Sam squinted. His eyes went in and out of focus as his brain tried to comprehend what he was seeing.

There was a thick fog.

Elise asked, "What do you see?"

"There's a thick fog of some sort."

"Right. And what sort of day was it when the Dreamlifter made its watery landing?"

"It was stormy. I remember they were flying in a total whiteout because of the clouds."

"Sure. But at what altitude?"

"You're right. They broke through the cloud cover. On the ground, it was overcast, but the sea was a dark blue, nearly ultramarine in color, with sun rays flickering off its surface."

"That's right. That's what you saw on the FDR," Elise said, a slight grin forming on her lips. "What do you see here?"

"It's heavily overcast, with a thick fog setting in."

"Right. Only the fog isn't just now setting in. It's dissipating."

Sam said, "I don't understand."

"What color water would you expect to see if overhead were covered by thick, impenetrable clouds?"

"Dark. The water would take on a grayish-black appearance and be nearly impossible to distinguish." Sam grinned, curiously. "But I watched the FDR recording through the cockpit windshield, that water was beautiful. It was blue and crisp, and full of sunshine glistening off its surface."

"And it was all fake," Elise said.

"How?"

"A trick done by the cloaks and mirrors of a magician."

"How, Elise?"

"A combination of glycol and water."

"What?" Sam asked.

"Theatrical smoke on a grand scale."

Sam shook his head, and a grin creased the corners of his lips as he thought about the complexity of the simple ruse. "Someone, put up a smoke screen, and then, what, projected a small island and a runway directly over the top of it?"

"Yep."

"How did they get the projector so far above?"

"Drones, most likely. DARPA's using a similar technique for camouflaging troops as well as heavy military machinery."

"What shape would the drone be?"

Elise responded immediately, as though she'd seen one previously. "It usually takes the shape of a large sphere with hundreds of projectors."

CHAPTER TWENTY-FOUR

Ω————————Ω————————Ω

SAM'S FINGERS WORKED QUICKLY OVER his laptop's keyboard to bring up the image from the FDR video that he had captured on board the Dreamlifter.

He clicked on the image, and the entire screen lit up with the image of the metallic sphere.

He grinned. "Something like this?"

"Yes," Elise confirmed. "Something exactly like that. Why? Where did you get this?"

"Because that was on board the Dreamlifter."

Sam stared at the image in a new light. Despite appearing like something out of a bad science fiction movie, there were more than a hundred small protruding tubes. The purpose of which, he had no idea, but he now wondered if they could indeed be projectors?

He asked Elise, "What do you know about it?"

"Not much. It was a project DARPA was involved in nearly a decade ago when I still worked for the CIA. At the time, computer technology just wasn't powerful enough to make it work, but there's been recent speculation that the project has become possible with recent developments in computing."

"So it would seem," Sam said. Through narrowed eyes, he asked, "The question is, if we were doing it first, why was it built in Germany?"

Elise shook her head. "Only to be put on a cargo aircraft and flown to Quonset, Rhode Island?"

"Right." Sam took a deep breath as he remembered the scene from the Dreamlifter's cockpit of the artificial island and runway. The image was seamless. "And now we have reason to believe that regardless of whether or not we produced a successful version of the product, the Russians definitely have."

Tom stood up from the workstation and crossed his arms. "If the Russians already have the technology, why did they risk everything to steal it?"

Sam thought back to the mysterious theft of the specialized shipping container from the *Buckholtz*.

Could there be some sort of connection?

The door to the bridge opened, and Gene walked in. "I've been told the *Buckholtz* is ready to move and the tugboats are ready for the tow." He offered his hand. "I really appreciate everything you and your team did for us, despite the loss of the cargo."

Sam stood up and gripped the man's hand with a firm shake. "Not a problem. Sorry we couldn't save it. All the best with the repairs."

"It will be a big project, but much better than had the *Buckholtz* been stranded throughout the winter. If you ever need anything, I'm at your service."

"Thanks," Sam said. Then, turning his laptop around, he asked, "I don't suppose you've ever seen a machine that looks like this?"

Gene stared at the sphere. His eyes were dazed and hazy. All color was gone from his face. "Yes."

Sam expelled his breath silently. "Where?"

Gene opened his mouth, but nothing came out. His face twisted between horror and fascination. "Secured within the specialized shipping container."

"That doesn't make sense," Sam said. "That shipping container was 60-feet long and 8-feet wide. The image I just showed you was a perfect sphere."

Gene shrugged. "I was told it was for some additional equipment, but also as a ruse to prevent it being stolen."

Sam ignored the irony. "Who owned the device?"

"I'm sorry, Mr. Reilly. Even after its loss, I'm afraid I cannot reveal who the owner was. I've already spoken too much. The loss was a tragedy, but there's a lot more at stake, and I cannot reveal any more details."

Sam knew that Quonset, Rhode Island built submarines, so there was very little doubt in his mind about who the buyer was. Still, he couldn't work out why America would be sourcing such technology from a German manufacturer. And, more importantly, who would know enough to steal them.

"I'm sorry I couldn't stop the theft," Sam said. "Any news about who might have stolen the device?"

"No. Whoever was responsible certainly knew what they were doing."

Sam met Gene's eye. "So right now, all we have are those two bodies to go off of. We'd better hope the German Federal Intelligence Service can work out who they are and where they come from. They might just be the only lead we ever get."

Gene sighed heavily. "That might be a little hard."

"Why?"

The lines on Gene's face deepened and his lips set in a hard line. "The German Eurocopter which had retrieved the bodies crashed approaching Berlin. The helicopter exploded on impact, and there were no survivors."

CHAPTER TWENTY-FIVE

S AM PICKED UP HIS SATELLITE phone and dialed a number off by heart.

A woman answered on the first ring. "Mr. Reilly. I hear you've been making friends in Germany."

A small grin creased the edge of his lips at the secretary of defense's reference to the scuba diver who'd nearly killed him. "Plenty of friends, but they seem to bring with them more mysteries and fewer answers."

"Mysteries?" she asked. "About what?"

Sam filled her in on the two spheres that had been stolen through an elaborate, yet successful, plot to crash a modern jetliner and run a cargo ship aground. He finished by mentioning that the two unidentified bodies were most likely Russian, and how the helicopter carrying the German investigators had crashed and burned, destroying all evidence in the process.

When he had finished, the secretary of defense said, "And you're telling me this, why?"

"Both the Boeing 747 Dreamlifter and the cargo ship were bound for Quonset, Rhode Island, meaning, I'm guessing the spheres were on their way to our submarine fabrication yard at Quonset."

"I thought you said no one has admitted to what the spheres

were and where they were headed."

"No, but I figured that if two identical top-secret experimental devices that were en route to our submarine fabrication shipyard at Quonset under exceptional circumstances, you'd be pretty interested to hear about it?"

"What did the owner of the *Buckholtz* say?"

"It's proprietary knowledge. And his customer doesn't want that interrupted, despite the accident and subsequent... "accidental loss" of the specialized shipping container."

"The owner of a German-registered cargo ship doesn't wish to reveal his customer's secrets—as he should not—as we should not pry into the lives of our European counterparts."

"But I thought this might..."

"What?" she asked. "Concern the United States Department of Defense? This is about piracy at sea under the direct jurisdiction of the European Union. If they don't want you involved, then you're to accept it and sit this one out, do I make myself clear, Reilly?"

"Yes, ma'am."

Sam ended the satellite phone call.

Tom said, "What did she say?"

"She said it wasn't in the U.S. waters and both victims are part of the European Union—at least until the British formalize Brexit—so we're to sit tight and stay out of it."

Tom raised an incredulous eyebrow. "What do you want to do?"

"Is your father still the admiral of the submarine fleet at Pearl Harbor?"

"Yeah."

"Good. Let's go see him about what's going on and what needs to be done."

Tom grinned. "The admiral, my father, isn't the type of guy who's going to bend rules or break state secrets for his family.

So, what makes you think he'll talk?"

"Nothing, but it's the only lead we've got right now. Whatever secret technology just went missing was originally headed for Quonset, Rhode Island. Given they both went missing, and the parts were stolen, after someone went to the trouble to carefully have them transferred by separate modes of transport, I'm guessing, that constitutes a threat to national security."

"Right. Which means the secretary of defense would have jumped at the opportunity to interrogate you for information."

"Which she didn't."

"You're right." Tom shook his head. "Which means, she's lying and her hands are tied, or possibly, that she's lying because the U.S. government did something very wrong, and now it wants to cover it up."

"Either way, we'll get an answer from your father when we mention the story over a nice family dinner."

"He won't break state secrets," Tom said, emphatically.

Sam shook his head. "It's all in the telling. We're not there to pry out information—we're just catching up because we're in the area, all we're going to do is mention the two bizarre circumstances and watch his face."

"What reason do I give to tell my father that I'm in the area?"

"You need a reason to see your father?"

Tom gave Sam a look that implied not to go there and then shrugged. "Yeah. Don't you?"

"Touché."

Sam's father was a businessman who never took a day off, and family affairs needed to be penciled in as company meetings.

Tom said, "So what are we going to do?"

Sam opened up the internet and pointed to an amateur surfing competition in Oahu… "It looks like we're finally going on that vacation you've always wanted."

CHAPTER TWENTY-SIX

SOUTH PACIFIC, 100 MILES SOUTH OF THE GALAPAGOS ISLANDS

SVETLANA RAISED A PERFECTLY PLUCKED eyebrow as the captain of the *Vostok* approached her surveillance room, informed her that her room was being shut down for the next twelve hours, before locking her in the intelligence gathering room.

Buried in the bowels of the hull where the cold fish storage would have been — had the ship really been a fishing trawler — she was used to being locked out of the rest of the ship but being told her surveillance systems would be externally shut down for the next twelve hours was a new one for her.

She didn't argue with her captain. He outranked her, and after all, the *Vostok* was an intelligence gathering vessel, if he wanted it to keep secrets, who was she to argue? She could have screamed like a caged animal, but who would listen? After all, the entire surveillance room was covered in a nearly foot-thick layer of soundproof absorbing foam. To listen to the intricate sounds she received, her office needed to be completely isolated. At least it maintained a perfect temperature all year round.

Instead, she watched as each of the complex instruments scattered across the walls of her office, including, an array of technology for long and short-range listening devices, radar, sonar, and satellite hacking equipment, were each prevented from functioning.

She made a coy smile.

Her captain had gone to the trouble of sending divers overboard just to conceal her listening devices and hydrophones with impervious batons. The curiosity piqued her natural interest as an intelligence officer.

What was he up to?

An hour later she heard the obligatory clank of a submarine secretly docking with the hidden chamber at the bottom of the *Vostok's* hull.

A memory of the phone call she'd witnessed, in which her captain had spoken with an unknown person who'd offered to sell the USS *Omega Deep* and its invisibility cloak, flashed up in her mind.

Her heart raced.

Was it possible, as she waited in the dark, the *Omega Deep* was being transferred to her captain? Who would take it into the custody of the Russian Navy? She doubted it. If that was the case, why had he bothered to make sure she didn't record the truth?

None of it made sense.

She paced about for a few minutes, wondering what she should be doing. Her consciences twisted in conflict between honor for her country and her integrity with her captain.

In the end, her country won out.

All her external instrument arrays were covered by divers before the submarine approached. But not her internal recording devices.

She grinned.

There was something about a government that knew the value of spending just as much time spying on their own personnel as others.

She smiled, placed her headphones on her head, and pressed play.

CHAPTER TWENTY-SEVEN

SVETLANA CLOSED HER EYES AND listened.

Her hidden listening device relayed what she needed from within the ship. She heard the voice of a man say, "My best man was killed in the process of retrieving the second device." Svetlana's well-trained ear recognized the voice, but couldn't place it.

Her captain appeared unmoved. "That's unfortunate, but it's not my problem."

"It just became your problem," the stranger replied. "He was paramount to the mission."

The next voice she heard was her captain's raised voice. "And what about my fucking submarine?"

The stranger sounded nonplussed, answering almost in a whisper. "What about the submarine? It's there, where we said it would be."

"No, you didn't!" The captain slammed his hand or possibly the stranger's head against the steel bulkhead wall. "We paid for the submarine to be delivered to us. Where is it?"

"I gave you the location, didn't I?"

"Sure, but you said you couldn't move it."

"No. That's right. It seems not everyone thought it important to abandon their ship."

The captain swore and threatened to renege on their original deal.

The stranger said, "You're not going to do that."

"Why shouldn't I?"

"Because I've brought you a small piece of the material used to line the hull."

"You brought me a piece of *blackbody?*"

"Yes."

"I thought the U.S. military got the last piece?"

"They did. That's how they built the Omega Cloak. What's more, I have the detailed engineering schematics for how they did it."

"And that's all I need to camouflage my entire ship?"

"Yes and no. I think you'll find the device is a little more unstable than given credit for…"

"All right. But what about my submarine?"

"It appears someone's insisted on staying on board and changing the access codes."

"So, override them!"

"I'm afraid you underestimate the Americans. They didn't just spend nearly 30 billion on research and development only to turn around and lose it!"

"So what are you going to do?"

"I'm happy to keep working the problem… but…"

There was more silence before the stranger spoke again. "I've heard that some of your crew are still trained in some expert forms of interrogation, not necessarily recognized since the KGB's changeover to FSB during the collapse of the Soviet Union."

Her captain didn't remark on the stranger's slur on what she knew he believed to be the Soviet Union's glory days. Instead, her captain merely said, "So what is the location of this missing submarine—for assistance purposes only, of course."

"Of course."

"Where?"

"At the gateway to the 8th Continent."

CHAPTER TWENTY-EIGHT

---Ω---

SOMEWHERE OVER THE NORTH PACIFIC

TOM LISTENED TO THE NEAR-silent drone of the Gulfstream G650's powerful Rolls Royce engines. They were softening, and he guessed, they were about to commence their descent into Oahu.

He picked up the satellite phone and dialed a number by heart.

A man picked up immediately. "Admiral Bower's office, Lieutenant Gibbs speaking."

"Good morning, sir," Tom said. "This is Tom Bower. Is the admiral available?"

The man appeared to recognize his voice. "I'm sorry, Mr. Bower, I'm afraid the admiral is unavailable currently."

"Can you tell me when he will be?" Tom persisted.

"I'm afraid not, sir."

"Right. When he gets into his office, can you please ask him to call me on my cell phone. It's a matter of urgency."

"Can I pass on a message, sir?"

"Afraid not. What I need to discuss with the admiral is private and needs to be done so in person. I'll wait until he's free today."

"He might not be available for quite some time."

"That's fine. We're staying at Holiday Inn at Waikiki. You can let him know we'll come to him once he's available."

"I'm very sorry, Mr. Bower…" there was the slightest of pauses on the line, as though the operator was covering the phone to speak to someone else. Then, without further preamble, he said, "Admiral Bower is out at sea on deployment, for an unknown duration."

Tom let out an audible laugh. "Lieutenant Gibbs, my father retires in two weeks. His last posting was to Pearl Harbor, at his request, so that he could oversee the transfer of the Pacific Submarine Fleet… so don't try and tell me he's gone out to sea."

"I don't know what to tell you, sir."

Tom swallowed down the frustration. "Just tell him that Tom has an urgent message for him, that can't go through the Emerald Queen of Spades."

"Who?"

"It doesn't matter. Just make certain he gets the message."

"Understood, sir."

He ended the satellite call.

Sam glanced at him with a wry smile on his lips. "The Emerald Queen of Spades?"

Tom shrugged. "What? It was the best I could come up with at short notice."

"But will your father get it?"

"Of course, he will. That's what he used to call the secretary of defense when she cheated at cards."

CHAPTER TWENTY-NINE

S VETLANA COMMITTED THE PRECISE COORDINATES of the 8th Continent to memory.

She would have liked to have written them down, but any reference to them would have provided insurmountable proof that she had indeed spied on her own captain. Instead, she waited, trying to mentally picture the location in her mind.

How could a continent have remained hidden there for so long?

It was another hour before someone unlocked her door, and an hour after that before divers removed the purpose-built covers to her hydrophones.

She immediately increased the range to their maximum.

There was little point.

Despite the signals of three other vessels she heard within her range, she knew none of them came from the submarine that had docked beneath them.

The *Vostok* continued to head south for the next twenty-four hours.

She opened the thick, soundproofed hatch and was on her way to the deck to enjoy her first view of the sky — albeit at night time — since she boarded the *Vostok* nearly a month ago when she heard the sound.

Quiet at first. Little more than a sibilant hiss as wind whipped through the array of radar and satellite dishes on the top of the *Vostok's* bridge.

A moment later, she spotted the fine mist of water, as it pummeled the deck. The warm seawater quickly turned to ice. Above her, she heard the sharp crack of the thick Perspex windshields that lined the bridge, being shattered by the icy pellets.

Her head snapped round to the right, where the end of the passageway was starting to freeze solid. An intricate web of ice started to form. Small stars of ice formed on the doorway. Part of the wall broke apart as though the entire thing had been struck by liquid nitrogen.

Svetlana turned to run.

Her breath misted and crystallized in front of her.

She opened the door to her surveillance room and slammed it shut behind her. Inside, the room was silent. The temperature remained unchanged, protected by the thick layer of soundproofing.

There she waited.

What the hell was that?

After twenty minutes, she couldn't take it anymore. She opened the latched door, which opened inwards.

On the outside of the door, was a solid wall of ice.

She closed the door and screamed, her voice lost, trapped, and alone.

CHAPTER THIRTY

ROCKPILE BEACH, OAHU, HAWAII

SAM WAS BREATHING HARD FROM exertion as he made it over the crest of the final wave between him and the relative safety of the deep blue water beyond the break. He sucked in the warm ocean breeze as it clipped the tops of the waves falling away behind him. Snapping himself up to sit on his surfboard, he glanced over his shoulder toward the sand at Rockpile Beach on Oahu's North Shore. He raked the surf with his eyes, trying to see where Tom had gotten to among the white-water rollers.

He relished the ache in his triceps and back muscles after his hard work getting back out. He and Tom had been doing some hard surfing this morning, blowing off some steam on the first day of a long-needed vacation. Rockpile was usually the domain of veterans and kamikaze surfers only, renowned as one of the meanest breaks in Hawaii—and so far, it had delivered just what Sam and Tom were after—big, heavy waves.

Half a minute later Tom crested a breaking wave near Sam, paddling hard, whooping and laughing as he slapped down on the calm side of the break. He eased up alongside his friend, smiling from ear-to-ear.

"Pull up a seat!" Sam said, returning his friend's good cheer.

"Oh man," Tom said, with a satisfied groan as he sat up on his board, "It's been far too long between waves."

"Couldn't agree more," Sam said, with one eye on the horizon, searching for the next wave, idly paddling himself with his hands by his side.

There were a half-dozen other intrepid souls out the back of the break, spaced intermittently across the take-off zone. There was a friendly vibe, the dangerous waves immediately placing everyone present in an exclusive club of high caliber surfers. Sam looked at Tom to his right, and then followed his friend's smiling gaze across to a pair of girls, shoulder-to-shoulder astride their boards, fifty feet to their left.

Without a word, Tom turned and paddled hard, racing toward a massive wave. Beside him the two girls paddled swiftly trying to catch it too. Sam knew he was too far back to catch the wave so he kicked hard and duck dived beneath it.

On the other side of the wave, Sam watched as Tom stood up, lurching forward as he raced down the face of the twenty-five-foot wave. On the same crest, the two girls were up on their boards, confidently riding the waves like pro surfers—which they probably were. Tom leaned forward, trying to carve his way into the barreling wave.

It looked good, but he didn't quite have the momentum to keep it and a couple seconds later the front of his board dug into the sea and he fell head over heels, disappearing beneath the surf.

Sam laughed.

A moment later, he watched as the two girls tried the same maneuver. One ended up the same way as Tom, while the other managed to make it stick, as she squatted down hard on her board and dipped her head.

Sam lost sight of her as the barrel broke.

He assumed she, too, had failed in her attempt.

But a couple seconds later, he spotted her head break free from the northern end of the barrel, as she carved through the surf, veering to the crest on her right, before flipping her board

180 degrees and returning back on the same wave in the heading south, riding it all the way to the shore.

Sam clapped, not that anyone could hear him. It was an impressive maneuver, and he guessed he was probably right about her being a pro surfer.

Far behind the breakers, Sam was content just to sit for a while and enjoy the peace and quiet. He was in no hurry. There was nothing about the ocean he didn't love, so he just soaked it all in for a while.

When Tom returned, he came up from a duck-dive under a wave, emerging between Sam and the two surfer girls. Sam watched him strike up a conversation with the nearest one, a brunette, athletic girl in a short-sleeved wetsuit. Just out of earshot he watched as she returned Tom's chatter, smiling with brilliant white teeth and giggling.

With that, Sam took off on his own wave and was suddenly soaring down the face of a beautiful azure wall of hissing, diamond-speckled water. He was exhilarated as his feet took up the weight of his body on his board beneath him. He flew out the front of the face of the wave as it opened up, tiny bumps on the flat water at the bottom of his run slapping underneath his board and testing his feet's ability to hold on.

He bent his legs and sprung himself with vigor back up the face of the wave, cutting in to attack the rise of the water and feeling it surge powerfully beneath him. Turning back once more, he settled into a groove just in front of the breaking white water and set his eyes on the point where the water meets the sand as far off in the distance as he could see. He adjusted his balance, hunkered down and placed his right hand tenderly on the wall of water curling upward beside him. He gripped the left rail of his board with his other hand and relaxed.

The wave enveloped him.

The sound of curling, sucking water eddied around him on all sides as he carved between the thick walls of the wave. For a few moments that hallowed place of bliss and connection between those most accomplished of surfers and the ocean was his, all his senses entirely ensconced, then, as quickly as it came—it was gone, and he was shot out the front into the air.

He was struck by the noise and dazzling light of the day. He was thrilled and refreshed. The wave crashed behind him, and he pushed hard with his back foot, turning up and over the soft shoulder of the wave as it ebbed in the deeper edge of the breakwater. He landed softly down on his stomach, lowering himself to the board once again, smiling to himself. He shook the water from his hair and started the long paddle back out to his friend.

Making the deeper water once more, Sam found Tom deep in conversation with the two girls, charismatically gesticulating and relaying some story of adventure. They all turned and smiled as he arrived.

"See that!" he said to Tom, still scintillated by the last wave.

"See what?" Tom asked.

"Oh, nothing. Great waves today hey?" Sam said to all three.

"Sam, this is Kathy and MC."

"Pleased to meet you both," Sam said with a half-wave of his hand and a smile.

"What are you guys doing for lunch?" The girl farthest from Sam asked. She was Polynesian, with the slim and athletic build of someone who'd been surfing since she could first stand.

The four got chatting, light conversation about the North Shore's various beaches. Testing one another's level of local knowledge as was the custom amongst surfers. It occurred to Sam that both these girls were incredibly beautiful and friendly. As they surfed a last wave back in, he assumed Tom was thinking the same thing as him—imagining a future of surfing, lying about and relaxing on the beach. A life free from the stress, hunger, and hardship of adventure and intrigue. He really did need a vacation.

It would be a pleasant way to spend a few days.

Of course, Tom was still dating Genevieve, and both of them needed to urgently meet up with Tom's father to discuss the unique theft of the twin spheres.

He shrugged.

The four surfers tossed their boards in their cars, then met up at a burger stand on the edge of the parking lot. They ordered burgers and sodas and took stools at a high table. They sat chatting like teenagers. Both Sam and Tom were enjoying themselves immensely.

"So what do you guys do anyway?" Kathy asked, taking up her burger with both hands.

"Well, I'd love to tell you, but it's highly classified," Tom answered, grinning.

Sam kept quiet, concentrating on the juicy burger being placed in front of him by the server.

"Ha-ha," she answered. She smiled, yet sarcasm dripped from her words. Tom instantly liked her. "No really, what is it? Real estate, insurance, oh wait I know — you're big pharma reps on one of those, what do you call it — 'conferences,'" she said, making the inverted commas signals with her fingers.

"I'm just kidding around," Tom said, "Really we're just two boring ocean scientists on the first vacation in a very, very long..." Tom trailed off, and Sam caught his eye. Both men stiffened in their seats, instinctively turning to their left — toward the mountain behind them.

At that moment, five Sikorsky VH-3D Sea King helicopters burst overhead, thundering along in a classic five-point star formation. The helicopters were flying low, 500-feet and their noise was overpowering.

Sam knew these aircraft well, and without delay attacked his burger and fries.

They were *white-tops* — meaning they carried the signature paint job of the nation's most technologically advanced, highly powered luxury helicopters. They belonged to the fleet of twenty-three aircraft known as *Marine One* – the helicopters used for the president and other high-ranking government officials. They always flew in a group of five or more. One high-value bird, and four decoys. Not only were they like a mobile board-room, appointed with state-of-the-art technology and luxurious fitments, they were armed with an array of high-tech assault and defense weapons.

Tom, catching the hint, immediately started savaging the food in front of him too.

All activity on the beach ceased in awe at the display in the sky overhead – the crowd at Rockpile was instantly immovably transfixed by the spectacle. The huge helicopters turned and took up a line over the surf break. Facing the beach, they hovered shoulder to shoulder. Two of the hulking birds broke ranks and came forward, touching down on hastily cleared out sand which whipped up in all directions.

The landing helicopters came to rest side-by-side, 150 feet apart. The rotors slowed in almost perfect unison, and from the two opposing internal doors, seemingly identical Marines in full dress uniform stepped down – taking up positions at attention near the stairs. The other three helicopters, still roaring overhead turned in three different directions and took up a high circling formation, a constant show of power and intimidation. Sam and Tom wolfed down their food and slurped their sodas empty, then started tidying themselves up.

From one of the helicopters, a tall, broad-shouldered man wearing a navy dress uniform, glittering with color bars and brass stepped down on to the sand. He was shadowed by two Marines, wearing the Marine Blue Charlie/Delta dress uniform and carrying assault rifles. Awkwardly, the trio traversed the sand toward the burger stand. Sam and Tom collected their personal effects from the table and shoved them into their half-turned down wetsuits. Both men stood up as the party approached their table. Half a french-fry fell from the open mouth of one of the utterly aghast girls the men were lunching with.

The dress marine stopped at their table. "Which one of you is Sam Reilly?"

"That would be me, sir," Sam replied.

"You'd better come with us. The president would like to speak with you immediately." The dress officer glanced at Tom. "You, too, Mr. Bower."

CHAPTER THIRTY-ONE

Ω————————Ω————————Ω

SAM BECAME SUDDENLY CONSCIOUS OF the dripping wetsuit, pulled down to his waist. He turned to the dress-officer. "Do we have time to get changed?"

"No," came the officer's curt reply. "Someone will offer you a change of clothes once we're airborne."

Sam glanced at the five Sikorsky VH-3D Sea King helicopters. They had probably chewed up several thousand dollars' worth of aviation fuel already, just in the time they'd circled. "Understood." He then turned to Kathy and MC. "Thanks for the surf. Hope you enjoy the rest of the day. I'm afraid duty calls."

MC cocked an incredulous eyebrow and gave a sharp smile. "Of course. Another salvage job?"

Sam shrugged. "No idea, ma'am. You have a nice day. It was a pleasure watching you two carve up the surf while we mere amateurs simply tried our best not to get killed in the process."

She smiled at the compliment. "Take care."

The dress-officer said to Tom, "Someone will be along shortly for your boards and vehicle."

"Okay, thanks," Tom said, handing his keys to the extended palm of one of the Marines. "It's the '56 Jeep."

"We know, sir," replied the Marine, taking the keys.

"I'm sorry for the interruption ladies." The dress-officer said.

"No problem, sir," Kathy replied. She then turned to Sam and Tom. "Ocean scientists, huh?"

Tom and Sam smiled and shrugged, "Thanks for lunch!" Tom said being hustled away by Sam to catch the trio ahead of them. "Duty calls."

The Marines broke free and double-timed it to the bird on the left, climbing in ahead of the door guard in full dress, who flipped up the stairs and climbed in, sliding the door closed. The Marine at the open door of the other chopper saluted the admiral as he took the back stairs ahead of Sam and Tom. Over his shoulder, the admiral said, "There's a cabin on your left, boys, get yourselves cleaned up and I'll see you in the main section in five minutes."

"Thank you, sir." Sam stepped up into the helicopter. "Any idea where we're heading?"

The president of the United States answered from inside with his renowned calm and authoritative voice, "Pearl Harbor. We have a lot to discuss."

CHAPTER THIRTY-TWO

A FTER GETTING CHANGED OUT OF their wetsuits in the tiny lavatory cabin, Sam and Tom entered the main passenger area of the helicopter wearing jeans and white t-shirts. The whole room was fitted out with the same tan leather and plush pile carpet as *Air Force One.* They both immediately noticed how stunningly quiet and free from vibration the helicopter was.

As they looked toward the back, tired-looking aides and staffers, in civilian clothing, cradled laptops and tablets, talking quietly among themselves. Most of them looked like they hadn't had a chance to change their clothes in the last thirty-six hours. In the rear sat Margaret Walsh, the secretary of defense, General Louis C. Painter, the chairman of the joint chiefs of staff, and the president of the United States.

Sam and Tom sat down, facing the secretary of defense and the admiral. A waiter came and placed glasses of cold water with ice in small wells in the fuselage-side armrest of the recliners, and offered both men coffee. They both asked for black, and the waiter disappeared. The admiral smiled awkwardly as the three men sat in silence, waiting for the secretary to look up from whatever it was she was typing. Sam and Tom looked out their windows at the other helicopters flying in formation with them. After a minute, the secretary snapped her laptop closed and took off her glasses, letting them hang on the cord around her neck. "Listen. I'll get right to it. We need your help."

Sam nodded. He wouldn't have been summoned by the president if they hadn't. His mind raced to their original reason for approaching Tom's father for information. Had the secretary of defense somehow intervened?

Sam opened his palms in a conciliatory gesture. "We're here to help, anything we can do, ma'am."

The secretary nodded. "I'll let the president inform you of the problem. What he's about to say, only three other people on Earth are fully aware of, so it is with serious gravity that we're taking you both into our confidence. As such, nothing you are told is to ever be repeated."

"Understood, ma'am," Sam and Tom replied in unison.

The president said, "As you already know, a British Boeing 747 Dreamlifter crashed under unusual circumstances nine weeks ago. After that, the *Buckholtz,* a large container ship ran aground at Neuwerk Island. Both of these seemingly random events were orchestrated for the most serious purpose of stealing some of the most advanced stealth and chameleon technology ever produced."

Sam nodded. He'd already gathered that. What he didn't know was why American technology was being built offshore, and what the president wanted him to do about it, so he remained silent.

"What you probably don't know is that since then, the Chinese aircraft carrier, the *Feng Jian* was sunk by what they are insisting was an American nuclear attack submarine."

Sam studied the president through narrowed eyes. "What circumstances, Mr. President?"

"The *Feng Jian* pursued what appeared to be one of our nuclear attack submarines into a region of the South China Sea known as the Labyrinth because of its dangerous submerged reefs and atolls. When the submarine reached a dead end, it appeared to hover out of the water, and race across a coral reef.

Just when they thought for certain it was nothing more than a holographic projection, the strange vessel launched a torpedo. The *Feng Jian* couldn't maneuver within the narrow channel and was struck, causing it to sink into the shallow waters."

Sam asked, "So what fired the torpedo?"

"We don't know. It wasn't one of ours, but it might have been based on our technology."

"Really?" Sam asked. "What makes you think that?"

The president sighed heavily. "The *Feng Jian's* radar crew reported they were unable to see any sign of the submarine, thus suspecting it to be nothing more than a projection."

"But what did they see?" Sam persisted.

The secretary of defense clicked on an image on her laptop and then turned it around to show Sam and Tom.

"This," she said.

Sam swallowed. It was a perfect replica of the strange sphere they had seen on the FDR recording of the Dreamlifter's cargo hold.

"It was one of ours?" Sam asked.

The president scowled. "It might have been. Or someone else certainly wanted it to look that way."

Sam said, "*Jiè dāo shā rén.*"

The president looked confused. "What?"

"It's an old Chinese military strategy," Sam said. "It means, *to kill with a borrowed knife.* The concept was to trick a third party to attack, using the strength of an ally, instead of one's own army to win a battle."

A series of worrying lines loomed on the president's forehead as his frowned. "So far, we have a crashed British aircraft, a German cargo ship aground, and now a Chinese aircraft carrier torpedoed. The question is, risk of war threatens our nation, who is most positioned to gain from such a war?"

Sam said, "I'm sorry, Mr. President, my expertise is more in the area of ocean salvage and archeology. My guess is you have plenty of military advisers who might offer better opinions…"

"I'm asking your opinion, Mr. Reilly," the president said, tersely.

"When Tom and I dived the internal hull of the *Buckholtz,* we were attacked by another scuba diver. In the struggle, he was killed instead. The diver was wearing a dry suit known to be manufactured for the Russian elite Foreign Intelligence. German Federal Intelligence Service investigators retrieved the body. Unfortunately, the Eurocopter used in the transfer crashed en route and incinerated on impact, destroying the remains."

The secretary asked, "What are you suggesting?"

Sam expelled a deep breath. "I believe the Russians are behind this attack."

The president said, "That's impossible."

"Why?"

The president frowned. "Because the Russians were the ones who gave us the technology."

CHAPTER THIRTY-THREE

S AM FELT HIS WORLD SHATTER.

He closed his eyes, trying to concentrate and put things into logical order. The greatest superpowers in the world had all been thrown into direct conflict. It was impossible to believe that the world was going to race toward WWIII and even more unlikely that the Russians were now helping them by providing advanced stealth technology.

Sam opened his eyes and met the president's eye. "I don't understand, sir."

The president grinned. "China wasn't trying to force their opponents to fight one another. You were on the right track, though. In this case, nothing makes enemies work together like the sudden appearance of a greater foe."

Sam listened, but unable to get where the president was leading, remained silent.

The president continued. "Did you know that during the Cold War, at the Geneva Summit in 1985, President Ronald Reagan and Soviet Premier Mikhail Gorbachev agreed to pause the Cold War and come to each other's aid in the event of an alien attack?"

Sam laughed. "You're kidding, sir?"

"No. It's the truth. Gorbachev confirmed it in an interview in 2009."

Sam cocked an incredulous eyebrow. "Are you telling me we're under attack from an alien race?'

"No, no. Of course not. But all the same, the Russians, along with anyone else, would come to us to help defeat a mutual enemy."

"So, who's the enemy?" Sam asked.

"They don't know."

The slightest of smiles formed on Sam's lips as he waited for the president to explain.

The president met his eye. Conflict twisted his face into a grimace of indecision, as though deciding how much to tell. In the end, it appeared, he opted for the truth. "There's an insurrection."

"And the Russians came to us for help?" Sam remained skeptical. "There's been rebellions before."

"This is different."

"How?"

"Military secrets and technology are being stolen from the Russian government. Advanced submarine technology is being sold to a third party. A growing league who have infiltrated governments throughout the world and are slowly building a secret society—hiding in the oceans."

Sam thought that sounded a little far-fetched. "What makes you so confident the Russians are telling the truth?"

The president set his jaw. "Because we have the same problem, and so does Britain, Germany, and France."

CHAPTER THIRTY-FOUR

Ω————————Ω————————Ω

AFTER FOLLOWING THE COAST SOUTH, the Sikorsky VH-3D Sea King, banked to the left, suddenly deviating inland.

Sam thought about the implications of the news. "The Russians sent you the spheres to try and find the mole?"

The president nodded. "After the loss of the Boeing 747 Dreamlifter, they had Germany send the second sphere by cargo ship. When the *Buckholtz* ran aground, we knew we were in real trouble. Two days later, when we heard the *Feng Jian* was sunk, by what appeared to be an American nuclear attack submarine but gave off a radar image of a sphere, we knew our time was running short."

"Elise said that DARPA was working on the spheres nearly a decade ago, back when she was still working for the CIA. How did we let the Russians beat us to it?"

The president smiled. "Who said they beat us?"

"So, the sphere that attacked the Chinese aircraft carrier…"

"Was most likely one of ours," the president finished the statement.

Sam glanced at the secretary of defense. "What does your intelligence team think this league's reasons are?"

She spoke without hesitation. "It appears they want to encourage WWIII."

"Why? Won't that just destroy them in the process?"

"We believe they have an underwater habitat. Somewhere large, where they believe they might survive the fallout of such a war."

Sam said, "How long have we known?"

The president answered. "Nearly five years."

"Five years!" Sam just about swore. "Why haven't we done anything about it?"

"We did." The president turned to his secretary of defense. "Perhaps Painter had better explain to you what we've been trying to do."

Sam glanced at General Painter, the highest-ranking officer in the U.S. military, and direct military advisor to the president and the secretary of defense. "Sir?"

"More than a decade ago we commenced research and development into a perfect submarine. Something entirely undetectable."

"Go on," Sam said, knowing that stealth was the golden aim of all submarines.

"Recently, the project reached its successful fruition with the discovery of the material known as *blackbody,* found on a 13,000-year-old meteorite, we were given the medium needed to make a truly undetectable submarine."

Sam knew plenty about the strange element, known as *blackbody.* Microscopically, it was similar to an atomic sponge, capable of soaking up all surrounding sub-atomic particles. The ancient Master Builders knew about the material and had devised a method of controlling the stones, to protect the earth from extinction, after the magnetic poles rapidly switched positions, causing catastrophic changes to the weather.

The material was highly unstable and capable of destroying the world if mishandled. It horrified him that his government would try to use such a material to advance its military. Even so, it also amazed him. As far as he was aware, the last of the unearthly element had been destroyed. "Where did you obtain it? I thought the entire meteorite had been thoroughly mined?"

Painter nodded. "We discovered the meteorite, found near Göbekli Tepe in the Southeastern Anatolia Region of Turkey, broke in two upon entry into our atmosphere. Originally, it was assumed the second piece broke up in the atmosphere, but after a long search, it was discovered in a field near Portland Oregon."

"And you took it to produce the ultimate submarine?"

"Exactly. It was called the USS *Omega Deep,* and to date, it was the most advanced submarine on Earth. The submarine was launched nearly three months ago now and was on a mission to find this secret league's underwater habitat."

The Sea King turned on to its final approach to a helipad at the Joint Base Pearl Harbor-Hickham.

Sam frowned. "You said it was the most advanced submarine on Earth?"

Painter nodded. "I'm afraid we've lost it."

"How?"

"We don't know. It might have been a mechanical malfunction, it might have imploded, it could have run aground into a submerged mountain, an accident with a torpedo bay…" Painter sighed heavily. "Or…"

"What?" Sam asked.

It was the president who finally answered. "There's a chance its commander has intentionally stolen the submarine and its technology."

Sam was mortified. "Who was its commander?"

The president spoke directly to Tom, "I'm sorry son, your father was in command."

The Sea King landed adjacent to the main administration complex of the submarine command. It was hard to hear anything above the scream of the helicopter's powerful engines. The pilot finally shut them down, and Tom's voice became audible.

"No way, my father never would have betrayed his country. The U.S. Navy was the closest thing to God to my father. There's no way he would have betrayed it."

The president put his hands up in a conciliatory gesture. "We know. Your father has served his country for more than four decades. No one is really suggesting he's behind this, but we can't rule out the chance that someone on board did."

Sam asked, "How many on board?" Sam asked.

The secretary of defense answered without hesitation. "There were 192 submariners, men and women, the absolute cream of the crop—they were hand-picked by Admiral Dwight Bower, himself."

Tom took a deep breath, exhaled slowly and pushed his hand through his hair. "How long can they survive if the submarine's lying on the seabed somewhere?"

"Painter?" The secretary intoned, turning to the secretary of defense.

"Around 120 days, give or take. She's equipped with a symbiotic drive which can theoretically support the homeostasis system on board indefinitely. The crew still need food and water though. She's equipped with a new cloaking engine which absorbs all sound, making her completely undetectable by sonar. She's also the fastest nuclear sub ever built, by a fair margin—which, unfortunately in this situation, significantly widens our search area."

"No distress beacons were recovered?" Sam asked.

"None."

"Well at least theoretically we have plenty of time, right?" Tom asked. "Assuming they're just stuck."

Painter turned to the secretary, waiting for her response.

"No," she said. "Time is something we don't have a lot of. We lost contact seventy-eight days ago."

"Seventy-eight days!" Tom said, exasperated.

"All right," Sam said, placating his friend. "So, what's the plan then?"

The president faced him directly and said, "Right now, we've exhausted our options, and we're looking to you and Tom to find a needle in a haystack, without knowing which ocean that haystack resides."

CHAPTER THIRTY-FIVE

Ω————Ω————Ω

THE U.S. NAVY UNDERSEA RESCUE mobile command center was housed in a basketball court, which had been appropriated for this specific mission. The large room was abuzz with people working round the clock to avert the tragedy. Sam took in the sight of more than a hundred people, who worked across an array of desks, laptop computers, communication stations, satellite feeds, and in a private meeting, liaising with people from submarine search and rescue throughout the world in private meetings.

The president of the United States, the secretary of defense, and the chairman of the joint chiefs of staff disappeared to attend a briefing with the COMSUBPAC—Commander, Submarine Force, U.S. Pacific Fleet, leaving Sam and Tom in the hands of the commander of the U.S. Navy Undersea Rescue Unit.

A man in his mid-fifties greeted Sam with a firm handshake. "I'm Commander Benjamin Woods. I'm currently in charge of the search and rescue operation for the USS *Omega Deep*. I've been involved with the deep submergence rescue program since the 1980s, having originally trained on the DSRV-1 Mystic, back when she was still in service."

"Sam Reilly," he said, shaking the commander's hand, "And this is Tom Bower."

The commander greeted Tom with a hard smile. "Pleased to meet you, sir. I knew your dad for nearly four decades. He's a good man."

Sam was pleased that Woods hadn't yet written Tom's father off as deceased.

Commander Woods said, "Chairman of the joint chiefs of staff, General Painter, has briefed me to bring you up to speed with the project so far. I'll fill you in what we know and don't know. Then, we'll send you back to the *Maria Helena* to head off a secondary search and rescue plan. That way we're not doubling up, and I pray you come up with more than we have."

"Understood," Sam said. "Where do we start?"

Commander Woods said, "I'll start by telling you exactly what we know about the USS *Omega Deep* and what happened when she disappeared."

Sam listened as he was filled in on the Omega Cloak's unique capabilities, what tests its commander had already performed, and what, if any, were the submarine's known faults.

When they were finished, Commander Woods started to point out the senior officers heading up the investigation from their respective branches, including seismic listening posts, real-time satellite imaging, sonar and radar bases throughout the world. In addition to the U.S. Navy's team, there were civilians too. Scientists, meteorologist, hydrologists, naval engineers, and submarine specialists, who were all there to provide expert advice. Sam noted, with surprise, that they weren't all American. A team from the British Submarine Parachute Assistance Group and also ISMERLO — International Submarine Escape and Rescue Liaison Office were there to help.

"Any questions?" the commander asked.

Sam made a wry smile. "Yes. I thought this would be more protected?"

"You mean regarding the experimental side of the *Omega Deep*?"

"Exactly."

"The two of you and I are the only ones in this building who know the truth about the submarine."

"What does everyone else think they're looking for?"

"Oh, they know that a *Virginia* class block VII nuclear-powered fast attack submarine has gone missing," Commander Woods said with a suppressed smile. "But they don't know about its Omega Cloak. As you can imagine, that's heavily classified. You've been brought up to speed because of your need-to-know status, and the fact that the secretary of defense was adamant that you both had explicit first-hand knowledge of the material, *blackbody,* which she thought you might use to your advantage."

Tom asked in a whisper, "How are they supposed to find the submarine without knowing about its unique invisibility capabilities?"

"It doesn't matter. Those capabilities were designed to make it undetectable. The fact that its disappeared hasn't changed that."

Sam persisted, "Still, how can the world find it, if they don't know what they're looking for?"

"If the Omega Cloak is still activated we'll never see that submarine again. It's as simple as that. All this," Commander Woods glanced around the packed mobile command center, "is in the off chance we get lucky, and the Omega Cloak is no longer activated."

Sam continued with the practical issues of the rescue. "If we find it. Then what?"

"The U.S. Navy Undersea Rescue Unit has a Pressurized Rescue Module known as PRM-1 Falcon." Commander Woods glanced at them, and, seeing recognition in their eyes, continued. "The PRM-1 Falcon can be loaded onto a waiting Boeing C17 Globemaster III and flown to any location on Earth in under 24-hours. From there, it can be installed onto a vessel of opportunity—known as a VOO—and delivered to the location of the distressed submarine."

"All right," Sam said. "What are your prime theories about what happened to the *Omega Deep?*"

The commander answered immediately from a previously determined list. "We've narrowed it down to one of two possibilities."

"Go on."

"One: the submarine ran aground on an unmapped submerged valley, ripping a hole in her hull, and flooding her." Commander Woods pointed out a number of known submerged valleys in the region where the *Omega Deep* was last sighted. "This would explain why no communication buoys were ever received identifying her location."

"And the second possibility?" Sam asked.

"She's been stolen. Either by her CO or any other member of her crew. In which case, she's probably already been sold to the highest bidder, and we've lost $30 billion dollars' worth of research and development and the greatest naval advantage over the world's oceans we've ever had."

Sam thought about that for a moment, staring at an enlarged world map nearly five feet tall and stretched out against the wall. He studied the areas already searched, and the known submerged reefs, valleys, and mountains. He pointed to the Atlantic. "What about over here, off the Continental Shelf?"

"Too deep," the commander dismissed the suggestion. "No chance the submarine would have collided with anything down there."

"What about a malfunction causing her to dive uncontrollably?"

"Impossible," Woods was emphatic.

"Why?"

"An implosion anywhere in the Atlantic would have been picked up by more than a dozen seismic listening posts on either side of the ocean. Heck, even Wisconsin's hydrophones would have picked it up." Commander Woods sighted. "In fact, none of our seismic listening posts have detected any acoustic anomaly throughout the submarine's last known coordinates, or anywhere around the world, which means it's unlikely the submarine has reached its crush depth and imploded. If that had happened, almost anywhere in the world, we'd have heard it."

"All right," Sam said, accepting the point. "You said that the *Omega Deep* was last sighted on the surface of the Norwegian Sea. At the time, satellite imaging showed my own ship, the *Maria Helena* in the same vicinity, searching for the downed British Boeing 747 Dreamlifter, and also the *Vostok,* a Russian fishing trawler, suspected of being an intelligence gathering vessel."

"That's right. Do you know where the *Vostok* went afterward?"

"It didn't follow the *Omega Deep,* that's for sure. It would have been impossible."

"All the same, do you know where it went?"

"It remained in the Barents Sea, Norwegian Sea, and the North Sea for another month—under the pretense of deep sea fishing, and then headed south, toward the Atlantic Ocean. I can have one of my aides find its current location for you."

"Thanks. Now, you said the commander of the *Omega Deep* confirmed that he would cancel the original mission, and focus on assisting with the search of the wrecked aircraft?"

"That's right."

"How did Admiral Bower do that?"

"Through a secure, coded transmission."

"Is it possible anyone else might have made the transmission."

Woods considered that possibility for a moment. "It's unlikely, but I suppose, it could be possible if they were able to gain access to Admiral Bower's secret codes."

"So, as you say, it might not have been Admiral Bower who's betrayed the U.S. Navy?"

"It's definitely a possibility," Commander Woods said, happy to deflect from the more likely possibility that Tom's dad was guilty of treason.

Sam said, "What was the original mission?"

Woods said, "It was a series of tests, to see how undetectable the submarine could be."

"Have you checked those locations?"

"No. It's highly unlikely the submarine would continue on with the original mission, isn't it?"

"You didn't search the original route?" Sam asked, incredulously.

"Of course not. Why would we? The *Omega Deep* was given the express order to surface and engage in all efforts to search and rescue the crashed Boeing 747 Dreamlifter."

"And it never occurred to you that he refused the order only to continue on with the primary mission objective?"

"No." Woods smiled in that almost condescending way, which said, that's a stupid waste of time even thinking about that. "That's daft. Think about it. You don't refuse a direct order from the president of the United States only to pursue your original mission objective, testing and displaying the formidable power of..." he paused, turned his gaze from Tom's hardened gaze, and said, "I'm sorry Mr. Bower. I knew your father well. He was a legend in these parts, and I don't believe he has betrayed his country. But the fact is, the USS *Omega Deep* received express orders to help with the search and recovery of the crashed Boeing 747 Dreamlifter, but instead, activated its Omega Cloak, and disappeared. So we have to assume someone on board is no longer following the president's orders."

"Do you have a copy of the original route the *Omega Deep* would have taken had they been ordered to continue with their primary mission objective?"

Woods thought about it for a second. "Yeah, sure. Why?"

"Because right now that seems like the only lead we have. It's a massive longshot, but it is the only lead we have."

Woods opened his mouth as though he was about to argue the point, and then meeting Sam's eye, thought best of it, and brought the image of the original route up on a 100-inch LCD screen mounted to the wall. The digital image encompassed North and South America across to the coastal regions of Mediterranean and Russian ports… "You're not going to be able to see anything from here."

"Why not?"

"Because if the *Omega Deep* continued to utilize her cloaking technology, there's no way you're going to identify her from satellite images."

"What about DRAPES?"

Commander Woods thought about that for a moment and then grinned. "Not a chance in hell."

During the Cold War, the U.S. Navy laid a fixed network of underwater hydrophones on the ocean floor called the Sound Surveillance System, known as SOSUS, to detect Soviet submarines transiting from their bases to patrol areas in the Atlantic and Pacific Oceans. Listening arrays placed in strategic chokepoints that those submarines would necessarily have to transit, like the waters between Greenland, Iceland, and Scotland—the so-called GIUK Gap—notionally let the United States know every time a Soviet submarine entered the North Atlantic, allowing the U.S. Navy to direct its own ships or submarines to track them. In 2016, that system was updated, and extended throughout more of the world, in a program named the Deep Reliable Acoustic Path Exploitation System.

Sam was incredulous. "The Omega Cloak is that good?"

"No." Woods smiled proudly. "She was better. Part of what made the *Omega Deep* special was her sound absorbing hull. Whatever sound she produces, is completely absorbed. No way our hydrophones could pick her up, even if we knew exactly where she was to focus our listening arrays."

Sam nodded, and studied the route, trying to determine any location where the submarine would have been forced to surface and might have thus been spotted using satellite imaging. The course spanned a long route from the British Isles, south into the Mediterranean, through the Dardanelles Strait, Bosporus Sea, Black Sea, and Sea of Azov within Russia. From there, it returned, making it out of the Mediterranean Sea, and across the Atlantic, through the Panama Canal and on toward the Pacific.

Sam stopped. "I can see why you're keen to keep this experiment under wrap. You would have many upset nations, including some of our closest allies by admitting that you penetrated their coastal regions under stealth."

Woods made a thin-lipped smile. "As you can see, our allies wouldn't be too impressed either. But it was paramount to the experiment's success that we tested it with high fidelity."

Sam's eyes ran across the route along Northern Africa, down the Skeleton Coast, across the Atlantic, and finally landing on Panama. His eyes narrowed. "Was this the end of the experiment?"

Woods shook his head. "No."

"So, what was supposed to happen here? Was the *Omega Deep* meant to surface and report, or go somewhere else?"

"No, there was more to the experiment."

"Where?"

"She was to cross through the Panama Canal and head southwest, on to Australia, before turning north, and returning to Pearl Harbor."

"Can you please bring up the more detailed map for me?"

"Sure." Woods clicked a new icon, and the second map appeared, with the route superimposed in red. "But I doubt it will do you much good."

Sam studied the new map. "How did you plan to get it

through the Panama Canal?"

"Oh, that took some planning, but in the end, we decided to coincide it with a particular date we planned to have an old *Iowa* class battleship transverse the Panama Canal for a historical event."

Sam said, "I wasn't aware they even fit through the Panama Canal?"

"They do. Only just. The *Iowa* class battleship is the largest vessel in the world that's allowed to make the crossing. At 108.6 feet, she only just squeezes into the 110 feet wide Panama Canal."

"How would that have helped you squeeze the *Omega Deep* through? The Panama Canal's water-tight locks are 1050 feet in length, with a useable length of 1000 feet. No way you're going to get a battleship and the *Omega Deep* through in one go."

"No. Of course not. The engineers at the Panama Canal insisted that we pay for two allotted spaces, so that they could have a dry run after the *Iowa* class battleship made its traverse, that way they could see if there were any faults and then repair them, before another large vessel, such as a cargo ship crossed."

Sam grinned. "And in that dry run, you were going to bring the USS *Omega Deep?*"

"Exactly."

"Was there any way you could have spotted the submarine had it passed through the canal?"

"Not if it maintained its Omega Cloak and its crew didn't want to be spotted. Originally, there was a plan… but obviously things have changed."

"What was the plan?" Sam asked, eagerly.

"During the filling of the third lockout, someone on board the *Omega Deep* was going to release a helium-filled balloon in the shape of an American flag. To any casual observer, it would appear that the balloon had just floated into the area, but it would be a confirmation the submarine had passed through the region."

Sam said, "Do you have recorded footage of that date."

"We don't personally," Woods said. "But there's a live feed from the top of the lookout tower. They keep records. I can bring those up if you want?"

"Yes please."

Woods raised an eyebrow. "You don't think the crew decided to rub our noses in the fact that they stole $30 billion dollars' worth of military hardware, by giving us a sign, do you?"

"As you said, it's unlikely, but stranger things have happened."

Commander Woods searched the Panama Canal's security records on his laptop, entering the exact date and time the USS *Omega Deep* was supposed to travel through the canal and pressed search. The recording of the live feed came through.

The image captured the *Iowa* class battleship leaving the water lock, and Woods fast-forwarded the section until it showed the battleship leaving and an empty water lock, now thirty feet lower.

Wood glanced at Sam and pressed play. "Here you go."

Sam watched as the heavy steel, watertight locks closed and the empty lock filled with water until it was another thirty feet higher. Through squinting eyes, he searched the surface of the lock. Shallow ripples showed a local breeze teasing the empty water's surface.

Wood's lips formed a hard line, as he went to press stop on the recording. "I'm sorry. They weren't there."

Sam's response was an immediate, almost visceral, cry. "Stop!"

"Why?"

Tom said, "Look at that!"

Wood's eyes fixed on the image on the laptop.

There, in the middle of the empty water-tight lock, was a

balloon rising out of nothing. Woods paused the image and zoomed in on the balloon. It was shaped like a flag and covered in the stars and stripes of the American flag.

CHAPTER THIRTY-SIX

S AM WATCHED AS COMMANDER WOODS slammed the laptop screen shut.

There would undoubtedly be a lot of questions he couldn't answer if anyone else in the room spotted the anomaly.

To Sam and Tom, Woods said, "Come with me."

Sam grinned and followed the commander out of the U.S. Navy Undersea Rescue Unit's mobile command center, crossed an open field and entered a new building. Inside they headed through a series of secure passageways, toward the main command center for COMSUBPAC—the Pacific Submarine Fleet's headquarters. The three men walked in silence. They all knew the consequence of such a finding, but no one could have expected what it meant.

At the end of the hallway, two marines in dress uniform guarded the soundproofed door.

Woods approached the door, but one of the marines blocked his progress.

"I'm sorry, sir," the marine said, "I can't let you in. The presidents in a meeting."

Woods spoke with the quiet authority of a man with nearly four decades of command. "He's going to want to hear what I have to say."

224 | OMEGA DEEP

The marine looked like he was going to protest, but then said, "I'll just be a minute, sir."

The marine knocked on the door, entered, and returned a few moments later. "You're right to go through."

Sam and Tom approached the door.

The marine stared at them, wondering if he should question more, before the commander said, "They're with me at the president's express orders. He'll want to hear what they have to say, too."

Inside, the president, secretary of defense, and chairman of the joint chiefs of staff were sitting around a series of leather lounges. The president greeted them and motioned for them to take a seat.

Sam and Tom took a seat.

Commander Woods closed the soundproof door and took a seat.

The president said, "You've found something?"

Woods opened his laptop. The image still depicted a balloon a few feet off the surface of the water within the Panama Canal. "Yeah, what do you think of this."

There was a collective, audible exhale throughout the room as the president, secretary of defense, and chairman of the joint chiefs of staff took in the significance.

The president spoke first. "So, that confirms it. The USS *Omega Deep* did reach the Pacific."

Woods cocked an incredulous eyebrow. "You're not surprised, Mr. President?"

"No. Far from it," the president replied. "I would have been, but some recent information has come to my attention, and we were already just about certain the *Omega Deep* was now in the Pacific."

"What news, sir?" Woods asked.

"I believe Mr. Reilly requested one of the tech engineers to locate the Russian-owned spy vessel, the *Vostok?*"

"That's right," Sam confirmed.

The president expelled his breath. "Well, it was found."

That came as no surprise to Sam. The Russian intelligence gathering vessel disguised as a fishing trawler was a poor national secret. He had no doubt that the U.S. Navy would make short work of finding its present location.

"Where is it, sir?" he asked.

"The South Pacific, roughly two hundred miles south of the Galapagos Islands."

Sam made the connection immediately. Could it be that their Russian counterparts had achieved what the entire U.S. Navy couldn't, and located the USS *Omega Deep?* The thought intrigued him as well as terrified him.

"Have they found the *Omega Deep?*" Sam asked.

"No," the president replied. "We're unsure what they were doing there, but it's almost a certainty they've had contact with our missing submarine."

"Why?"

The president addressed the secretary of defense. "Perhaps you had better explain it to him, ma'am."

The secretary nodded. "The *Vostok* appears to have succumbed to an accident, rendering it lifeless. The entire ship is currently drifting helplessly."

"Any survivors?" Sam asked.

She shook her head. "It doesn't look like it from any satellite images, but we'll find out as soon as we put someone on board."

"What did the Russians say?"

"Nothing."

Sam's eyes narrowed. "You haven't told them?"

"No."

"You going to tell the Russians?"

"Hell no."

"Why not?"

She bit her lower lip. "We want to work out what went wrong first."

Sam stared at her, noticing her tentative response. "What's wrong with the ship, ma'am?"

"Everything." She smiled. "The entire ship's turned to ice."

"You mean it's crashed into an iceberg?"

"No. I mean, the entire thing's been turned into ice. Like someone picked it up as they would a toy and left it in the freezer for a month until it became a block of solid ice."

"You're kidding me?"

"No."

Sam expelled a deep breath but kept his mouth shut firm, his mind, pensive.

The secretary was the first to break the silence. "You know exactly what this means, don't you?"

Sam nodded. "It means the *Vostok* has been experimenting with *blackbody*."

"Exactly," the secretary said.

The president said, "So you see now why we weren't surprised to discover the *Omega Deep* had crossed the Panama Canal and entered the Pacific."

Sam asked, "But where did the Russians get another piece of *blackbody* from? I thought the last of it had been used on the *Omega Deep's* hull?"

The general answered that question. "The *Omega Deep* kept a single block of the unique material as a back up to power part of its redundancy sound absorbing system. It would appear that someone from the *Omega Deep* has been in contact with the crew from the *Vostok*. Maybe they dived the stricken submarine and salvaged the *blackbody,* which someone on board the *Vostok* used to experiment with, resulting in their deaths."

Sam recalled how the original experiments with *blackbody* proved the material to be highly unstable, causing nearby subatomic particles to compress on themselves, becoming denser and in the process, colder. If the chain reaction was left unhindered, it would ultimately end in freezing everything around it—and in the ocean, that would most likely lead to ice and snow.

He said, "When will your team leave?"

"Any minute now. We're still gathering the members of an elite team to investigate the *Vostok*. Also, we're taking no chances of someone else finding the *Omega Deep,* so we've deployed an aircraft carrier to the region—the USS *Gerald R. Ford.*"

Sam asked, "Who were you thinking of sending to investigate the *Vostok?*"

The president leveled his gray eyes at him and said, "You."

CHAPTER THIRTY-SEVEN

Ω

GALAPAGOS ISLANDS

SAM CHARTERED A PRIVATE AIRCRAFT—a Cessna Citation CJ3—from Hawaii to the Galapagos Islands. The aircraft banked to the south, revealing an island surrounded by azure waters, as the pilots set up for their final approach onto San Cristóbal. It was the easternmost island in the Galápagos archipelago, as well as one of the oldest geologically.

According to his briefing notes, the island's official Spanish name, "San Cristóbal" comes from the patron saint of seafarers, St. Christopher.

The reference made Sam feel that it was a good omen in their quest for the lost submarine, Tom's father, and 192 U.S. submariners.

The Cessna landed on the short runway, its pilots easing her gently onto the blacktop and braking hard, before taxiing to the newly built hangar.

Across from him, Tom remained sound asleep.

Sam waited until the pilots shut down the engines and then woke Tom up. "We're here."

Tom sat up, unclipped his seatbelt, and glanced out the window. It was a warm day, with a crisp blue sky, but the ocean breeze kept the temperature to a balmy 85 degrees Fahrenheit.

Tom smiled with appreciation. "Nice place."

"Don't get too enamored with it. We've got a pleasure cruiser waiting for us at the beach to take us away from the Galapagos Islands, due south, to the *Vostok*."

Tom shrugged. It wasn't the first time Sam had teased him with a nice work environment only to be torn away to the middle of nowhere. "Tell me again, why the USS *Gerald R. Ford* is en route to the location, but we have to hire our own yacht to get there?"

"Plausible deniability," Sam said. "The secretary wants us to investigate without involving the U.S. Navy."

Tom nodded. "That way if the Russians discover their vessel's been damaged, the secretary doesn't have to explain why she kept it secret."

"Exactly."

"How long until the *Maria Helena* gets here?"

"Another two days."

Sam grabbed his gear, and he and Tom made their way through the airport. Outside, a local tour guide met them with his Jeep and drove them the short distance to the harbor.

"San Cristóbal Island," the guide said, "is composed of four fused volcanoes, all extinct. It is home to the oldest permanent settlement of the islands and is the island where Darwin first went ashore in 1835."

The Jeep took them east along the coast to Puerto Chino. Sam took in his environment, devouring the sights like a Thanksgiving feast. The island was host to a number of unique flora and fauna, including, frigate birds, Galápagos sea lions, Galápagos tortoises, blue and red-footed boobies, tropicbirds, marine iguanas, dolphins and swallow-tailed gulls. Some of its more famous flora included the Galapagos rock-purslane and cut leaf daisy.

The ride ended quickly, and Sam and Tom climbed out with their duffel bags.

Anchored in the bay was a Prestige 620 pleasure cruiser, named, *Matilda.*

Its naval architecture was a combination of rich teak and ultramodern carbon fiber flybridge and cabin. It was powered by twin 700 HP Volvo Penta D11 IPS900 engines, allowing the pleasure cruiser to reach a cruise speed of 18.1 knots.

A local tourist operator met them at the harbor, and the operator ferried them out to the yacht in a small tender.

Once onboard, Sam and Tom quickly checked over the yacht. She was kept in pristine condition, and originally there for a rich guest who would arrive in another two weeks. Sam had promised to have the yacht back in a matter of days with plenty of time to spare.

Confident the yacht was in a safe condition, Sam pulled up the anchor, and Tom set a course due south toward the last known location of the now drifting, stricken, *Vostok.*

It took nearly twenty-four hours to reach the *Vostok.*

Sam switched off the sports cruiser's autopilot and took control of the helm. He eased the yacht in a slow cruise around the much larger Russian vessel. From the outside, it certainly looked like it had once been a fishing trawler. Of course, that's what it was supposed to look like. It no longer mattered, the entire vessel was now frozen solid. Whatever secrets it once knew, would never be told. Thick ice caked its deck, and several pieces of the overhead rigging had collapsed under the weight.

Tom expelled a breath. "It's a wonder the entire ship didn't sink under the weight."

"Yeah, that surprised me, too. I suppose it shows that the internal hull is hollow and not filled with water for its live holding tanks—otherwise, that too, would have frozen solid, and then the entire thing would have lost its buoyancy."

After the second reconnaissance trip, Tom said, "Should we tie up alongside the trawler?"

Sam shook his head, "I don't like the idea. If something

changes and the *Vostok* goes under, I'd rather it not take our little pleasure cruiser with it."

"Agreed. But what other choice do we have?"

"We could take the little runabout across."

"Sure, but then what do we do with *Matilda?* The water's too deep to anchor out here, and there's only you and me, so someone's going to have to stay on board."

Sam shrugged. "It's okay. You can stay here. Just bring me closer to the *Vostok,* and I'll climb aboard. Keep your eyes out for me on deck. I'll give you a wave when I'm done."

"You want to go and explore a frozen ghost ship by yourself?"

"No. You have a better idea?"

"Not really."

"Okay, so that's the plan, then."

Tom adjusted the twin throttles as he gently maneuvered *Matilda* in beside the Russian trawler. Sam, standing on the bow, waited until the two ships were nearly touching and then leaped across onto the lower aft deck of the *Vostok.*

CHAPTER THIRTY-EIGHT

SAM'S FEET LANDED ON THE icy deck and slipped out from under him. His back struck the solid ice with force, winding him. He gritted his teeth, rolled onto his side, and carefully stood up. His boat shoes were poorly designed for walking on ice.

Over his portable radio, he heard Tom say, "Are you all right? That looked like it hurt."

Sam thought he could hear the slightest snigger, as Tom tried to restrain his amusement. "I'm fine, Tom. The deck's a little slippery, that's all."

"Okay, let me know if you need me and be careful."

"I will."

Sam's eyes raked the icy ghost ship. He tried to imagine what it would have been like. Someone must have experimented with the *blackbody*, and then minutes later there would have been an icy storm. By the time anyone knew what was happening, they were most likely already frozen.

Just in case, he shouted, "Hello. Is there anyone alive here?"

There was no response.

He didn't expect there to be.

But just in case, he shouted again, "I'm coming aboard to help."

Next to the frozen fishing lines was a fish-hook. The handle was nearly six feet high and made of wood, with a sharp metal u-shaped hook and spike on the end. Its hook was joined with the rigging by ice, but it didn't take much for Sam to free it.

Sam gripped it with his gloved hand. He was thankful he'd had the foresight to bring a thick jacket and snow gloves but forgot about crampons, or at least something more practical than his boat shoes.

He pointed the spike into the ice and used the tool to brace himself as he made his way across the open deck.

It took him several minutes to reach the bridge.

Ice throughout the ship had started melting, and the internal stairwell leading to the upper bridge had a small stream of water running down it. Sam carefully climbed the stairs until he reached the main door. Like everything else on board the stricken vessel, it was frozen shut.

He took the fish-hook and used the spike to chisel away at the thin layer of frozen ice. The ice was already thawing and came apart easily enough.

Sam carefully opened the door.

Inside, were the bodies of several sailors snap frozen in time. Sam took in their appearance in an instant. Despite being frozen, he could make out some of the tell-tail signs of seasoned fishermen, including heavily callused hands. For a moment, he wondered if the U.S. Navy had gotten it wrong, maybe the *Vostok* was indeed a fishing vessel?

He glanced at the instruments. The digital course plotters, radar, depth sounder, and engine readings were all destroyed. He would have loved to know where they were heading. At the back of the navigation table was a pair of Admiralty charts for the region. There were a few penciled notations and some comments regarding continental shelves, deep reefs, and other high yield fishing spots.

Sam put them back. They were nothing more than a simple

ruse. After all, why would a Russian fishing trawler need to travel all the way to the South Pacific to find its catch? No, this was an intelligence gathering vessel, despite its clever façade.

So far, all he'd found confirmed what they already knew about the *Vostok*. What he needed to do was locate where the crew had been conducting their experiments with the *blackbody* material. And that meant getting below decks.

He carefully made his way back down the icy cascade of the internal stairwell.

Sam scoured the frozen deck for a means of accessing the areas below the deck. It seemed like someone had almost gone out of their way to remove all evidence of the multiple decks below. On his second lap of the main deck he spotted the little hatchway near the bow. It was frozen over with three or four inches of ice, but visible.

He chipped away at it using the fish-hook, the same way he had done with the doorway to the bridge. Sam was getting better at the technique, and within about fifteen minutes he'd broken through the edges of the hatch, allowing him to dig the hook into the hatch and pry it open.

It was dark inside.

Sam retrieved a small flashlight from his jacket and shined it into the hold. A vertical ladder led at least ten feet into the deck below. He felt like he was entering the frozen cool room at the butchers. At the bottom of the ladder, he swept the room with his flashlight.

The place looked like it was one giant hold for live fish. Of course, there was no water and no fish. It was most likely more of the subterfuge used by the Russians to promote their image of a legitimate fishing trawler and not an intelligence gathering vessel.

At the end of the hold, there was a closed doorway that appeared to lead toward the stern.

Sam turned the door handle. It was a little stuck but gave way with a little bit of forceful encouragement.

The door opened, and it led to a single passageway that ran the length of the ship. Sam slowly made his way aft, shining his flashlight into every room he passed. This section of the ship appeared to have been more affected by the icy event, with every wall and room covered in thick ice, at some parts more than a foot deep.

He heard the crackle of Tom's voice in his portable radio. "Sam. You've been there for nearly an hour. Is everything all right?"

Sam depressed the microphone and replied, "All good over here, Tom. It looks like a frozen ship. No survivors. No answers."

"Are you ready to come back?"

"Soon. I'll do one more reconnaissance sweep, and then I'll come and get warm."

"Give me a call when you're ready."

"Will do."

Sam turned to make his way back to the original hold and up the ladder.

He gripped the first rung of the ladder and stopped.

Behind him, he heard the sound of someone chiseling away at the ice. Sam stepped back down the ladder and shone his flashlight around the room. The sound continued to echo in the hold, but he couldn't quite make out its precise location.

He closed his eyes and listened.

The sound was distinctly coming from the portside of the dark hold. Sam shined his flashlight in that direction and stopped to listen.

The chiseling sound stopped for a few moments.

Sam felt his heart race.

Had his mind been playing tricks on him?

Then it started again.

Sam snapped the flashlight around, fixing it straight at the origins of the noise. The sound had stopped, but Sam audibly gasped, because in its place a hand now penetrated the frozen floor, extending upward with a metal chisel.

CHAPTER THIRTY-NINE

S VETLANA HEARD THE STRANGER'S VOICE and froze.

"Hello, I'm here to help," came a confident man's voice. "Are you all right?"

"I'm down here," she said in fluent English, without a trace of her Russian accent. She waved her hand through a hole she had broken in the ice above her head.

"Okay, just step back. I'm going to break through. Is anyone else alive down there?"

She felt her chest constrict at the question. Did he just imply that no one else survived the disaster? "No. It's just me. What about everyone else?"

"I'm sorry, I haven't found any other survivors."

That confirmed it. She was the only survivor. Svetlana stepped back into her surveillance room and listened as the stranger struck the icy roof of her confines with something heavy. Broken pieces of ice fell through the gap and into her room.

As the second piece ricocheted off the wall and fell onto her shoulder, the revelation of her circumstance struck her as vividly as if she'd been dumped in icy water. The stranger had an American accent. She was the sole survivor from a Russian spy vessel, and she was in trouble.

Svetlana glanced at her surveillance monitors. She pocketed a small USB drive with all the valuable information she'd gathered, including the internal recordings of her captain and the submarine commander who'd offered to sell the *Omega Deep*. She still felt that the information was valuable, certainly important enough to risk her life to keep.

What frightened her was who to provide it to. Someone within the Russian Foreign Intelligence had betrayed her government, trading in their secrets for money. The question was, how high up was the insurrection? If she returned to Russia for a full debrief, was she walking straight into the hands of the very people who were involved in the conspiracy?

Perhaps it was better that her government continued to believe she went down with the *Vostok* until she could study more of the information on the USB stick. There had been hundreds of hours of continuous sound recordings inside the *Vostok*. Somewhere in there were the answers she needed before she knew who to report to.

She then removed her laptop's hard drive, slid it into a slot on her desk, and flipped a switch. A brief humming sound of the degaussing machine wiped and destroyed the drive. She suspected if the U.S. Navy had boarded her vessel, they would most likely guess without any trouble what the ship's true purpose was, but at least there wouldn't be irrefutable evidence.

A few minutes later, the stranger broke through the opening.

She looked up and saw his arm reach down into the narrow opening of ice.

"Give me your hand," he said. "I'll pull you up."

Svetlana took one last look at what had been the highlight of her short-lived career in espionage and gripped his hand.

The stranger pulled her up through the narrow ice hole without any effort, and in a matter of seconds, she was standing in the bogus fishing hold.

"My name's Sam Reilly," the stranger said, offering her his

hand.

She took it. "Svetlana. Thanks for getting me out of there."

He had a nice face with a carefree and kindly smile, full of even white teeth, and piercing blue eyes, that reminded her of the depths of the ocean.

"You're welcome," he said. "How long have you been trapped?"

She thought about it for a minute. "About two days, I think."

"You must be starved. You're lucky you're not frozen. Come on, my friend and I have a yacht. You'd better come aboard and have something to eat and get warm. We can notify the authorities and get you back home."

"Sounds great," she said.

She couldn't believe her luck. The *Vostok* must have been spotted by local sailors or tourists. Of course, that luck would only last so long. The U.S. Navy would investigate as soon as her rescuer notified the authorities.

It didn't matter. She would have to work out a way to deal with that. Svetlana hardened her resolve. If she needed to, she might have to kill the man who'd come to her assistance — only if she had to.

She followed him up the ladder onto the deck.

Into a portable radio, Sam said, "Tom, do you want to come alongside now with the *Matilda*. I have one survivor."

Svetlana glanced to the west, where a wealthy pleasure cruiser was making its way toward them. She smiled. What were the chances that she should be picked up by a wealthy tourist on vacation and not a U.S. Navy patrol?

The pleasure cruiser pulled up alongside the hull.

Sam said, "Here, give me your hand, and I'll help you across."

She reached the side railing of the *Vostok* and stopped. "I'm sorry. Can you please wait a few minutes? I just realized I forgot something that I really need from down below."

"All right," Sam replied. "No problem. Can I give you a hand?"

She made her best smile, tilting her head to the side in that coquettish way that came unnaturally to her, and said, "I'm fine. I'll just be a minute."

Her eyes met his.

She bit her lower lip, hoping that he would buy it. If not, she wondered whether she would need to dispose of him? She had no doubt she could kill him by surprise, inside the dark confines of the *Vostok's* hold, but what about the other men on board the pleasure cruiser? How many were there? Would she be able to take them out, too?

No. It would be best if Sam just left her alone.

The stranger said, "All right. I'll just wait here. Let me know if you need anything."

She smiled. "Actually, can I borrow your flashlight."

"Sure," he said, handing it over to her.

She took it. "Thanks. I'll just be a minute."

He smiled warmly. His voice filled with the insouciance of a rich tourist, happy to just be where he was. "Take all the time you need."

She nodded and made her way quickly across the icy deck and down the first ladder. She picked up the metal hammer that was left on the forward hold, the same one she'd been using to chip away at the ice. From there, she made her way to the aft section of the hull, where she found another trapdoor. It didn't take long to break through the ice and open the hatch.

This one led to the bottom of the *Vostok's* hold, where the bilge was dry. No water had made its way into this part of the ship, and as such, despite the freezing conditions, there was little ice. Svetlana switched on the flashlight. She shined it across the bilge. The hull was made of thick steel, designed to protect against icebergs in the Arctic Sea above Russia.

Several thick steel pipes penetrated the hull. These were called seacocks, with an oversized lever like the handle of a tap and were designed to release bilge water when the ship was in dry dock. They were larger than they needed to be, but that was because they served a secondary purpose.

In the event of being captured or boarded, the seacocks could be opened fully, causing the hull to flood within minutes, sending all they had to hide to the bottom of the sea.

Svetlana didn't hesitate. She reached the first seacock closest to the bow and opened its lever. Seawater gushed into the bilge hold with the pressure of a fire hydrant. She made her way quickly toward the stern, opening each one, before quickly climbing the ladder to the main living quarters deck.

She shined her flashlight into the hatch and was pleased to see that the water was rising fast. Much faster than she expected. For an instant, she wondered if she'd gone too far opening all the seacocks and the *Vostok* was about to sink while she was still below decks.

Svetlana put the thought out of her mind. She would have done it anyway, even if it killed her. The information on board, particularly about whatever strange material her captain had purchased which ultimately froze the ship, would have been enough to incriminate her government. No, she would have sunk the ship anyway.

She started to run, racing across the icy passageway, and climbed up the deck.

Behind her, seawater had already reached the hatchway and was now flooding the passageway. She grabbed the ladder and started to climb.

Before she reached the top, a hand reached down to grab her.

It was Sam's. She took it, and he pulled her up.

"Quick!" he said. "The *Vostok's* about to go under!"

She didn't need to be told twice.

Svetlana ran across the icy deck. The *Vostok* was sitting much lower in the water, and its fishing deck was already at the same level as the sea, with the gentle crest of the ocean's swell lapping along the icy deck.

Next to it, the bow of the pleasure cruiser, which was previously much lower than the *Vostok*'s deck, was now above it, meaning that they would need to climb to reach it.

She felt the *Vostok* sink beneath her as she jumped to reach the bow.

Another stranger grabbed her and pulled her up over the railing onto the pleasure cruiser. Behind her, Sam made the large jump, gripped the railing and pulled himself up and over, onto the expensive teak deck of the pleasure cruiser.

The pilot of the *Matilda* didn't wait for introductions, but instead threw the yacht into gear, and powered the engines.

It took seconds for them to break away from the stricken *Vostok*.

Svetlana took in a deep breath, reveling in the warmth of the tropics as she watched Russia's most technologically advanced intelligence gathering vessel slip beneath the waves, and disappear into the depths of the South Pacific Ocean.

She exhaled. She had pulled it off.

Sam Reilly turned to face her, his piercing blue eyes fixed on hers, as though he could read her thoughts.

"What?" she asked.

"Nothing." He grinned as though it had nothing to do with him.

"What is it?" she persisted.

"Do you want to tell me why you just opened the seacocks and intentionally sank your vessel?"

CHAPTER FORTY

───────Ω───────

SAM STUDIED HER RESPONSE.

Her full lips formed a coy smile that he was almost certain was well practiced, rather than natural. She tilted her head and squinted her eyes. "Excuse me?"

A wry smile formed on his lips and his eyes narrowed. "Did you just open the seacocks?"

Conflict twisted her face into a grimace of indecision. For a moment Sam thought she was going to lie, but instead, thinking better of it. She answered with the truth or a very near version of it. "Yes."

"Why?"

"We're a scouting trawler. Some of the places we go aren't strictly legal for international fishing, and some of the locations and in-depth fishing analysis are the company's intellectual property. I figured the best thing I could do was to sink the ship. It's not like it was going to be repaired. Besides, it would have served as a dangerous hazard to any other would-be rescuers."

Sam knew she was lying, but that suited him fine. "Oh, okay. Maybe next time, don't open all the seacocks, or your vessel might drag you under before you get a chance to get free."

She put her palms upward in a placating gesture. "Okay, okay. I'll remember that. I'm sorry, I don't know what I was thinking. Are you all right?"

"Fine." Sam stood up, recalling his manners, he said, "You'd better come down below and get warm. Are you hungry?"

"Famished."

"Well, we'd better find something for you to eat, too."

Sam stepped onto the flybridge.

He said, "Tom, meet Svetlana, the only survivor from the trawler."

Tom had taken the *Matilda* back to an idle and cut the engine. The swell was calm, and there was no point heading anywhere until he knew where they were heading. Tom glanced at Svetlana, "Pleased to meet you. I'm Tom. Make yourself at home. There's food in the fridge there. Sam will grab you some warm blankets. Let me know if I can do anything for you. You've no doubt been through a lot."

"Thank you," she replied, taking a seat and wrapping a warm blanket around her.

Sam opened the fridge. It was stocked with fresh seafood and a variety of sandwiches with fresh meats. "Hope you're not allergic to seafood, that's all we appear to have stocked. Wait… it looks like we have premade sandwiches too."

"I'll take the sandwiches, thanks." She took a large swig of water from the cup.

Sam put out a plate of seafood and one with sandwiches. "Help yourself to whatever you like."

"Thank you. You've been very kind."

"Not a problem." Sam said, "We have a satellite phone on board. Do you want to use it to call someone?"

Svetlana finished drinking her cup of water. "Soon. There's a lot of people to call. I'm not really sure who protocol dictates I should contact first. This is the first time I've been on a ship that's sunk."

"I bet you're the only person who's been on a ship that froze in the tropics," Sam said. "I don't suppose you have any idea what's caused the accident?"

"Not a clue. I work in the dark hull, beneath the waterline. My expertise is in bathymetric imaging, which normally refers to sonar-generated 3D mapping of the seafloor, but I was employed on the *Vostok* to study fish life and their environments."

"Interesting," Sam said, impressed by how easily the lie rolled off her tongue. "And you have no idea how that whole crazy freezing thing happened?"

"Sorry. Like I said, I was below decks at the time. Luckily, the room I work out of is insulated with soundproofing to prevent any sound intrusions from affecting the hydrophones I was using. As a consequence, I survived, while my crew all died."

"That was fortunate. Pity we'll never know what happened."

Svetlana shifted uncomfortably in the leather lounge, uncertain if she was being reprimanded for intentionally sinking the *Vostok,* and thus destroying any evidence of what happened. She appeared to regain her composure quickly and asked, "What are you and Tom doing here?"

"Fishing."

"Really?" she sounded incredulous. "Where did you come from?"

"San Cristóbal, Galapagos Islands."

"That's nearly two hundred miles north of here."

Sam shrugged. "We like offshore fishing."

"Well, you won't have much luck out here. There are more than two thousand feet of water below our keel, I wouldn't think there'd be a lot of fish out here, and I'd know, I'm an expert fish finder."

"Right," Sam said, and they both knew each other was lying.

"How long will you stay in the area?" she asked.

"Two more days. Possibly three. We're waiting to meet up with my ship."

"Your ship?" she cocked a delicately trimmed eyebrow. "I

thought the *Matilda* was yours?"

"No. Just a rental. My ship's on its way."

"What's sort of ship do you own?" she sounded impressed.

"It's an old icebreaker, actually." Sam smiled, ready to end the game of secrets. "But it's been refitted to work in ocean salvage. Her name's the *Maria Helena*. You might have heard of her?"

"Really?" she said, unable to conceal her interest. "What's she doing out here? I hope you don't expect to salvage the *Vostok*?"

Sam laughed. "No way in hell. As you pointed out, we're in more than 2000 feet of water here. There's nothing onboard the *Vostok* to entice me to drag her out."

Svetlana asked directly, "So, what are you looking for?"

"A missing nuclear attack submarine called the USS *Omega Deep*."

Her face paled. "What makes you think it's out here?"

"Nothing. I was hoping you might be able to tell me where it is."

"Why?" She couldn't contain her concern now. "What makes you think I know anything about a missing submarine?"

Sam smiled. "Well, for a start, you were in the process of tracking her when your strange weather event occurred."

CHAPTER FORTY-ONE

Ω ———— Ω ———— Ω

SAM STUDIED HER FACE IN silence.

Svetlana was attractive, not just beautiful, but striking. Earlier, she had flirted with a coy and coquettish appearance that didn't match her obvious intelligence. That façade had been stripped back like the curtains at the opera, revealing a cold, calculating, hardness in her gaze. Her lustrous dark hair was smartly tied back in a single plait. She wore no makeup whatsoever. She had intelligent, smoky blue-gray eyes and a strong nose. Her jaw line was prominent, with high cheek bones, leading to a rosebud mouth and full lips that now appeared set with defiance.

She didn't deny the truth, nor did she refer to it. Instead, she said, "Now what?"

"Now, we wait until my ship arrives. When it gets here, it will be with a support vessel. You may, if you choose, decide to join our support vessel, which should be able to accommodate you, and find a means of transport so that you can return home."

Her eyes narrowed. "And what will you do?"

"Tom and I will continue to search for the *Omega Deep*."

"You're in the U.S. Navy?"

"No. Like I said, we work in ocean salvage. Our ship's racing here as we speak and when it gets here, we intend to find the submarine if it has indeed ended up on the seabed somewhere."

"You're civilians?"

"Yes."

"What's a nuclear attack submarine to you?"

"We're Americans. You could call it patriotic duty to help. We have the technology, and we're going to try to help, if we can—as we would, if there was any other stricken submarine of any nation. Of course, for us, the *Omega Deep* is personal."

"Why?"

"Its commander just so happens to be Tom's father."

Sam had a bite of a roast beef sandwich. In the excitement of the past few hours, he hadn't realized he'd neglected to eat lunch.

Svetlana was the first to break the silence. "So, you're willing to let me go?"

"Of course," Sam said, his face a show of mocked indignance. "What sort of people do you take us for? As soon as we meet up with our support vessel, you can go aboard, and see what they can do to help you get home."

"Don't you want to interrogate me and find out if I know where the *Omega Deep* is?"

"No. You already said you didn't know."

"And you believe me?"

"Sure."

"Why?"

"Because I know how its cloaking technology works, and we can't track it, so there's no way for you to track it."

"But you knew the *Vostok* came into recent contact with the *Omega Deep?*"

"Yes."

"How?"

"The way your vessel froze all of a sudden. It's a problem with the highly unstable material *blackbody*, which I presume some of your crew were experimenting on. Given that the *Omega*

Deep had the last known supply of the rare element, it's only natural to assume that you made contact with it or someone who'd made contact with it."

Svetlana said, "Thanks for letting me know. I had no idea what went wrong. I was in my surveillance room, and my array of hydrophones were concealed, while a submarine mated with our dock beneath the keel. Our commander purchased something from that submarine — by the sounds of things, it was this strange material you talked about, *blackbody*. You have to believe me, that's all I know."

"Okay, I believe you," Sam said, with his customary insouciance.

Svetlana said to Tom, "I'm sorry about your father."

Tom frowned. "I still believe there's a chance my father might still be alive."

"I hope you're right. Thank you, both of you," she said. "What's your support vessel?"

Sam smiled, "It's the USS *Gerald R. Ford.*"

CHAPTER FORTY-TWO

SVETLANA'S RESPONSE WAS VISCERAL. "NO, you can't leave me with the U.S. Navy."

"Why not?" Sam asked.

He noticed her composure suddenly shatter.

"You have no idea what's going on, do you?"

"No."

"You think I'm frightened of your navy?"

"Aren't you?"

"No."

"Then what are you frightened of?"

"It was recently discovered that advanced military technology and government secrets are being passed through senior officer's hands. I was sent to join the *Vostok* in an attempt to discover who was involved from our side."

Sam made a wry smile. "You're worried about what your own people will do once they find out you're still alive."

"Yes."

"You want to appear dead forever?"

"It beats actually being dead forever."

"What would you do?"

"It depends. I have information. If I can work it out, and

discover who's responsible, then I can return to Russia. But until I know who's responsible, I will be returning to a trap."

"What do you need?"

"I need a computer, and I need you to keep me a secret for a few more days."

"I can't give you connection to the internet," Sam said, emphatically.

"I don't need it. I just need to review some data I already have."

"How do I know I can trust you?"

"You can't." She smiled. "But while we're out at sea, without access to your satellite phone, there's nothing I can do. In fact, it's probably the safest place for you to keep me."

"You've already admitted that you work in intelligence gathering for a foreign country. Your entire training and purpose is to spy and gather information that might be used against my country. Why should I help you fix problems in your own government?"

She set her jaw firm. "Because I heard that whoever infiltrated my government has penetrated yours, too."

Sam expelled his breath. She had hit a raw nerve. This was precisely what the president had feared.

"Go on."

"And what's more. Whoever betrayed me was involved in the sinking of the *Omega Deep*."

Sam met her eye.

Against his better judgment, he said, "All right. You have three days until the *Maria Helena* arrives. You can stay aboard until then."

CHAPTER FORTY-THREE

———Ω———

T HE NEXT TWO DAYS PASSED quickly.

On the morning of the third day, the *Matilda* rendezvoused with the USS *Gerald R. Ford*. Svetlana remained below decks, while Sam went on board to have a meeting with the secretary of defense who had flown there directly to discuss their progress in person.

At a length of 1,106 feet, with a beam of 206 feet and 25 decks, the USS *Gerald R. Ford* made the *Matilda* look like a bath toy. Sam ran his eyes across the vessel. He'd been on the same aircraft carrier previously, shortly after she was first launched, but somehow every time he came onboard he was amazed by the sheer size of it. To him, the aircraft carrier, with more than 75 aircraft and a complement of nearly 4,000 servicemen and women, the place always appeared more like a small city, than a ship.

He was taken to a strategic planning room. With its leather chairs and mahogany table, the place looked more like the boardroom of a Fortune 500 company than the meeting place for military strategists.

The officer who had escorted him asked him to take a seat. Sam took a seat and a moment later, the secretary of defense entered the room, closing the door behind her.

"What did you find?" she asked, without preamble.

"On board the *Vostok?*"

"Yes. On board the *Vostok*. Why else do you think you were sent here?"

Sam ignored her derision. "She was frozen solid."

"Any survivors?"

"No," Sam lied.

He didn't trust Svetlana, but he had accepted her case that they shared a common enemy. Someone had infiltrated a high level of both their governments and militaries. It was a long shot, but if she could find out who, then he was betting it would be worth his time to give her the opportunity to do so.

Besides, the secretary of defense had already admitted they believed they had a leak in the U.S. government.

The secretary fixed her emerald green eyes on him, as though she could see his discomfort. "What did you find, Mr. Reilly?"

"Like I said, ma'am, the entire place was frozen solid. I broke into the iced-over frigid bridge. The digital systems were all destroyed by ice, and their Admiralty charts were nothing more than a ruse, identifying deep shoals and reefs known to be good for longline fishing."

"Did you retrieve anything of use?"

"No, ma'am."

"Why did it sink?"

Sam sighed. "It was listing to port heavily. I believe the melting ice had flooded the bilge. The *Vostok* sank within an hour of boarding it. I nearly got caught below decks."

The secretary scrutinized him with her piercing green eyes. "What aren't you telling me?"

Sam smiled. He'd never been a good liar, and even the best couldn't lie to the secretary. "I can't tell you yet."

"You don't trust me?"

"No. I don't trust anyone."

"Will this lead you to the *Omega Deep?*"

"It may."

"All right." She asked, "How long do you need?"

"Another week. Then, one way or the other I can reveal what I know."

"Okay. After that, I'm bringing you back in, and I expect you to give me a full, unadulterated report."

Sam stood up. "Understood, Madam Secretary."

"Sit down, Mr. Reilly," she said. "You're not finished, yet."

Sam swallowed but remained silent.

"I have someone here who has something that may help you find the *Omega Deep*." She pressed an intercom and said, "Please send the professor in."

Sam turned to see Professor Douglas Capel enter the room, an astrophysicist and astronomer—the same man who'd first identified the strange material now known to be *blackbody*. Sam stood up to greet the professor.

Professor Douglas Capel said, "Hello, Mr. Reilly. It's good to see you again."

Sam shook his hand. "You, too, professor."

The professor was tall for his generation, standing eye-to-eye with Sam. Wiry gray hair sprouted from his head and made his eyebrows look like those of a mad scientist. The same hair sprung from his ears like coiled antennae. His skin was surprisingly smooth in contrast. His blue eyes twinkled with good humor. A ready smile, somewhat crooked, gave him the appearance of smirking below a large, well-shaped nose.

Both men took their seats.

The professor handed Sam a metallic suitcase. "Madam Secretary has brought me up to date with our problem."

Sam met his eye. "And you've found a solution?"

"I've found a tool that might help you, but first you'll need to locate the rough location of the USS *Omega Deep*."

Sam asked, glancing at the metallic case. "What have I got

here?"

The professor smiled. "Radioactive isotopes."

"Of course," Sam said, willing to accept anything.

"As I'm sure you will remember from your high school chemistry, an isotope is an element that contains equal numbers of protons, but different numbers of neutrons in their nuclei, and hence differ in relative atomic mass."

"Sure," Sam agreed.

"In that case, you have naturally occurring cadmium, which is composed of 8 isotopes. For two of them, natural radioactivity has been observed, and three others are predicted to be radioactive but their decays were never observed, due to extremely long half-life times."

"Right." Sam squinted as though it would help him put everything together. "And how is this going to help me locate the *Omega Deep?*"

"It won't. You'll need to find the rough location of the submarine, but this should help you locate the otherwise invisible hull."

"Go on."

"Cadmium is in a class of isotopes, known as primordial isotopes." The professor pulled his glasses forward to meet Sam's eye, and seeing little understanding there, made a dramatic sigh, as though a complaint on the state of science education these days. "Primordial isotopes were present in the interstellar medium from which the solar system was formed and were theoretically brought together during the Big Bang."

Sam simply said, "Of course."

"This is important for you because when we were running tests on *blackbody*, we discovered that it had an extremely powerful affinity to the unstable isotope of cadmium. These have been coated with ultraviolet materials, meaning that they will be easy to see under UV light."

Understanding finally cleared the mist of Sam's confusion.

"When we find the rough location of the *Omega Deep,* we can scatter some of these particles into the water, and… what… they will be drawn to the hull of the *Omega Deep.*"

"That's exactly right."

"How much range?"

"Definitely up to 10 miles. But it might be longer."

"I've also included a device you'll need to mount onto your keel if you want to track it."

"Thank you, professor."

The professor, realizing that he'd been dismissed, stood up and said, "Good luck, Mr. Reilly."

The professor left, and a navy officer entered the room. Without preamble, the officer handed Sam a second metallic suitcase and left.

Sam's eyes swept across the two suitcases and landed on the secretary of defense. "Do you want to tell me what the second one is for?"

"As you're aware, China and Russia are both up in arms regarding the USS *Omega Deep.* Everyone is searching for the submarine. As much as I hate to admit it, there's a significant chance Commander Dwight Bower has gone rogue. Are you following what all of this means?"

Sam said, "I need to find that submarine and fast before it escalates to World War III?"

The secretary spoke slowly and clearly, so there could be no confusion. "If we ever locate the *Omega Deep*—we're going to have to send her to the bottom for good. There are too many secrets on board that the world can't know. Too much of a risk that Dwight Bower's gone rogue. We need to destroy it."

"Are you sure we don't want to try and salvage it?" Sam asked.

"Afraid not. It's too dangerous now. The Russians and the Chinese have both sent their own aircraft carriers into the region."

Sam opened the suitcase. There were three magnetic beacons with a single switch at their center. "What do I do with these?"

"They're homing beacons. Attach them to the hull and flick the switch."

"What will happen?"

"You and anyone you want to keep alive will get as far away as possible. As soon as the USS *Gerald R. Ford* picks up the homing signal, it will launch a pair of torpedoes. In the end, you'll have less than five minutes between flicking the switch and the complete destruction of the submarine."

"What about the crew of the *Omega Deep?*"

The secretary of defense's face twisted into a grimace of indecision. "It's been more than 130 days since the *Omega Deep* left its harbor. They had enough food to keep them for 90 days. I think one thing's for certain, Mr. Reilly. We're never going to see the crew of the USS *Omega Deep* again."

CHAPTER FORTY-FOUR

TEN MILES WEST OF THE SKELETON COAST, NAMIBIA

SONAR TECHNICIAN BELINDA CALLAGHAN'S HEAD hurt.

Not just her head. Her entire body was sore. She had blisters on her hands, her tongue was dry, and her skin was burned. Even just breathing took effort. She tried to roll onto her side, but that only hurt more, and she still couldn't see anything.

Where was she?

She felt the ground beneath her back move. It was enough of a surprise to jolt her into action. She tried to sit up but struggled to find her balance. She was lying on some sort of rubbery canvas. Again, the ground seemed to move underneath her. Her original fear that she was being attacked by some sort of giant snake had now been quelled, but as yet another ripple of movement knocked her onto her back again, she was still no closer to determining where she was or what had happened to her.

Belinda gritted her teeth, utilized every piece of energy she could muster and sat up fully. Still, all she could see was yellow. She reached the edge of the shallow wall and pulled herself up onto it. Her eyes peered over the edge.

A carpet of ultramarine blue blinded her vision all the way to the horizon.

I'm in the middle of the fucking ocean!

The sudden understanding of her location didn't provide her with any relief. The fact it didn't fill her with terror, just proved how lethargic her mind was at the moment, and that it was unable to process what she was seeing.

How did I get here?

She considered the last few things she remembered. She was at her station on board the USS *Omega Deep*.

There was an accident.

Something happened.

The *Omega Deep* ran aground!

They all had to escape via their submarine escape immersion equipment — SEIE — she glanced at the side of the life raft. It was part of the SEIE suit. That's why she was on her own. But how long had she been out at sea? Something seemed wrong. What happened after she and the rest of the crew surfaced? That's right, they were attacked. Everything was coming back to her in incoherent bits and pieces.

She closed her eyes.

There was a cave. A massive cave. And a sandy beach with a small aircraft at the end of it. Large trees reached for the top of the world in an ancient forest. There were delectable fruits, wild animals, and a small freshwater river with plentiful fish that ran straight through the heart of it. Something about the place made her feel warm.

It felt like some sort of utopia.

A prehistoric Eden.

How long had the rest of the crew been there? Did they all make it? She couldn't remember. But something went wrong. What went wrong? Why did they ever leave the place? Her heart started to race, and her chest felt heavy at the memory.

She opened her eyes.

That's right. They were attacked.

By wild beasts! Monsters as big as cars. Some covered with

giant spikes. Others were more than ten feet tall and capable of jumping twenty feet at a time.

Her memories seemed so incredibly real yet at the same time, entirely impossible.

She put the thought out of her mind and returned to reality.

How did I get here?

"Hello there!" someone shouted in the distance. "Is anyone alive?"

She squinted.

Was that someone calling for me or just my imagination?

"Hello!" the voice was getting closer. "Are you alive?"

The sound was too clear to be anything but real.

Belinda tried to answer. "I'm here!" Her voice was a dry croak. Relief and hope and dread were jamming her tongue into the roof of her blistered mouth.

The voice continued as though the owner hadn't heard her. "We're coming about. Yell if anyone is alive."

She tried to yell. But the sound came out as an inaudible hiss. She fumbled with her safety vest. There were several attachments. One of them was a whistle. She fumbled with it until she could get it into her mouth, and then blew multiple short, sharp, whistles.

"I hear you!" the voice replied. "We're going to come get you."

Belinda rolled onto her back. A dark shadow blocked the burning sun. Her eyes went in and out of focus, trying to make sense of the sight that towered over her. Then she spotted someone waving their hands.

A man climbed down to greet her with a bottle of water.

"Are you all right?" the stranger asked.

"I am now," she replied with a level of enthusiasm she didn't quite feel.

The stranger opened the bottle of water. "Here drink this."

Belinda took a small gulp of water. It burned her blistered mouth but seemed to soothe her dry throat.

She looked at the man who rescued her. "Thank you."

"You're welcome. Where did you come from?"

"I don't know. I was on a submarine. We must have struck some sort of underwater mountain. There was a hull breach. And the submarine flooded…"

"You're American," the stranger said, noticing her accent.

"Yes."

"Where were you when the shipwreck… submarine wreck occurred?"

"I'm not certain exactly. But somewhere in the South Pacific Ocean."

The stranger stared at her. Even in her confused state, she spotted the incredulity in his face. "I'm sorry, that's impossible."

"Why?"

"You're ten miles out, off the West African coast. No way you could have drifted all that way."

CHAPTER FORTY-FIVE

THE *MARIA HELENA* MADE ITS rendezvous with the *Matilda* at 8:15 a.m. Genevieve had flown the Sea King out to San Cristóbal to pick up a company skipper for the *Matilda,* who took possession of the vessel, and by 9:00 a.m. exactly, the *Maria Helena* was making its way due south.

At the navigation station on the bridge, Sam Reilly stared at several neatly-arranged Admiralty and bathymetric charts.

Next to him, Matthew and Veyron examined the map.

"What makes you certain the *Omega Deep* is headed this way?" Matthew asked.

Sam answered without hesitation. "Because that's where I would go."

"Really?" Matthew was surprised by his confidence. "Why? That submarine could be anywhere in the world right now. Given what we know about her, we have no reason to even believe that she's lying on the bottom of the sea somewhere with a wrecked hull."

Sam said, "Because Commander Dwight Bower's original orders involved taking the USS *Omega Deep* into the South Pacific to test her maneuverability."

"Sure," Matthew accepted that, "But the South Pacific is

massive — in fact, most of her seabed has never been charted — so what makes you think you can guess where she went?"

"I know it's a long shot, but it's all we have."

"Where exactly are you thinking?" Veyron asked.

"Here," Sam said, pointing to a series of submerged valleys.

Veyron studied the submerged valley. He had a doctorate in submersible technology and a second one in mechatronics. There was little he didn't know about how a submarine, like the *Omega Deep*, might handle.

After a few minutes, he shook his head. "I don't think it would have gone here."

"Why not?"

"Too dangerous. Commander Bower would never have risked it."

"But I ran the submarine through a simulator of the same submerged valley with identical dimension. It was hard but doable."

"Sure. But I read the report on the *Omega Deep's* upgraded systems. It wasn't running with sonar — it would have been relying on visual navigation, using its new digital video sphere system."

"Its what?" Matthew asked.

"More than two hundred tiny video cameras are imbedded into the hull of the *Omega Deep,* allowing it to provide a real-time 360-degree view surrounding the submarine, as clear as though they were looking out the window."

Sam's eyes narrowed. "And you think that technique would be intrinsically more difficult to navigate by the previous systems, such as inertial navigation, GPS, and sonar?"

"Not more difficult, simply unknown," Veyron replied. "And I've met Tom's dad. He's no fool. Like all good commanders, he would have known that arrogance with new technology was lethal. So he would have taken them farther south…"

"Where?"

Veyron studied the next map, which extended into the waters south of New Zealand and out toward South America and Cape Horn. "Here. There's an ancient valley system extending hundreds and potentially thousands of miles. They start off wide and continue to get smaller, giving the crew of the *Omega Deep* time to practice. That's where I would have gone."

Sam said, "That's great. Now we just need to narrow it down to an area of more than a million square miles."

Veyron put his hands in a placating gesture. "Hey, I'm just saying what I would have done if I was commanding a new experimental submarine like the *Omega Deep.*"

Sam said, "Thanks, Veyron."

The satellite phone rang.

Sam picked it up.

It was the secretary of defense. She said, "Where are you headed?"

"South. Somewhere near New Zealand. Veyron thinks the *Omega Deep* headed to a series of known submerged ancient valleys to perform maneuvering tests. Possibly, something went wrong, and the submarine ran aground."

The secretary said, "That's impossible."

"Why?"

"Because we just found the crew of the *Omega Deep!*"

Sam felt his heart take off at a gallop. "Where?"

"In a series of individual SEIE suit life rafts scattered along the Skeleton Coast of West Africa."

"Was everyone rescued?"

"We only recovered about two thirds of the crew."

"Tom's father and the XO, James Halifax are missing too." She paused. "There's a chance they're still out there in the Atlantic, and it's just a matter of time before we locate them. Or…"

"What?"

"Or, it just proves they were responsible for the theft of the *Omega Deep*."

"All right. What are the crew saying happened?"

"None of them can remember. They were following a private submarine—an Orcasub—into a valley, but something went wrong. They all seem to be giving conflicting stories. Some say the submarine's hull was breached and flooded. Others say they made an emergency exit using the SEIE suits. Others say they surfaced and abandoned the submarine for life rafts after mechanical faults and the two most senior officers went below to scuttle the submarine. You have to remember they were all sleep deprived and dehydrated, so they aren't quite making any sense yet."

"How bizarre. Was there any similarity between their stories?"

"Not really. Except…"

"Except what?"

"You wouldn't credit it, but almost all of them made some reference to being in paradise only to be attacked by what they are calling monsters."

"Monsters?" Sam asked. "What sort?"

"They were described as being beasts as large as cars. Some looked like bears—others were covered in scales and spikes. I would have dismissed the lot of them, if it weren't for the fact that it was the only general theme they all shared."

"Bizarre. Did you find drugs in their system?"

"Drugs?"

"Yeah. Amphetamines, cocaine, LSD? Something that might account for their shared hallucinations."

"Not yet. They were only picked up an hour ago by local fishermen. One of our vessels currently stationed in the Mediterranean is on its way to meet them."

Sam said, "All right. Let me know what they find. We're going to keep heading south. Let us know if you learn anything, and we'll circle around Cape Horn and head into the Atlantic to help. Just one more thing…"

"Shoot?"

Sam made a thin-lipped smile. "Did any of them give a rough location of the wreck site?"

"Yeah, but we're pretty certain its wrong."

"Why?"

"Because they said they were in the South Pacific Ocean at the time. But that's impossible. There's no way anyone would have survived floating on a single-person raft all the way from the Pacific around the Cape, and across the Atlantic, is there?"

Sam swallowed. "Not a chance in hell."

CHAPTER FORTY-SIX

Ω

SAM FOUND SVETLANA WORKING ON the laptop Elise had loaned her in the meeting room on the first deck. It's hard drive had been wiped beforehand, and it had no connection to the satellite internet. At the end of the room, Genevieve reviewed maintenance logs for the Sea King and caught up on some other paperwork, which was more of a pretense for what she was really doing, which was guarding Svetlana. No one had told her that Genevieve was Russian. Right now, they wanted to play all their cards as close to their chest as possible.

To Svetlana, Sam said, "Any luck finding who was involved?"

She took a sip of her coffee and said, "Some, but not enough."

"What do you know?"

"The man who came to visit the *Vostok* while I was locked in my surveillance room was an American. What's more, the very same man visited the *Vostok* nearly three months ago, just before she was assigned to the Arctic Circle. One of the men who took him for a tour of the *Vostok* was my commander who's now dead, but the other one I can find, and right now I have no way to find out if he was another American or one of ours."

Sam said, "If you give me a copy of the image of the man's face, I can have Elise find out for you. If he's one of ours, she'll have it on the navy's human resources database. And if he's one of yours, she will probably have it on the navy's foreign intelligence databases."

Svetlana eyed him, as though conflicted by how much to trust him. "Sure. I've got a copy on this USB stick. You can give it to Elise if you still don't want to trust me with wireless connectivity."

Thanks, Sam said, taking it. "I think that's best, for everyone." Then, turning to Genevieve, he said, "Do you mind running this up to Elise and asking her to urgently locate the identity of the man on the right."

"Sure," Genevieve's eyes darted between Sam and Svetlana and back again. "Are you sure you're all right down here?"

"Fine," Sam replied amused by her concern.

Genevieve had already mentioned that just because the Russian spy wasn't armed, didn't make her any less dangerous.

Returning his gaze toward Svetlana, he said, "Elise is a genius. It won't take her long to find out whose face that belongs to."

"Elise is in intelligence gathering?"

Sam evaded the question. "Sort of."

"CIA, FBI, or Military?"

Sam laughed. "It's none of your business, but if it lets you concentrate on the task at hand, I'll let you in on a secret."

Svetlana smiled, as though she was willing to wait patiently for whatever it was Sam was going to reveal to her.

Sam said, "Elise works with me. She's a computer geek and one of the best hackers in the world. She's not for sale. She only works for me because it entertains her, and if I don't find her enough interesting challenges, she disappears."

Svetlana smiled, amused by the thought. Then, returning to her problem, said, "What about the American?"

Sam grinned. "I don't suppose he was just coming on board as a guest?"

"No way in hell. You forget the *Vostok* was our prized information gathering vessel. There's no way someone would have allowed an American to come on board."

"What do you think he was doing there, three months ago?"

"I think he was offering to sell the *Omega Deep* to the commander."

"But the *Omega Deep* hadn't even launched yet."

"Think about it, Mr. Reilly. You're a smart guy. Where are the crew of a submarine from the whole world over, a few weeks before they're deployed to a potentially 3–6-month tour of duty?"

"They're on leave."

"Exactly." Svetlana smiled, revealing perfectly even white teeth.

Tom walked into the room.

Sam said, "Hey Tom, do you have the crew list for the *Omega Deep* on you?"

"Yeah, I think the Secretary emailed it to my phone. Why?"

Svetlana answered. "Because we need you to use it to see if someone who boarded the *Vostok* three months ago was on it, who I believe might have been in the process of trying to sell the *Omega Deep* to my commander." She froze the image and zoomed into the face. Turning the laptop toward Tom, she said, "This man."

Tom glanced at the screen and frowned. "I don't have to check the list."

"Why?" she asked.

"Because I already know who that is."

Sam said, "Who?"

"His name is James Halifax, and he's my father's XO."

CHAPTER FORTY-SEVEN

SAM CONTACTED THE SECRETARY OF defense and updated her with the news of who most likely betrayed them.

When he was finished, Sam asked, "Any news from the survivors?"

"It was LSD."

"What?" Sam asked, confused.

"You said to check their urine for traces of illicit drugs. We did. There were high levels of LSD."

"In all of them?" Sam asked.

"Every single one of them. Someone wanted them to give a strange account of their disaster, that would confuse our search."

"It would appear so."

Sam asked, "How much longer until we have the Chinese and Russian navies on our tail?"

"They're running about 24 hours behind you. The Russian aircraft carrier crossed the Bearing Strait a few hours ago and the Chinese aircraft carrier will reach Hawaii in about 4 hours."

"All right, so while we keep heading south, we'll keep that advantage, but I don't have a clue what we're going to do while we search for the *Omega Deep,* if it even is in the Pacific Ocean. Like you said, no matter which way you look, it's almost impossible to think that the survivors have all traveled from the South Pacific Ocean in small life rafts."

"About that."

"What?"

The secretary said, "It appears some of the survivors might be telling the truth."

"How so?"

"They said they ran aground in the South Pacific Ocean, so we had the life rafts tested — to see where the microbes and sea life originated."

"And?"

"As expected, there were many types of marine algae, protists, plankton, and bacteria."

Sam almost shouted, "What did you find!"

"*Bacillus pacificus.*"

"That's only found in the tropical, warm waters of the Pacific Ocean."

"Yes."

"And our only lead takes us farther south. There's no way we're heading the right direction."

"I know. It's not necessarily helpful, but at least you know you're in the right ocean. We're sending the USS *Gerald R. Ford* back to escort you. Good luck."

Sam put the satellite phone down.

Svetlana asked, "What now?"

"The life rafts were contaminated with the bacteria *Bacillus pacificus,* which is only found in the tropical waters of the Pacific Ocean."

"Does that definitely rule out the South Pacific?"

Sam said, "It does unless you can find some warm water there."

"How warm?"

"At least 85 degrees Fahrenheit."

"What will you do?" she asked.

"I'm not sure." Sam shook his head with incredulity. "To make matters worse, we now have aircraft carriers from Russia, China, and America all racing to converge on our location."

She leveled her gray eyes at him. "You know if you play this wrong, you're going to set us up for World War III, don't you?"

Sam nodded. "I know."

Elise walked into the room. "I know who the third person was in that photo you sent me, Svetlana."

"Who?"

"Luka Kuznetsov."

Svetlana swore in her native language.

Sam said, "You've heard of him?"

"Of course, I have. He's a senior official in charge of military research and development." Svetlana swallowed hard. "And he's also the president's brother-in-law."

Sam understood the implication immediately. Either Luka Kuznetsov was trying to buy the submarine for Russia, and there was a traitor within the U.S. Navy, or Kuznetsov was a traitor to Russia. Either way, it begged the question, was the president of Russia involved? Then he thought about the attack on the Chinese aircraft carrier, which was made to look like it had come from an American nuclear attack submarine.

"You know what someone's trying to do?"

"Yeah, face the world's superpowers off against each other."

"The question is, who would gain the most from it?"

"Beats me," she replied. "What will you do now?"

"I don't know. It's clear the USS *Omega Deep* might be the only thing that stands between us and war."

Sam studied her, he had fallen into the easy way of communication he had with the rest of his crew, even though she was a known Russian spy. It was dangerous territory, but she had plenty of information to offer him, and he had no reason, or place to get rid of her at the moment.

He asked, "What do you want to do?"

She shrugged as though it wasn't her problem. "I think right now that I'm the only thing stopping World War III from taking place."

"How?"

"We need to get to the *Omega Deep* before anyone else."

"How? We've already been through this—our original theory of where the submarine ended up has now been totally shot."

She sighed heavily. "I might be able to help if you give me your bathymetric and Admiralty charts."

Sam studied her through narrowed eyes. "Why should we trust you?"

"Because I have the coordinates for the wreckage of the *Omega Deep.*"

"What? You knew all this time? Why didn't you tell me?"

"How could I trust you? Besides, we only know now that finding that submarine is in our mutual interest, as possibly the only solution to avoid a clash between the world's greatest superpowers."

Sam dismissed his sense of betrayal. After all, he reminded himself he was dealing with a Russian spy. Instead, he turned the problem at hand, and asked, "Where?"

Svetlana grinned. "Somewhere inside the 8th Continent."

CHAPTER FORTY-EIGHT

Ω———————Ω———————Ω

THE SUBMERGED 8TH CONTINENT, 500 MILES SOUTH OF NEW ZEALAND.

THE *MARIA HELENA* REDUCED ITS speed to a gentle cruise of just four knots.

Sam shook his head in disbelief. The coordinates Svetlana had given him had taken them to what appeared to be an ancient landmass, now buried in just 50 feet of water. The rough waters and large swell of the Southern Ocean were replaced by the perfectly still waters that concealed the 8th continent.

If you drew a line between New Zealand's North Island and South America, and then cut it in half, and headed 500 miles due south, one would reach the strange place.

With the exception of Veyron, who was checking the towed monitoring array that would allow them to track the UV-emitting cadmium that Professor Douglas Capel had provided, the rest of Sam's crew and Svetlana stood at the bridge. With Matthew at the helm, adamant that no one except himself would touch the wheel while the *Maria Helena* explored such uncharted areas. Sam and Tom simply studied the calm sea out through the windshield. Elise studied her laptop, which constantly received updated bathymetric data and correlated it with any location that might be concealing the USS *Omega Deep*. Svetlana studied the new-found land, her eyes sweeping the flat surface of the sea in awe, while Genevieve kept an eye on Svetlana, almost daring her to do something dangerous.

Sam struggled to understand how the place had remained hidden for so long.

His mind turned to the Dutch explorer Abel Tasman who discovered Van Diemen's Land, now named Tasmania, in 1642 before returning on another voyage in 1644, when he passed the coast of a mighty landmass, naming it Nova Hollandia.

That landmass was later charted by British explorer Lieutenant James Cook, on board the HMS *Bark Endeavor,* and named *New South Wales,* before later being named *Australia.* Cook's charts depicted a coast very different to the one Abel Tasman produced. No one ever came up with a logical explanation for the discrepancy, but now, Sam wondered whether or not the Dutchman had in fact discovered the 8th Continent, back when it still existed above the water.

Could such a landmass have been destroyed in so little time?

Studying the bathymetric readings, Sam ran his eyes across the ancient river which opened up to a shallow underwater tabletop, covered in vivid and impressive coral gardens. A digital camera, designed for just such a purpose, was dropped overboard so that he could get a better visual of the submerged environment.

That image was displayed in color on a monitor next to the bathymetric readings.

Sam grinned.

It was a unique tropical playground that didn't belong anywhere near the Southern Ocean. Tropical fish filled the place, swimming in and out through the coral reef, which was awash with color.

Fifteen minutes later, the *Maria Helena* reached the exact coordinates Svetlana had given them. Sam studied the bathymetric reports, which provided a 3D image of the seabed below by using an array of hydrophones which combined to provide the sonar image of the seafloor.

Matthew steered the *Maria Helena* in a counter-clockwise search grid, in an outward spiral.

Sam stared at the digital image of the sea below. The water was so clear and the visibility so good that he could make out every intricate detail on the seabed.

He crossed his arms. "Anyone see anything?"

There was a general murmur of "No."

Tom said, "Shall we use the good professor's cadmium?"

Sam's face hardened. "Typical. We find a wonderful new coral ecosystem, and already we want to poison it with cadmium."

Tom shrugged. "According to the professor's instructions, nearly all of it should be absorbed by the *blackbody* paint on the *Omega Deep's* hull."

"That's only if we're within 10 miles, close enough for the two elements to find their natural affinity with one another."

Tom met his eye. "I don't think we have a choice. It's not good, but it's still only a small amount of cadmium and a lot less destructive than nuclear radiation if we can't find the *Omega Deep* and this thing goes bad."

"Agreed." Sam switched on the powerful UV lights and camera which would track the movement of the cadmium. The monitor showed very little, except the brief outline of the seabed. He depressed the button on the local VHF radio microphone and said, "Veyron, can you please release the first canister of cadmium?"

"Understood. Releasing the cadmium."

Sam watched as the heavier-than-water cadmium sank into the water. He involuntarily held his breath, as he watched the toxic element drift slowly to the south, before eventually getting caught on a rising submerged atoll, which prevented it from going any farther.

He cursed. "All right. Anyone got another idea?"

Svetlana said, "It seems to me that the material worked. It showed us that the USS *Omega Deep* is out there, presumably somewhere to the south of us."

"You're right," Sam said. "Matthew, can you please take us across that reef?"

Matthew's eyes ran across the bathymetric image of the reef, taking note of the exact depth at its highest point, and landing back on Sam's determined face. "It will be shallow, but we should have a few feet to spare beneath our keel."

"All right, let's see what's on the other side of that reef."

Matthew eased the twin throttles gently forward, and the *Maria Helena's* bow slowly edged toward the reef.

There was a concerned silence on the bridge, broken by the depth-sounder's warning. It came on whenever the keel suddenly got within five feet of the seabed below. Matthew eased the throttles into reverse, slowing their forward momentum to a near standstill.

The *Maria Helena* drifted forward across the shallow reef, revealing a narrow valley or ancient river, running southeast, at a depth of fifty feet.

Sam's lips curled slightly upward in relief. "We've crossed over."

"Of course, we have," Matthew replied. "You don't really think I would have put the ship into any danger just because you wanted me to follow one of your whims, do you?"

Sam and Tom laughed.

Matthew was, by far, the most conservative member of the crew. It was a good trait to have for a skipper. And his high aversion to risk often came to clash with Sam's carefree, risk-taking behavior.

Sam returned to the task at hand. "All right, Veyron. Can you please drop the second canister of cadmium?"

"Understood, releasing it now."

Sam stared at the UV monitor and smiled as the cadmium

followed the ancient river along its southeastern course.

Matthew didn't need to be asked to follow. Instead, he shifted the throttles forward, and the *Maria Helena* began her pursuit.

The cadmium followed the river for nearly fifteen minutes before its weight finally caused it to catch on some coral. Sam stared at the UV monitor, as the fine particles thinned until there was nothing left to follow.

But it was obvious now that the submarine would have had trouble leaving the ancient valley, so they continued, taking the same route the USS *Omega Deep* had before them.

The submerged valley below opened up into a large open space, nearly a mile wide and ending in a concaved atoll, which rose nearly all the way to the surface.

Sam said, "This is it. There's no way the USS *Omega Deep* would have cleared that reef."

Matthew eased the throttles into reverse and brought the *Maria Helena* to a standstill. Sam ran his eyes across the bathymetric readings.

The seabed was full of sand.

Nowhere to hide a submarine so large.

Sam swallowed, feeling disappointment weigh him down. "I don't get it. I was certain it was here."

Svetlana glanced at the monitor and said, "What about here?"

He looked directly where she was pointing. There was a shallow curved indent in the sand that ran nearly 600 feet in a perfectly straight line. It very well could have been where the *Omega Deep* had originally run aground. There were even large piles of sand where scuba divers had obviously gone to the effort to free the submarine from its buildup of sand.

Sam said, "I don't believe it. We're too late. Someone's already beaten us to it."

Svetlana made a winning smile. "I wouldn't bet on that."

"Why not?" Sam asked.

She pointed to the almost negligible increase in water temperature surrounding the aft end of the depression in the sand. "That looks to me like the thermal runoff from their active nuclear reactor."

Sam met her gaze. "You think the *Omega Deep* is right in front of us, hiding in plain sight?"

"Yes."

Sam grinned, turned to Tom, and said, "Come on. There's only one way we're going to prove whether your dad's submarine is down there."

CHAPTER FORTY-NINE

―Ω――――――――Ω――――――――Ω―

SAM STOOD INSIDE THE MOON pool at the bottom deck of the *Maria Helena* and donned his wetsuit and scuba gear. The dive was shallow, less than 80 feet—closer to 50 to the top of the submarine if it was there—and they had no need to be down there very long, so he and Tom didn't go to the trouble of setting up their closed-circuit rebreathers. Instead, opted to dive with a standard single dive tank containing 210 Bar of compressed air.

He checked his Heckler & Koch MP5 and secured it to his right thigh. The 9mm submachine gun was one of the preferred weapons among military special forces around the world, for its durability, reliability, and accuracy—even after prolonged periods of water submersion. It functions according to the proven roller-delayed blowback principle, making multiple subsequent shots highly accurate.

Veyron glanced at him with a wry smile. "You're expecting trouble?"

Sam shrugged. "No, but I thought I should come prepared anyway. That way I'm less likely to find it."

"Not a bad principle."

Sam stood up on the diver's platform at the edge of the moon pool. The water was so clear, he could now clearly see the outline in the sand where the *Omega Deep* had almost certainly been at some stage.

In his left BCD pocket, he kept a pair of night-vision goggles. It was an absurd thought, but he and Tom had decided to bring them, just in case they were to find survivors inside the stricken vessel. By now, he imagined the entire system would be shut down and dark, to preserve energy.

That's if it was even there.

The 30-billion-dollar question as to whether or not it was still there, remained to be seen.

He and Tom quickly checked each other's equipment.

Elise entered the room, a worried crease across her brow, which was out of character for her. Without preamble, she said, "I just got off the phone with the secretary of defense. The USS *Gerald R. Ford,* the Russian aircraft carrier, and the Chinese Type II aircraft carrier will all converge on this location in under an hour."

Sam glanced at his watch, making a mental note of the time, and said, "All right. That just means Tom and I had better be back here well within that timeframe."

Elise said, "The secretary also wants me to remind you of the second package you were given."

"You can assure her I haven't forgotten." Sam motioned to the inbuilt pouch on the right-hand side of his buoyancy control device, where two of the HF magnetic homing devices were stored. "If the *Omega Deep's* down there, it won't be for much longer."

"Okay. Stay safe and get back here as soon as you can."

"Understood." Sam turned to Tom. "You're all set."

"Set and ready to go."

"All right."

Sam pulled his full-faced dive mask over his head and stepped into the moonpool.

The water was warmer than he expected, more like diving in the tropics than the Southern Ocean. He descended to 20 feet, making certain that he cleared the rest of the *Maria Helena's* keel.

He glanced at his dive gauges. Everything appeared to be working correctly.

"You still good, Tom?" he asked.

"Never better," Tom replied cheerfully. "Let's go find the truth before World War III starts above us."

"Agreed."

Sam released some more air from his buoyancy control device, making him markedly neutrally buoyant.

He descended another twenty feet before his hand reached something cold and made of steel.

"Tom!"

"What is it?"

"I'll be damned, but I think the submarine's not missing."

"It's not?"

"No. It's just hidden very well."

Sam ran his hand along the cold, invisible steel, as he and Tom descended on the port side of the hulking dormant submarine.

At the base of the indiscernible object, he dug his hands deep into the sand and covered the top of the submarine with it. The sand scattered over the clear surface, slowly revealing the shape of the submarine's conning tower.

He ran his hand along the hull on his way down to the seabed, making certain that he didn't accidentally crash into an invisible exterior of the naval predator. He grabbed some more sand and started back toward the sail deck, hoping to discover the USS *Omega Deep's* registration plate—and definitive proof that he had the right submarine.

Sam thought about the horrible task he'd been given. He needed to destroy the submarine, there was no doubt about that, but first he had to be certain.

His gaze extended outward, along the sandy seabed, across a small coral reef that caught his attention. It was a colorful mixture of deep reds, greens, and purples. Vibrant and exuding life. His right hand felt for the homing beacons in his BCD storage pack.

What a terrible waste.

Behind him, he heard Tom yell, "Holy shit!"

Sam snapped his head around, instinctively reaching for his knife, as though it might protect him from a shark or something.

Instead, he was confronted by a much larger predator—the USS *Omega Deep.*

Her Omega Cloak, a technological masterpiece had been unraveled like a magician's cape, revealing her in all her glory.

And confirming that someone was still aboard.

Sam followed Tom down to the port side of the massive sunken sub. He watched as Tom swam out in front of him, dwarfed by the scale of the black monster that lay silent on the seabed. The submarine was matte black, and its exterior fuselage featureless. Sam noted the absence of the usual rubber anechoic tiles which reduce sound reflection and transmission. Somehow though, the whole ship seemed to still absorb light completely.

The divers approached the stern of the submarine and located the escape trunk hatch. Unlike its predecessors, the *Omega Deep* was fitted with two escape trunks, one on each side—each with horizontal access doors in place of the vertical escape chutes fitted to previous craft.

Tom shined his flashlight inside the narrow opening before going inside.

Sam said, "Are you sure you want to do that?"

"No. But I don't think I could live with myself if I don't. A third of the crew is still missing. I have to know the truth before we destroy what should have been my father's legacy."

"All right. I'll come with you."

"It's all right, Sam. Prepare the magnetic homing beacons. I'll be back out within a few minutes."

Sam followed him inside. "No way. We go together. You've got ten minutes. Not a second more."

Inside, there was a backlit numerical keypad which lit up red when a hand was close by. Sam entered the override code supplied to him by the secretary of defense's office and the keypad color changed from solid red to flashing green. The pad flashed while the escape trunk filled with water, equalizing the pressure gradient on both sides of the door. After two minutes, the number pad turned solid green, and the escape hatch opened outwards.

Tom ushered Sam in with a wave of his gloved hand and Sam entered the lockout trunk. A ten by six-foot room, the escape trunk can accommodate 22 swimmers without gear, or 10 fully-loaded Navy SEALs. Sam smirked at Tom, who somehow managed to fill most of the rest of the space with his massive frame, weapon, and diving kit. They closed the hatch and locked it off. Sam operated the pump switch on a simple control panel to empty the room. The two men stood and doffed their headgear as the water around them drained out of grates in the floor. Once the hatch was empty, they relieved themselves of their dive gear completely and checked the status of their weapons.

Sam pulled night vision goggles for both of them from his pack, and they placed them on checking the ambient light settings. With a nod to Tom, Sam killed the lights in the hatch and they unlocked the door, opening it outwards on the count of three. They came out as two, one high and one low sweeping their carbines in opposite directions through the sections of fire to clear the immediate egress point. Using hand signals, Sam indicated Tom loop around the far side of the ordnance racks and meet up at the distant end of the room.

The air was thick with moisture, smelling of musty condensation. There were small puddles here and there under the racks of storage in the center of the room. The room was empty of other people though—that much was clear from the outset.

In the same fashion, the pair cleared room after room in the forward section of the submarine, finding everything intact and as it should be.

"The forward section of the boat's been flooded at some point," Sam said, relaxing a little and switching on the overhead lighting.

Tom removed his night vision goggles and ruffled his own messy brown hair. "Yeah, the starboard escape trunk door's off, and the chamber's a mess. Some kind of firefight."

"Cause of the sinking maybe?"

"I'd say boarders more likely."

"No one here now. What do you think?"

"I think we should clear the rest of the ship."

They moved back to their insertion point, replaced their night vision goggles and started clearing the rest of the boat. It was as if the crew had just stepped out for a moment, leaving everything as it was. Bunk racks were tightly made with personal effects stowed under the mattresses. All ancillary systems were functioning, and there was power to all areas of the submarine. Sam was surprised at the headroom inside the newly built vessel. The last submarine he had been on was an *Ohio* class which had an ever-pervasive ceiling height of six feet, at the maximum. The *Omega Deep* had ample height for your average professional basketballer.

They kept the lights off and moved through the ship room by room. The command center was empty with all systems on standby. The pair moved forward again, into the nuclear reactor room. The systems all indicated in the green, and in perfect order. Using his override login again, Sam ran a diagnostic on the batteries and backups, all of which showed operational and on standby.

He was at the reactor's main interface console when he felt it. The uneasiness of being watched. Tom knew it too. Sam sensed him take two steps back and flick the safety on his carbine. Sam slowly moved his hands to his own MP5.

"You won't be needing those, gentlemen. I'm the only other living soul on this vessel at the moment."

In night vision, the specter of the emaciated, heavily bearded old man was all that much eerier. He had a heavy, fatigued shuffle, and was leaning heavily on the apparatus surrounding the companionway. The man made his way into the glow from the monitor in front of Sam. With facial features negative in the green glow, hollow black eyes with iridescent white irises that stared out into the gloom.

"Dad?" Tom asked.

"In the flesh," the old man answered.

CHAPTER FIFTY

COMMAND CENTER, USS OMEGA DEEP

TOM TOOK HIS FATHER'S RIGHT hand in a firm grasp. There was strength in Commander Bower's return grip, but it was borne of tenacity and emotion, not the latent power Tom was used to feeling there. The skin of the hand was dry, raspy and tough—Tom could sense the bony features. He looked his father in the eye and placed his other hand on the commander's left shoulder—it was the closest they ever got to a hug.

"Been down here long Dad?"

"Long enough, son. Long enough."

Looking at his father, Tom could see the strength and suffering in his face. Tom was overwhelmed with compassion and pride for this man, commander of the most advanced undersea weapon in the history of the world, his mentor. A man reduced to an emaciated state in the pursuit of his duty and never for a moment wavering in his resolve to serve—at any cost.

"It's really good to see you, Sir," Tom paused. "What happened?" he asked.

"It was a double-cross. My XO, James Halifax. Whoever he was working for is well-funded and highly organized. They had a dummy sunken hull the size of a *Seawolf,* and from it, transmitted the secret distress code."

"There's a secret distress code?" Tom asked.

"Yes, there is. Detectable by sonar, there's a U.S. Navy captain-to-captain, coded distress message sent over a particular bandwidth. It's Commander Security clearance and above, intended for use only in the case of a stricken submarine," The captain hung his head, shaking it morosely. "I'll be damned if I know how he got a hold of it."

"What about the rest of your crew?" Sam asked.

"Halifax disabled the C02 scrubbers and flooded the ventilation with smoke grenades. He set off the alarms and ordered the evacuation. Combined with our loss of power, once the wheels were set in motion—the crew couldn't get off fast enough. They were squeezing twenty at a time into the escape trunks."

"What happened to them at the surface?" Tom asked.

"God only knows. I fear the worst."

"Where were you?"

"I remained behind to change the main computer's codes and stop them from stealing the *Omega Deep*."

"Good thinking," Sam grinned. "Why didn't you send an emergency locator buoy to the surface?"

Tom knew the device used a satellite phone to send an encrypted message back to the head of the Navy in Wisconsin…

"I did," Commander Bower said. "Multiple times. My only guess is that they've covered the top of the submarine where the buoy is deployed from."

"What about trying to get to the surface?"

"You mean taking an escape suit and trying to reach the surface?" Commander Bower asked.

"Sure. You're only in fifty feet of water. It wouldn't have been difficult."

"Yeah, but what was I supposed to do then?" the commander asked. "Look where we are. We're a hundred and eighty miles off shore here. I'm an old man Tom — I wouldn't last three days."

"So, you stayed here and starved."

Commander Bower nodded. "I've hung in as long as I could."

"Like you said Dad, long enough."

"Sir, do you think we can get this submarine underway again?"

"We'll need more than the three of us, but I don't see why not. Halifax's efforts were more subterfuge than actual sabotage. Over the past six weeks, I've rectified faults and restored power to the propulsion intakes, the ventilation circuits, and ballast pumps. As far as I can tell, she should be good to go, all I need is a crew."

"How many do we need?" Sam asked

"Bare minimum five for basic operations, seven if we want to fire anything from the ship."

Sam ran his eyes over the sophisticated system.

Commander Bower said, "Where possible, every system has been fully automated, which has reduced crew numbers. Even so, we're going to be limping into Pearl Harbor with a crew of seven."

Sam said, "We have aircraft carriers from Russia, China, and the USA all about to converge on our location. I've been ordered to destroy your submarine if I can't make it disappear before they get here, so it's your call, can it be done?"

Commander Bower grinned through a thick beard. "You're damned right it can be done."

A crisp, audible ping, came from the passive sonar station — once the confines of the lower decks distant from the Command Center — and Sam glanced at the monitor. It showed a submarine approaching from nearly 800 feet away, making no attempt to cover up the sound of its propulsion as it raced ahead.

The passive sonar made another sweep, revealing only two possibly enemy targets. One was a surface vessel, which Sam knew was the *Maria Helena,* while the second one was the

296 | OMEGA DEEP

unidentified submarine, which appeared to be making a straight line toward the *Maria Helena.*

Sam swore.

To Commander Bower, he asked, "How long before one of your torpedoes are available to fire?"

The thick creases of the commander's face appeared to deepen and harden with concern. "Five or six minutes at least. They're not armed."

Sam said, "You and Tom get onto it, now!"

He watched Tom and his father disappear to the main torpedo room at the speed of much younger men.

Sam picked up the VHF radio, depressed the mike and said, "*Maria Helena,* you've got an incoming submarine!"

CHAPTER FIFTY-ONE

Ω————————Ω————————Ω

ON BOARD THE *MARIA HELENA*

SVETLANA HEARD THE RADIO AND raced to the active sonar monitor.

The outline of a large predator submarine lit up the screen. At a glance, she knew it was too short to be an American, French, or British nuclear attack submarine. Its hull was too wide to be a nuclear bomber, too. It looked similar to one of Russia's new *Yasen* class nuclear-guided submarines, but even that seemed unlikely. The outline was similar, but it was making far too much noise. In fact, that's what hit her as wrong about the submarine—it was making too much noise to be any submarine built in the past three decades!

Unless it wanted to be heard?

But why?

So it definitely wasn't one of ours.

Matthew seemed to spot the conflict twisting in her face. His voice was confronting, and he asked, "Is that one of yours?"

"Afraid not," she replied. "It looks like one of our old *Typhoon* class nuclear submarines, but I can promise you it's not."

"Why not?"

"Because you can hear that thing from a mile away." She

made a thin-lipped smile. "Let me assure you — we didn't spend billions of dollars to produce a submarine that can be spotted by a salvage vessel. Besides, we sold the lot of them in the early nineties."

"Touché." Matthew grimaced. "But that doesn't reveal what it is doing here!"

Svetlana studied the shape a little more closely. "You know what. I do believe this is an old *Typhoon* class nuclear submarine, that has been heavily modified."

"How so?"

She pointed to the bow, where a sphere rose like a strange wart. "That doesn't belong there. If anything, it adds more noise and increases the size of the submarine's natural wake. My guess is that it's been retrofitted, but I couldn't even guess what purpose it serves."

That slowed him. His face pale and disturbed by her reference to the sphere, Matthew said, "I can."

"Really?" she asked, now curious. "What?"

"You'll see soon enough," he said, his eyes fixing on the sonar monitor. "The submarine appears to be surfacing."

Her eyes darted from the monitor across to the calm surface of the sea, half a mile off the port bow.

The submarine rose fast, disappearing from the view of the *Maria Helena's* array of active sonar transducers.

Nearly two minutes later, the submarine still hadn't surfaced. She turned to Matthew and Elise who were searching the bathymetric and sonar monitors. "Where did it go?"

Matthew increased the range and decreased the angle of the transducers. "We're working on it."

On the edge of the horizon to the starboard bow, a vessel appeared.

Elise flipped the radar monitor around to the side. "We have a battleship on the horizon."

"Where?" Matthew asked.

"Starboard side. Approximately two miles out."

Svetlana said, "Any idea whose battleship it is?"

"Not a clue," Elise replied, turning the monitor to face her. "You're the surveillance expert. What do you think this is?"

Svetlana glanced at the radar monitor. "That's a French, La Fayette Class Frigate. But I can't imagine what it's doing here."

"We'll know soon enough," Matthew said. "It's coming around to meet us."

The French Frigate raced toward them.

Matthew picked up the mike for the VHF radio. "Unidentified battleship, this is the *Maria Helena*. We're an American-owned civilian salvage ship, currently on a search and rescue mission, do you need our assistance?"

Svetlana rolled her eyes but remained silent. The French Frigate was nearly ten times their size and practically an indestructible battle-tank on water.

Like her, the French Frigate remained silent as it steamed across the horizon until she was perpendicular to the *Maria Helena*.

Veyron stepped up onto the bridge. "Anyone else notice we have a French *La Fayette* class frigate on our starboard?"

"It came to our attention," Elise said.

Genevieve raced up the steps to the bridge, breathing hard. "There's a…"

"We see it!" Matthew said. "Veyron, you'd better prepare the countermeasures."

"I'm on it!" Veyron shouted.

Genevieve said, "I'll prepare the torpedoes!"

Svetlana turned to Matthew. "Countermeasures and torpedoes? I thought you were a civilian vessel?"

Matthew shrugged. "Sometimes we work in some pretty unfriendly locations. Consequently, we have a pretty advanced weapons and defense system."

Svetlana swallowed. "I doubt it's going to do anything against a Frigate."

"Yeah, I don't suppose they will," Matthew replied. "I'm still hoping an outright confrontation can be avoided."

Toward the forward third of the Frigate a 100 mm TR automatic gun rotated on its turret 90 degrees until it lined up square with the *Maria Helena*.

"Diplomacy's out!" Svetlana shouted. Fear rose in her throat. Her heart pounded in the back of her head. "What weapons have you got?"

She didn't hear a reply.

Instead, the 100 mm TR automatic gun began to fire.

The barrel lit up with flame, as its multipurpose artillery pieces fired at a rate of 78 rounds per minute.

Svetlana closed her eyes, accepting her death.

But it didn't come.

She turned to Matthew, "What the hell happened! How could they have possibly missed?"

"Don't look too relieved. It was a ruse. A holographic distraction!"

"What?"

Matthew said, "The La Fayette's not real."

"It isn't?"

"No. That submarine must still be out there."

Svetlana scanned the horizon.

She placed the headphones on her ears and listened. Instinct taking over, she instantly turned the array of sounds into useable information, giving her a visual image of the submarine nearby. She closed her eyes and listened.

In the distance, she heard the blast of a torpedo entering the water, followed by the whir of its electric propeller, and the closing of the submarine's torpedo hatch.

A moment later she spotted the torpedo.

It was half a mile away, running just below the surface, it could have been a shark if it wasn't running so damned fast.

Matthew responded surprisingly quickly.

He depressed the mike for the shipboard PA system and said, "We've got a live torpedo approaching at 270 degrees!"

Veyron shouted back. "Countermeasures in the water!"

Svetlana glanced out the portside, where an AN/SLQ-25 Nixie torpedo decoy raced to meet the incoming torpedo.

She grinned and held her breath.

What sort of civilian salvage vessel carried torpedo decoys?

The torpedo wasn't to be distracted. Instead, it glided past the decoy, undeterred, racing straight for the *Maria Helena.*

Svetlana said to Matthew, "You got anything else in that bag of tricks?"

Matthew set his jaw with disbelief. There were tiny tremors where all color was gone from his face. He depressed the mike to the shipboard PA system. "The torpedo's gonna hit us hard. Everyone off the boat!"

Svetlana opened her mouth to argue. Her eyes darted from Matthew to the incoming torpedo. The sight confirmed what she already knew — they had run out of time.

They had seconds to get off the *Maria Helena.*

Elise was already out the starboard door.

Svetlana followed at a sprint.

Matthew shouted, "Jump!"

Svetlana Jumped.

Behind them, the torpedo ripped through the *Maria Helena's* hull.

By the time Svetlana's feet touched the water, the time-delay detonator fired and the torpedo exploded. Its blast ripped through the *Maria Helena* as though it's steel bulkheads were made of plastic.

CHAPTER FIFTY-TWO

G ENEVIEVE'S HEAD BROKE THE SURFACE first.

She ran her hands through her short brown hair, wiping it out of her eyes. She opened her eyes. Parts of the *Maria Helena* were scattered throughout the sea for hundreds of feet. The bulk of what was left of her hull was now being pulled down by her stern. Gone. After braving some of the worst storms in history, their trusted ship had made her way to the bottom in a matter of seconds. The ship had been Genevieve's home, her reprieve from a previous life of violence, and a place she shared with a crew who were closer to her than her own family.

A moment later, she spotted with relief, the heads of the rest of that crew as they surfaced and Svetlana, the Russian spy — who, by now, she had to admit, was unlikely to have been involved in the attack.

If there had been more time, she would have wept. Instead, her blue eyes gazed on a surfacing submarine, less than half a mile away. Squinting, she spotted someone on the conning deck. He gripped something in his hand. It was too far away to see it clearly, but she had no doubt about what it was and what the submariner's intentions were. If there had been any doubt, it was removed a second later, when the machinegun opened fire.

Seawater sprayed into the air where the shots fell short of their desired targets.

There wasn't time for a debate about their options. In fact, they didn't have any options. On the surface, they were unable to defend themselves. Even if they had weapons, they would have been of little use against a nuclear submarine.

Genevieve shouted, "We have to reach the *Omega Deep!*"

"It's nearly sixty feet down!" Svetlana said. "It's too deep!"

"There's emergency regulator mouthpieces attached to compressed air inside the lockout trunk," Genevieve said. "If we can reach that, we'll be all right."

Another round of shots fired closer.

Genevieve started hyperventilating.

Svetlana said, "Sixty feet it is then!"

A third set of shots raked the water, progressively approaching their heads.

Genevieve took one last deep breath and dipped under the water.

She kicked hard all the way to the bottom. Sam had marked the top of the lockout trunk with a red marker, so that it could be spotted, despite the Omega Cloak.

Her chest burned with that unforgiving and relentless desire to take a deep breath.

Reaching the horizontal opening, Genevieve entered the code into the keypad and the outer hatch swung open. She swam inside and fumbled around in the dark for the mouthpiece. Her right hand made its connection and she shoved it into her mouth and took a deep breath.

The air was cold and sweet.

Next to her, Matthew shined a waterproof flashlight that he must have had in his pocket. Genevieve handed her mouthpiece to Svetlana who was the last to enter the lockout trunk. Genevieve made her way to the opposite end of the trunk to locate another regulator mouthpiece.

When all five of them were attached to the internal breathing apparatus, Genevieve closed the external hatch and vented the water, leaving them inside a dry chamber.

The lockout trunk filled with air, expelling the last of the seawater. When the pressure equalized with the internal hull, Veyron turned the lock, and the watertight hatch opened up.

Sam Reilly looked up from inside with a grin. "Welcome aboard."

CHAPTER FIFTY-THREE

Ω————————Ω————————Ω

INSIDE THE COMMAND CENTER OF THE USS *OMEGA DEEP*

SAM BROUGHT THE REST OF his crew up through the forward passageway into the Command Center.

They were bruised and battered, but in remarkably good shape given that the *Maria Helena* had been torpedoed seconds after they jumped overboard. Genevieve had a small laceration above her right eyebrow that she appeared not to have noticed and no one had any fractured bones as far as he could tell.

Genevieve spotted Tom at the helm, where he and his father were quickly working their way through a series of checklists to start up all the submarine's system.

She came up and gave him a passionate kiss on his lips.

It was short and sharp. They both knew there was plenty of work to do if they wanted to live much longer.

Tom said, "I was worried about you."

Genevieve shrugged. "It takes more than a torpedo to kill me."

Sam laughed. In her case, she probably meant it. She was probably the toughest person he'd ever met, male or female, and certainly the most naturally deadly.

Commander Bower ran his eyes across the gang.

Sam introduced everyone to the commander.

Commander Bower said, "I believe I've met your entire crew, except Svetlana," the commander said before his eyes landed on Svetlana. "I don't think I've met you before — what do you do?"

"She's a spy," Sam said, matter-of-factly.

"Oh good. One of ours?"

"Afraid not. She's Russian. Actually, she was in the process of trying to track your submarine."

"Of course," Commander Bower said, cheerfully. "How did she end up here?"

Sam sighed. "It's a long story."

Svetlana glanced at the sonar monitor. "We've got incoming!"

Sam said, "Another torpedo?"

"No, depth charges," she replied.

There was nothing the *Omega Deep's* countermeasures could do about it.

Commander Bower said, "Brace for contact!"

A nearby depth charge rocked the *Omega Deep.*

The commander glanced at an array of instruments, forgetting about the spy on board his experimental and most secret submarine.

Another depth charge rocked the hull. Sam thought for sure the hull would be ripped apart any minute.

Sam asked the commander, "How long can she take this?"

"All day, if she has to. Those depth charges are being intentionally dropped too far away to cause any real damage."

"Why?"

"Because Halifax doesn't want to sink the *Omega Deep* any more than I do. He needs it still afloat if he's to sell it."

"They know where we are?" Sam asked.

"Sure they do."

"How?"

"A man named James Halifax, my old XO, betrayed me. He sold the *Omega Deep* to the highest bidder but hasn't been able to break the security code I placed on the computer's main system. He's been back and forth a few times, hoping he could starve me into submission. My guess is he's marked the outer shell of the submarine with something so that he can identify her, despite the *Omega Cloak* still being active."

Another depth charge exploded nearby. This one was much closer.

Sam said, "All the same. I'd rather not wait around here a moment longer than we have to. Can we get this thing underway?"

Commander Bower grinned. "You bet your ass we can!"

CHAPTER FIFTY-FOUR

SAM LOOKED IN THE REAR-view-mirror at the top of his console at the commander, who seemed twenty years younger as he buzzed from station to station in the control room, checking readouts and making minor adjustments on the touchscreens. The task of leading this crack team of mariners was invigorating him, breathing new life into his emaciated form.

The commander had given Matthew a crash course in submarine piloting. Though substantially different to a surface ship, mastering the craft shared similar principles, so was not altogether alien to him.

Veyron had taken the copilot's chair. The shifting of ballast and executive monitoring of all major systems was a no-brainer for him. Gravitational dynamics was his passion, so he quickly learned the parameters of the operations, and even started to test the boundaries. He flicked through all the menus on the screens and familiarized himself with the layout of the submarine systems. He customized a desktop for himself, prioritizing his access portal to the various functions of the ship under his control.

Every command was given to the pilot team by Commander Bower and repeated back to him as the movements and adjustments were completed. Sam watched the old captain's excitement as his ship came back to life around him.

Svetlana manned the sonar systems, Tom the navigations, and Genevieve—weapons systems. They all shared the command center together. It was a bull-pit, a war room.

Once Commander Bower was satisfied everyone had a rudimentary ability to operate their assigned stations, he brought the ship alive, section by section.

He monitored the nuclear reactor systems himself, ensuring the powertrain held up after the grounding.

"Okay people, here we go." He said to the assembled crew.

The ship started to gently shudder as the commander transferred thrust to the jet propulsion systems. *The Omega Deep* was heavily connected to the seafloor, and they needed to break the suction of the soft sandy bottom in order to move the ship up into the water. He set an initial power as a baseline and waited, monitoring the readouts on the screen before him. He called orders to Veyron and Matthew, asking for adjustments of the ballast, rudder, and bow planes. He sought to extract every bit of movement he could from the ship, without stressing her hull too much. He had been aboard this ship since it was three giant pieces in a Massachusetts hangar by the slipway. He knew exactly how much she could and couldn't withstand. With his hand gripping the edge of the control island, he felt his ship's pulse as the power started to build.

They all waited. Commander Bower stood as a solid rock of determination, unmoving.

Taking his right hand to the screen the commander directed more power to her thrusters. The shuddering of the ship built to a humming crescendo. Again, he waited. It was a huge mass of steel he was trying to move, he wanted to do it as gently as possible—and his sixty-five years had given him patience.

He increased power to the starboard jets and steadily increased throttle at the stern. He was trying to unlock *Omega Deep* from the seat into which she listed with her 9,000 tons without destroying her driveline. Clouds of mud and sand started to swirl around the ship, clouding the vision from the remote cameras at the stern. The hum in the ship built to a discordant vibration.

Alarms on the consoles in front of Veyron and Matthew started lighting up red, one after the other. Reverberation shook the trembling room like an earthquake. Veyron jettisoned the last of the ballast, waiting expectantly for the ship to shoot to the surface like a rocket. The commander stared maniacally at the screen below him as he leaned over the main console island which stood in the middle of the room.

The ship rattled and ground against itself, vibration thrashing everything.

"Come on baby!" Commander Bower yelled above the cacophony.

The others shared momentary glances and looked about for anything that might disconnect itself from the ceiling and drop onto them.

The ship continued to heave against itself, like a jumbo jet under brakes at the start of a runway. She seemed as though she would tear herself apart. The thunderous noise of the water moving away from the mighty jets and the trapped energy in the boat were rocking her and her crew in a thousand directions at once.

Finally, the sea bottom relented and released its grip on the massive submarine. The fuselage issued a mighty metallic groan of relief, and the tension was relieved as she pulled up and away from the bottom.

"Hooray!" The crew cheered as one.

Sam looked at the commander and thought the old seaman might cry in joy and relief, as he pulled back the power to the reactor.

Veyron flooded ballast into the ship as fast as he could, and Matthew battled to catch and carry the ship as she jumped to life undersea.

Tom stood and climbed out of the navigation station. He turned to congratulate his father on the extrication.

It was at that moment the proximity alarm on Svetlana's screens lit up in concert with a wailing siren, and the ship automatically deployed her counter-measure device against an incoming torpedo strike. In days gone by, decoys were deployed against torpedoes, but these days American submarines used high-tech *Countermeasure Anti-Torpedoes* (CAT's) that seek and destroy incoming ordnance. CAT provides a rapidly deployable kinetic energy, hard-kill solution to use against torpedo threats. Launched in an instant, it homes in on the enemy torpedo and destroys it through proximity detonation and/or collision.

"Contact, starboard, 150 feet and closing!" Svetlana called.

Sam scrambled back to his station, roughly mashing the headset against his right ear as he dropped into the seat. "Torpedo!" he said, "Brace for impact!"

The torpedo chasing the *Omega Deep* was relatively small, intended to disable her by puncturing her hull — but not destroy her. The artificial intelligence in the CAT's onboard computer triangulated a trajectory as far from the submarine as possible, yet close enough to confuse the targeting device on the incoming weapon.

Self-propelled, the *Omega Deep's* CAT closed proximity on the incoming deadly underwater missile. Nearing the attacker, it released a sonic shockwave which produced both sound and an underwater wake. This confounded the hostile torpedo's homing system, breaking its lock on the *Omega Deep* and successfully nominating itself as the target of choice. A few seconds later the two torpedoes made contact, and both weapons initiated their explosive systems.

Boom!!

A shockwave slammed over the *Omega Deep* from the starboard side, and the tubular vessel rolled violently 30 degrees to port, knocking the commander off his feet. He fell hard to the floor, striking his head on the counter as he went down.

In the same moment, the attacking torpedo tore into the CAT. Inside the broad casement of the CAT, a series of magnesium fueled fireballs in excess of one million degrees Fahrenheit each erupted one after the other, the last of which also ignited a charge equivalent to 500kg of C4 explosive. The torpedo's TNT warhead detonated. The remainder of the missile changed course by 45 degrees, and exploded into four pieces, each now white hot and pliable as a rubber ball.

If what was left had struck the *Omega Deep*, it would have merely glanced off her armored side. As it was, the pieces traversed another 300 feet of water, sinking and disintegrating, brittle under the rapid temperature change. The whole event took less than four seconds.

In the command center on the *Omega Deep*, a siren mercilessly throbbed and the crew held on to their stations with both hands. Matthew pushed all his controls against the inertia of the explosion and pushed the submarine back over.

"Evasive maneuvers!" The commander called from the floor, reaching up to the counter-top to pull himself to his feet. "Elise, how much water do we have?"

"One forty feet sir, in another 600 yards east we can dive though. There's a drop-off over two thousand feet."

The commander hunkered over the powertrain control screen and swiped thrust to the propulsion to 100 percent. The ship silently leaped forward into the free ocean before her. This was what she was made for—combat.

"Power at 100 percent. Pilot!"

"Yes sir," Matthew responded.

"Let's make for the drop-off, then take us around to due east, and down to a thousand or so feet. We'll skirt along the rim of the drop for a while and come about somewhere down the line. She's built for hard angles, let's put her through her paces."

"Copy that," Matthew replied.

"What's our top speed, sir?" Sam asked

"She's pretty comfortable at 40 knots," The commander answered. "Elise, let us know the moment we can dive."

"Will do, commander."

"Pilot, keep her as low as you dare. Keep at least fifty feet between us and the bottom, but beyond that, it's up to you."

"Aye sir, fifty feet," Matthew responded.

"Sonar, weapons, report!"

"Sir, one enemy sub," Tom started. "Computer identifies it as a Russian *Typhoon* class—whatever that is."

"A *Typhoon!* They were all supposed to be retired under the START treaty."

The Strategic Arms Reduction Treaty was a bilateral treaty between the United States of America and the Union of Soviet Socialist Republics on the reduction and limitation of strategic offensive arms. The treaty was signed on 31 July 1991 and entered into force on 5 December 1994.

Sam said, "I guess they were retired to the highest bidder because this looks like a perfect match."

"Range?"

"4100 yards, speed 27 knots. We're pulling away from her."

"Well she can't keep up, but she'll give us a run for our money. That's a monster of a sub—and God knows what she's armed with. They used to run Type 53's. And a bucket-load of ICBM's, but those are definitely accounted for. Weapons, what's your status?"

"Sir, we have fifteen more CATs, all four torpedo tubes are operational, and I've got Mark-48's live, locked and loaded in each one."

"We'll run for a bit. Then we'll come around on 'em. Sonar, do not lose that ship."

"I'm all over it," Svetlana replied.

"Copilot!"

"Copilot," Veyron responded grinning, apparently enjoying himself a little too much.

"How are my pumps and ballast?"

"All good sir, this tin can seems pretty tough."

"Let's hope so. I'm going to need your help to carry this boat around some hard angles if we're to outsmart this *Typhoon*."

"Let me know what you need sir. I think I'm getting the hang of her. You said it was a crash course, but this is a little extreme!"

"You're a natural Veyron, I can sense it already."

"Matthew?" the commander continued.

"All good sir. Plenty of power and she's a lot more responsive at this speed."

"Just don't rip the bowfins off of her and we'll be fine."

"Aye sir, I'll baby her all the way."

"Good man."

Commander Bower leaned in toward Sam's station with a hand on the back of his chair. "Hell of a team you got here, Mr. Reilly, hell of a team."

CHAPTER FIFTY-FIVE

───Ω───Ω───Ω───

ON BOARD THE UNIDENTIFIED ENEMY SUBMARINE

JAMES HALIFAX LOOKED AROUND THE deck of the *Arkhangelsk.*

It was a Russian-built behemoth of a craft, 574 feet in length with a massive beam of 75 feet. A nuclear submarine, built as a launch platform for the now extinct *'Sturgeon' Submarine Launched Ballistic Missiles.*

His financiers had purchased her at a steal from the shipyard Colonel in Severodvinsk. If you call fifty million U.S. dollars a steal, that is. She came equipped with twelve Type-53 torpedoes, which have always been in his opinion, some of the most effective ever produced. However, there were no cruise missiles, no SLBM's, no mines, nothing else. He was depending on his torpedo man all the way. So far, it was close — but no cigar. He cursed the United States' development of the CAT system — he should have the *USS Omega Deep* in his grasp already.

James Halifax looked around the control deck and smiled.

He marveled at how much technology the *Typhoon* class shared with the United States *Ohio* class submarines that he had served on, all those years ago. Crewed by Russians, and one of the safest war subs ever conceived, this ship ran as smoothly as anything he had commanded, and was a good deal wider in beam, which had its comfort advantages.

Out-of-work Russian ex-submariners were not in short

supply, and these staff had been discarded like so many micro-fiche operators when the subsequent *Borei class* was commissioned. They chatted among themselves, light-hearted and obviously glad to be back in the saddle one last time.

He went across the pressure hull divide into the sonar room and leaned in.

"How are we looking for the next torpedo?"

The pasty, gaunt, heavily bespectacled Russian replied in a thick Georgian accent. "They're still within range of the fifty-threes, but since we only have eleven of them left I'd like to be a little closer before we engage again. They're pulling away quickly, but the torpedo is much faster than they are."

"Lock one on as best as you can. I'd like to take the rear end off that thing and sink it to the bottom before they make the edge of the continental shelf and dive."

"They're already diving hard."

"So, hurry up God-damn it!"

The sonar operator lifted a microphone handset and passed the message in Russian, including co-ordinates for the programming of the torpedo. The scratchy voice on the other end came back, arguing with the sonar man. The conversation ended abruptly, and the sound of the torpedo launch bay doors rang through the hull as another Type 53 was issued.

The sonar man tracked the torpedo as it settled into the groove of wake left by the *Omega Deep.* It sensed turbulence in the water and snaked back and forth across the disturbed water layers that defined the previous location of its intended target. This time, however, it appeared that his enemy was waiting for him and the torpedo was destroyed by another CAT, this time at a range of 350 feet from the *Omega Deep.*

"God-damn it all!" the tall man barked at the screen.

The Russian sonar operator said nothing and stared at the green waterfall-style sonar monitor.

"Let me know when we're closer!" he yelled at the skinny

submariner.

"Yes, commander," he replied without moving a muscle.

Halifax stormed off, returning to the bridge and berating the men with orders to speed the ship up, seek out, and disable that damned submarine.

The sonar room light started flashing at the copilot's control station, and his phone rang. A moment later the proximity alarm began flashing silent bright red light through the command center.

After answering the phone in Russian, the copilot lifted the handset above his shoulder and looked to the tall man. "It's for you."

The sonar operator said, "We've got an incoming torpedo. It's running hot!"

"A torpedo?" Halifax replied. "Where the hell did Bower get a crew to fire a damned torpedo? Evasive maneuvers! Countermeasures, fire!"

CHAPTER FIFTY-SIX

———Ω———Ω———Ω———

COMMAND CENTER, USS *OMEGA DEEP*

SAM GLANCED OVER SVETLANA'S SHOULDER at the sonar monitor.

Their Mark-48 torpedo raced toward the enemy submarine. He found himself unintentionally holding his breath, as the 650-pound warhead raced through the water at a speed of 55 knots. Two interceptor CATs were fired from the enemy submarine.

The first one failed to make contact, but the second one struck their Mark-48, causing it to detonate instantly.

The subsequent shockwave rocked the *Omega Deep*.

Sam met Commander Bower's hardened stare. "How long to load and fire another torpedo?"

"Too long, I'm afraid," the commander replied. "The enemy ship has a full complement, which means they'll be able to get off multiple shots for every one of ours. We can't keep this up. Our best bet is to break free of these shallow waters, and dive."

"Could we fire multiple torpedoes at once?" Sam asked.

"Afraid not. If we had a full team, we might be able to shift them quickly, but with our skeleton crew, it would be impossible. Our only hope is that we can reach the open ocean, dive beyond their crush depth."

Sam said, "I have a better idea."

"I'm listening."

Sam pointed to the navigation table. "Can you take us into this narrow valley?"

Commander Bower raised a thick eyebrow. "Anywhere, in particular, you want to go?"

Sam pointed at a small grotto about half a mile in. "Right there."

"No way the *Omega Deep*'s going to enter that cave."

"I don't plan for it to." Sam said, "The question is, can the *Omega Deep* be piloted into the valley?"

The commander inputted the route into the digital route-planner. "It will be a tight squeeze, and we'll need to slow right down, but it can be done."

"Good. Let's do it!"

"We'd be nuts to go in there. We're lining ourselves up to get trapped. This valley zigzags wildly. It will be hard for them to target us, but harder still for us to get a shot off."

"That's okay," Sam said. "I've got no intention of firing another shot."

Commander Bower's lips curled in a wry smile. "What are you thinking of?"

Sam stood up and started to don his scuba gear. "Letting the USS *Gerald R. Ford* do the job for us."

CHAPTER FIFTY-SEVEN

T HE *USS OMEGA* DEEP TACKED hard to the starboard side, entering the narrow valley.

Inside the dark confines of the lockout escape trunk, Sam felt the inertial shift of the monstrous submarine to the side. He imagined the massive predator, racing through the narrow straits like a race car. A rally to the death, the modified Russian *Typhoon* class nuclear submarine was hard on their tail.

Three minutes later, it shifted again.

Sam imagined it was like trying to thread a needle. Only, in this case, the eye was the width of a football field, and the thread was nearly half the field wide and twice as long.

He flooded the lockout trunk.

When the internal pressure equalized with the outer seawater, the lock-out trunk hatch opened.

He adjusted his buoyancy control device until he was neutrally buoyant and swam out the horizontal escape trunk.

The *Omega Deep* was moving slowly. Less than four knots, as it weaved its way through the narrow-submerged valley. He prayed the larger *Typhoon* class submarine trailing them would have to reduce its speed even more.

Sam stared at the ground below.

The *Omega Deep* steered to port, its bow thrusters whirred

326 | OMEGA DEEP

into life, as the massive vessel turned on its axis, to slip through the hair-pin turn.

Below him, Sam saw the entrance to the grotto that he'd spotted earlier.

He swam down, taking refuge inside the dark opening.

Once there, he removed the two magnetic homing beacons from his buoyancy control device and waited. It was a total of eight minutes before he spotted the round bow of the *Typhoon* class submarine.

He waited.

The enemy submarine looked massive in the narrow valley. It edged slowly toward the hairpin, making the maneuver almost at a complete standstill.

Sam swam round its swollen steel belly and placed the two magnetic homing beacons to the side of the predator's hull.

The beacons turned from red to green, confirming they were armed.

Sam let go and watched as the enemy submarine slowly pulled away. He'd done all that he could do. Now it was up to the weapons team on board the USS *Gerald R. Ford* to do the rest.

CHAPTER FIFTY-EIGHT

Ω——————Ω——————Ω

ON BOARD THE USS *GERALD R. FORD*

T HE WEAPONS OFFICER SAID, "THE *Omega Deep's* on the move, ma'am."

The secretary of defense looked up from her laptop. This was it. Her heart leaped into her throat. "How can you tell?"

"The homing devices we gave Mr. Reilly just became active, and they're moving."

"You've located the coordinates of the signal?"

"Yes." The weapons officer showed her on the bathymetric maps the *Maria Helena* had made when Sam had first surveyed the area. "The signal is coming from inside this narrow valley, here."

She raised an eyebrow. "Why are they heading deeper into the remains of the 8th Continent?"

"We don't know ma'am. The signal's going to pass the region that the *Maria Helena* charted within another ten minutes."

"Can you get a lock on them?"

"Yes, ma'am."

"What speed is she doing?"

"Four knots." The weapons officer then explained, "The channel is so narrow, the *Omega Deep's* having to make very slow maneuvers."

She sighed. "Interesting. What are they trying to do?"

"We don't know. And we've no way of knowing for certain if we'll maintain our line of sight to the target once they get much farther."

"All right. If she's moving, she's no longer under our command."

The weapons officer asked, "What are your orders, ma'am?"

Her emerald eyes flashed with defiance. "Fire with everything you've got!"

"Understood, ma'am."

The secretary of defense stood up from her desk at the back of the bridge. She casually wandered to the port side and stared out the windshield.

The ship rang out with the constant ring of the automated warning bell—meaning that torpedo doors were opening and the torpedoes were now live—and on the port side of the hull four torpedo bay doors opened.

Inside a total of four separate Mark-32 shipboard torpedo launchers—armed with three Mark-46 torpedoes—rotated 80 degrees silently and trained at its target.

Her mouth was set hard, and her eyes flashed defiance. She felt tears come to her eyes. She blinked them down, telling herself that she was sorry for the loss of the *Omega Deep* and the substantial technological advancement that the submarine represented. But in her heart, she knew that she was mourning the loss of the crew from the *Maria Helena.*

"Goodbye, Mr. Reilly."

In the shallow water, long strips of whitewater remained where the torpedoes raced toward their target.

CHAPTER FIFTY-NINE

Ω—————————Ω—————————Ω

ON BOARD THE *ARKHANGELSK*

JAMES HALIFAX GLANCED AT THE sonar monitor.

The lines in his face seemed to deepen and darken in the bare light. His mind was twisted in a battle of logic, unable to accept the inevitable outcome. There were four torpedoes approaching his submarine simultaneously. They were inside a narrow valley, with nowhere to maneuver. And they could release just two CATs.

The *Countermeasure Anti-Torpedoes* could only take out one torpedo each. The math came out the same way no matter which way he looked at it.

They were going to be hit.

The question was, could they sustain such a hit, and survive?

His rational mind knew the answer, but eons of evolution have made it difficult for the human mind to be rational when it comes to determining their own demise.

Halifax said, "Weapons! Deploy the remaining CATs."

"Understood, sir. Launching the remaining countermeasures."

"Pilot!" Halifax watched the sonar monitor where their CATs and incoming torpedoes were on a collision course. "On my mark, I want you to turn full starboard rudder."

"Aye, sir."

"Ballast," Halifax shouted. "On my mark. I want you to blow everything, let's see if we can get some cover in that reef."

"Aye, sir."

Halifax watched as two of the incoming torpedoes detonated on impact with the two CATs.

"Pilot, full starboard rudder."

"Aye, sir. Full starboard rudder."

Halifax shouted, "Ballast. Full blow."

"Aye, sir. Full blow."

On the sonar monitor, he watched as the remaining two torpedoes rounded the nearby explosion, undeterred, and dipped into the channel, in preparation for their final run.

What the hell happened?

There was nothing more he could do.

It was as though his submarine was emitting a homing beacon, to which the two torpedoes were now locked.

Halifax gritted his teeth and gripped the grab bar on the side of the command center.

There was no reason for it.

He knew there was no way the torpedoes would miss their mark now. It was impossible his submarine could withstand the hit.

Halifax opened his mouth to scream.

But the sound never had the chance to escape. In a split second, the first torpedo ripped a hole through the hull, followed two-thirds of a second later by the second one. Their time-delay explosion, fired a full second later, causing the submarine's hull to implode.

CHAPTER SIXTY

Ω

OPEN WATERS, 8TH CONTINENT–TWO MONTHS LATER

USS GERALD R. FORD'S BOW SLICED the water of the South Pacific Ocean at a cautionary 10 knots. At 110,000 tons, the aircraft carrier, seemed almost indifferent to the large seas, as her bow cut through the water.

It was a little after midday when the aircraft carrier appeared to reduce speed for no more than a few minutes, before picking up its original course, and head toward New Zealand, to participate in a series of war games. In the great expanse of the Pacific Ocean, such a deviation in course and speed was nearly imperceptible. Yet in that time, a single yellow object was discarded into the deep water below.

The little yellow private submarine hit the water with a slight jolt, resting on the surface for no more than a couple minutes before sinking into oblivion beneath the waves.

Sam Reilly gripped the joystick in his right and gently pushed it forward.

The submersible's multiple electric thrusters immediately started to whine and the Orcasub, slipped farther under the waves, at a measly 6 knots.

It was three weeks after Sam and Tom had arrived, unexpectedly to their own funerals, after everyone had presumed they had died on board the *Maria Helena* or the imploded USS *Omega Deep,* both men were back at the edge of the submerged 8th Continent.

The very same place where everything had started when the *Omega Deep* had first sighted a little yellow Orcasub, and Commander Bower had made the catastrophic decision to follow the submarine.

Sam maneuvered the sports submarine, kind of a cross between an airplane and a two-seater submersible, the machine flew with precision, gliding its way through the narrow valley. They had set a course along a south to southwesterly direction along the remnants of an ancient submerged valley.

The submarine's exact dimensions were: 20 feet of length, beam 14 feet—with a 7-foot wingspan—and a height of 5 feet. There were two glass bubble domes positioned forward and aft of each other, where a single pilot and copilot were housed. The overall shape of the submersible was sleek, like a sports-car, or more accurately, a sports underwater airplane, with narrow wings and a V-shaped tail-wing. The two wings even had two large thrusters fixed to each wing, like jet-engines on an aircraft.

It was identical to the one that Commander Bower had tracked nearly six months earlier. Sam pulled back on the joystick, and the little submersible rose out of the higher cliffs of the nearly three miles wide valley, leveling out after its rapid ascent, across an ancient waterfall.

Emerging onto the tabletop of the 8th Continent.

The ancient river opened up to a shallow underwater tabletop, covered in vivid and impressive coral gardens. It was a unique tropical playground that didn't belong anywhere near where they were. Coral reefs provided homes for tropical fish, sponges, mollusks, giant manta rays, sea turtles, and giant clams. The diversity of form and color was the sort of thing that inspired humanity to explore beneath the waves in the first place.

A small pod of dolphins raced beside their submersible, swimming upside down and by its side.

Sam said, "Someone looks like they're enjoying their day."

"What's not to enjoy?" Tom replied. "They live in an undersea paradise."

The depth of the tabletop was roughly fifty feet, with a narrow chasm. Sam gripped the joystick, easing the Orcasub up to a depth of 100 feet.

Sam said, "We're approaching the place."

"I see it," Tom replied. "It's at your 3'Oclock position."

"Got it."

Sam slowed the Orcasub, as he approached the end of the chasm, taking it to a stop at the mouth of a large underground chamber, roughly twenty feet high by thirty feet wide. He switched on the submarine's overhead lights, which shined like two little bug-eyes from the top of the sub. The cave formed out of the mouth of a small rocky outcrop on the coral tabletop, like a monolith.

"You ready?" Sam asked.

Tom said, "Yeah. Take us in."

Sam dipped the joystick forward, and the Orcasub's propellers whined as he edged her through the mouth of the opening.

The tunnel descended steeper until they were at a completed dive. At 160 feet, the rocky passageway appeared to level out, before ascending again.

At 140 feet the passageway opened, and seawater ceased. The submarine surfaced into a gigantic, air-filled grotto that extended so far back, that neither Sam nor Tom could see where it ended. A giant light filtered through the top of the cavern, like the rays of the sun, glistening on the spectacular white beach.

Sam eased the Orcasub forward, until she became gently beached on the sandy beach. Confident that the submarine was securely grounded, Sam disengaged the hatch and climbed out. He removed his MP5 submachinegun and slung it over his shoulder.

He had no intention of taking any chances.

The wooden remains of a 16ᵗʰ century Dutch Fluyt with its distinctive pear-shaped hull—most likely used in early exploration of the southern seas—rested high up in the sand.

Toward the southern end of the beach, a Lockheed Model 10 Electra American twin-engine, all-metal monoplane, rested in near perfect condition, like the main feature of a rare antiquities museum.

Sam recognized the aircraft instantly.

And who wouldn't have?

The airliner had been developed by the Lockheed Aircraft Corporation in the 1930s to compete with the Boeing 247 and Douglas DC-2. The type gained considerable fame, not just for her renowned reliability, but as the one that was flown by Amelia Earhart on her ill-fated around-the-world expedition in 1937.

ΩΩΩ

Tom pointed at the plane and whistled. "How do you think something like that ended up in here?"

Sam shrugged. "It might have crashed nearby and been washed inside."

"No way," Tom dismissed the explanation without hesitation. "Impossible."

"Why?"

"Look at the tracks."

Sam ran his eyes across the tracks in the level, white sand. They started nearly 100 feet away, digging deep into the sand, and then turned 180 degrees, as though the pilot had set up for another takeoff.

The mystery made Sam grin. "All right. So, I suppose the more relevant question is how did an aircraft land on a beach that's now nearly 80 feet under water?"

"The island used to be above ground, but rising sea levels

changed all that?" Tom teased, knowing it was impossible.

"Not 80 feet…"

"Maybe the aircraft landed, and then, later, a volcanic event brought the beach to the bottom of the sea?"

"The volcanic event's a possibility, but it does little to explain why the tracks in the sand are still here, and the aircraft itself shows no sign of water damage."

"What about a vortex?"

Sam grinned. "What?"

"You know, like a type of whirlpool that intermittently sucks aircraft and boats alike deep into its confines, never to release them again."

Sam shrugged. "That's insane."

Tom said, "Come on, let's have a look inside."

It was a short walk, across the sandy beach to the wreckage of the antique aircraft.

Sam opened up the hatch toward the middle of the fuselage and made his way carefully to the cockpit.

Sam squinted, shining his flashlight into the barren cockpit.

There were no skeletons inside.

Instead, there was a single aviator jacket lying casually across one of the seats. Sam picked it up to examine. Sam felt his heart race. There, at the lapel were the letters, A. M. Earhart.

Sam expelled a deep breath of air and tried to remove the jacket, but something was preventing it from coming free. He leaned in and found what was causing the jacket to become snagged.

It was a Kodak 620 Duo camera.

CHAPTER SIXTY-ONE

Sam secured the 1930s era camera and what appeared to possibly be Amelia Earhart's aviation jacket inside the Orcasub, unwilling to risk losing or damaging either item. He had no idea about the recovery of such photos but was certain there would be a historical specialist who would be capable of printing the photographs stored inside.

"Strange place," Sam said.

"I'll say," Tom replied. "When you're ready, shall we penetrate farther, and see what this place is really hiding?"

"Sure, which way?"

Tom said, "I spotted a series of footprints in the sand, heading east. The path is well worn, so it looks like someone's frequented the place."

"Okay. Lead the way."

Both men were armed with MP5 submachineguns with multiple spare magazines. It felt strange to be searching an archeological site of such valuable history, with military weapons, but the news of a well-worn path reminded Sam that they weren't here for its rich history.

They needed to find out who was involved in the world-wide governmental insurrection and more importantly, if any of them were still alive.

It seemed naïve and unlikely that the submarine they had destroyed contained the last of their enemies.

The path rounded to the east, before entering a small passageway. Sam ran his hands across the black glassy stone.

"It's obsidian." His eyes swept the archway, all the way up to the top of the behemoth grotto. "Who do we know who has the technology to manipulate and shape obsidian in such a way?"

Tom set his mouth firm. "The Master Builders!"

"Exactly. They're not just manipulating the obsidian. Whoever built this place knew how to transfer light. That skylight overhead is still covered by 50 or more feet of water, and yet, it's shining down on this beach as clear as though it were a picturesque atoll."

Sam continued farther into the tunnel. It went for a couple thousand feet, descending the whole time, before opening up to an underground world. The ceiling in this new vault was so high that it could only be seen at the edges of the wall and not in the middle. As with the beach and submerged atoll, this place had a unique mechanism for providing an overhead light.

It shined so brightly that the entire place looked like daylight.

The passageway opened to a rocky escarpment that overlooked the entire place. There were trees and plants that were filled with fruits neither of them had ever seen, providing a rich fragrance throughout.

His eyes swept the near-mythical environment with wonder. It was impossible to tell where the place began and where it finished. It might have been a small country in its own right. Thick rainforests, including giant gum trees, more than a hundred feet tall, filled the area. There were massive open plains of grass, a freshwater river that split the ancient world in two, with multiple smaller tributaries and streams that ran off from it.

An 80-foot waterfall raged somewhere to the east, sending a fine mist down upon the valley. The sound of birds chirping echoed throughout.

Ancient megafauna drank by the bank of the river, including several monotreme species, including *Zaglossus hacketti,* a sheep-sized echidna, thought to be extinct from Australia for more than 40,000 years and once uncovered in Mammoth Cave in Western Australia. As well, an *Obdurodon dicksoni,* a seven-foot platypus spread out along the riverbank.

Sam scanned along the river bank, using his high-powered binoculars. He stopped at a burrowing *Diprotodon,* a hippopotamus-sized marsupial, most closely related to the wombat, which was thought to have become extinct 20,000 years ago in South Australia.

"What is this place?" Tom asked.

Sam shrugged. "I have no idea, but I feel like I've just entered a Jules Verne novel."

Tom laughed. "Now that you mention it, that's exactly what it is."

Like many explorers drawn to the underwater world, they had both enjoyed his early science fiction novel, *Journey to the Center of the Earth.*

Sam continued to search the area through his binoculars. Aside from the ancient flora and fauna, there were internal farmland areas with livestock, including cattle, pigs, sheep, and chickens. A rainforest. An entire biosphere. Light was being siphoned through the surface and redirected throughout the cavern.

But who was looking after the animals?

There were a series of interwoven, straight waterways. A labyrinth of aqueducts and irrigation. He followed them north until he spotted a series of houses. They appeared old, made out of sandstone, almost colonial in style.

But no people.

"Where is everyone?" Tom asked.

"No idea."

Sam ran his eyes across the colonial-style building, before reaching an opaline lake some distance behind it. There, several people were swimming. It was hard to tell from the distance, but Sam thought they appeared much taller than average humans. They looked to be at least seven-feet tall. They wore some sort of loincloth.

To himself, he said, "Well, I guess they are some sort of cavemen… and women?"

Then he spotted one of them come up from the surface of the lake, carrying a three-foot-long blue lobster, which he'd speared.

Tom said, "Zoom in over there. To the open grounds to the east of the colonial village."

"What is it?"

"Trouble."

Sam shifted his binoculars.

A dust trail showed a modern car racing along a dirt road. It pulled into a large square field. Someone got out of the car. He was too far away to see the man clearly, but he was wearing some kind of military uniform.

Sam moved his binoculars half an inch to the right and gasped.

There, in the large field, was an army—lined up on parade. They were carrying modern weapons and wore a blue military uniform.

"That's really something," Tom said. "Just when you thought you'd found utopia, there's some despot idiot who thinks he can rule it with a mighty fist."

"Yeah, we'll never learn from history," Sam replied. "All right, we need to get back to tell someone."

Sam lowered his binoculars and came face-to-face with a small car-sized echidna. Sam imagined the oversized spiky ant-eater, might have misinterpreted him as food. The creature snarled happily and charged toward him.

Tom fired his MP5 submachine gun in a continuous, rapid-fire burst.

The bullets appeared to do little to deter the beast, with foot-long spikes covering its entire body. Instead, it changed direction, charging at Tom.

Sam fired on the creature's hind legs.

The beast made a sharp whine, turned, and fled.

"You okay?" Sam asked.

"Yeah, never better. But we should get out of here while we still can."

"Agreed."

CHAPTER SIXTY-TWO

OFFICE OF THE SECRETARY OF DEFENSE, PENTAGON, VIRGINIA

S AM AND TOM TOOK A seat at the back of the large room. Despite its grand size, the office was surprisingly stark. With its blue carpet, a massive desk, and two small tables for meetings—four seats each. It wasn't the kind of place for a big, open meeting. Just a few generals and maybe a head of state or two. Secrets passed through this unpretentious, innocuous room day and night.

The secretary of defense sat down.

Speaking with authority, she said, "I've had those two items you believed came from Amelia Earhart sent away for analysis. The jacket was her exact size and might indeed prove to have once been hers."

"And the photos, ma'am?" Sam asked.

"Those, I'm told, will take some time, but our people are confident they can develop the photographs—so long as we don't rush the process."

"That's good," Sam said. "I'd love to know what's on them."

The secretary shrugged, as though their historical value meant little to her. She had more important problems to deal with in the present.

344 | OMEGA DEEP

As though reading her thoughts, Sam asked, "How did you know, ma'am?"

Her cheeks dimpled slightly and her eyes narrowed. "That the Master Builders were involved in the insurrection?"

"Yes."

"Because things are happening on a global scale, that aren't designed to aid anyone. Political strings are being pulled but not by the Russians, Chinese, or the Brits."

Sam cocked an incredulous eyebrow. "And that immediately drew your attention to a submerged world?"

"No. But I knew there was a secret navy operating in the seas, and the *Omega Deep* was the best way to locate it."

"That's why you created the *Omega Deep?*"

"Yes." She sighed heavily. "Like I said before, there's a war coming between the ancient Master Builders and the human race. Something we can't see, but it's coming. A race war, unlike anything we've ever seen between the human race and the Master Builders."

"At least we know who was responsible for the insurrection. Now that James Halifax is dead, we can at least close that door."

The secretary's lips thinned into a hard line. "I wouldn't be so sure."

Sam studied her attractive face. At nearly fifty years of age, she seemed more beautiful now than when he'd first met her more than a decade ago. As the leader of the U.S. military force, she possessed more power than any other person in the country, with the exception of the president of the United States. Her intelligent green eyes were filled with fear. It was a sight he hadn't seen there before.

He asked, "What do you know, ma'am?"

"Before the USS *Omega Deep* diverted from her orders, we received a message acknowledging the new orders from who we believed to be Commander Bower at the time. We've since learned that the message came from his XO, James Halifax."

"That's right," Sam said, having been through this line of thinking earlier.

"But the concerning thing here is that the message was written in a code used specifically for the very high echelon of command."

Sam sighed. "What are you saying, ma'am?"

"I'm saying, James Halifax didn't have the authority to access those codes."

Sam felt his world shift at the revelation. "That means someone else gave him the code."

She nodded. "And only five people in the world have that code. Commander Bower, the president of the United States, Chairman of the Joint Chiefs of Staff General Painter, General Potter – the head of the Army, and General Seymore of the Air Force."

"Which means, someone within that fine group of people, is currently betraying the United States of America." She swallowed. "Sam Reilly, I want you and Tom to make it a priority to find out exactly, who."

"How?"

"I believe the Master Builders are in the process of infiltrating high levels of government around the world, where they are waiting, biding their time, until they're ready to attack."

"And you think the 8th Continent might hold that secret?"

She nodded. "It's the only place where we know they've been. As soon as you're ready, I want you to start planning an expedition, deep into the submerged world of the 8th Continent."

"All right. We'll do it, but we might need another ship."

She smiled sympathetically. "I was sorry to hear about the loss of the *Maria Helena*."

"It's all right. My crew survived." Sam said, "That's all that matters. Ships can be replaced."

She stood up, as though the meeting was over. "I've spoken to the director of DARPA."

"And?"

"Congress has approved a twenty-million-dollar reward for the recovery of the *Omega Deep*. It's not a lot, but it should be enough to build a new ship."

Sam smiled. "That's very good of them."

"It's the least we could do after you recovered a 30-billion-dollar submarine," she said. "If you provide the lead engineer at the shipbuilding yard in Quonset, Rhode Island, with your unique specification, she said they would be happy to help put together your new ship, and Uncle Sam will pick up the tab."

"Much obliged, Madam Secretary."

She smiled, almost kindly at him. "What are you two going to do while your ship is being rebuilt?"

"We were thinking of taking a much overdue vacation."

"Sounds good. Where were you thinking of going?"

"Hawaii. There was some good surf we were trying to catch when this all came about."

"All right." She stood up and shook his and Tom's hands with a firm handshake. "Enjoy your vacation, but don't take too long. There's a war coming. Few people know about it, and even fewer still believe it, but mark my words, the human race might just be forced to get along, in its final battle for survival—against an enemy, we can't see."

"Thank you, ma'am. Will do."

She said, "Sam Reilly."

"Yes ma'am?"

"What did you do with that girl—the Russian spy?"

"Svetlana?"

"That's the one."

"You're aware that she can't return to Russia without being tried for treason after the loss of the *Vostok*, where she would most undoubtedly be convicted, and executed."

The secretary shrugged again. She was responsible for the lives and deaths of billions of people throughout the world. What did she care if Russia felt the need to execute one of its own. "Get to the point, Reilly."

"I liked her. She was intelligent, dedicated, and well meaning."

"Good God!" The Secretary's nostrils flared. "You've hired her, haven't you?"

Sam shrugged. "If it would make it easier for your moral compass, let's say she never survived the sinking of the *Maria Helena.*"

"Reilly!"

"Yes, ma'am?"

"You'd better hope she never made it back alive."

"Understood, ma'am."

Recognizing he was being dismissed, Sam stood up and made his way for the door, alongside Tom.

The secretary of defense said, "Mr. Reilly."

Sam raised his eyebrows. "Ma'am?"

"Be careful. Watch your back and keep your mouth shut."

"Yes, ma'am."

"We have a high-level traitor among us." She made a thin-lipped smile. "I'm glad you're still alive. We still have a use for your service."

"Thank you, ma'am."

Sam opened the soundproof door and stepped into the hallway.

A moment later, he felt the cold steel barrel of a handgun pressed hard against his neck. His pulse raced and his muscles tightened, but he made no attempt to fight against the solid arm around his neck.

The panicked stranger shouted, "Everyone back away, or this man dies."

CHAPTER SIXTY-THREE

S AM SWALLOWED HARD. "WE'RE NOT looking for trouble."

"Yeah, neither was I," the stranger replied. "I was just trying to do what I thought was right, and now look at me."

Sam remained silent.

The stranger motioned toward the door. "Is anyone in that room?"

"Yes," Sam replied, mechanically. "One person. Female."

"Can the room be secured?"

Sam genuinely thought about the question for a moment and answered, "Sure."

"Good."

Sam felt himself thrust into the office of the secretary of defense.

His captor moved with the calm efficiency of an elite soldier. There was nothing Sam could do to maneuver himself free of his restraint.

The secretary of defense's eyes widened with dismay. "What is the meaning of this?"

"Out!" the stranger said, emphatically.

Her emerald eyes grew wide with incredulity. "Do you have any idea who I am?"

"No," the stranger fired a single warning shot at her desk. "And I don't care. Get out of here or this man dies!"

The secretary of defense scowled. She straightened her suit and headed toward the door.

Her eyes met Sam's.

"Don't worry Mr. Reilly. He'll never make it out of the building alive," she said defiantly, as she stepped out through the door.

Sam watched her go. He noticed that she'd made no reference to whether or not he would make it out of the building alive.

His attacker latched the door behind her.

It appeared to be an ornamental door, made out of rich mahogany, but had two linings of lead, designed to stop the interference of listening devices from eavesdropping. The metal latch was solid. It would be impossible to kick in and it would take time for the marines, stationed nearby to retrieve a battering ram.

The stranger pushed him hard enough that he hit the floor.

By the time Sam was on his feet again, his attacker was pointing a handgun at him. It was a Glock 19. The weapon had no safety latch. It was designed to be used by law enforcement for its reliability and the immediate nature of its firing capability.

Sam glanced at his attacker.

The man was tall, a little taller than himself, at probably six foot-two. He had short brown hair and a strong jawline that women sometimes found attractive. He had a youthful appearance, like a man still in his early twenties, and the athletic frame of a soldier, with broad shoulders and muscular arms.

The man's piercing violet colored eyes fixed on him. "Where am I?"

Sam replied, "This is the Secretary's Office."

"What building?"

Sam squinted, surprise creeping in at his attacker's obvious confusion. "The Pentagon."

"The Pentagon!" The man's eyes flashed anger. "What the hell am I doing at the Pentagon?"

"I have no idea."

The man paused.

His focus was shifting fractionally in and out, his brows rising and falling a little, the shape of his mouth always changing, as if he was constantly thinking. As if there was a computer behind his eyes, running at full speed.

"I need to get out of here!"

"That might be difficult," Sam pointed out pragmatically. "We're near the center of the Pentagon. Already, there must be a hundred soldiers swarming toward this office. The building's going to be on lockdown. No one's getting in or out."

The stranger smiled sardonically. "Then we'd better move quickly. Because if I die, you die."

THE END

WANT MORE?

Join my email list and get a FREE and EXCLUSIVE Sam Reilly story that's not available anywhere else!

Join here ~ www.bit.ly/ChristopherCartwright

33446069R00206

Printed in Great Britain
by Amazon